# the
# turning

OTHER BOOKS BY PAULINE HOLDSTOCK

*The Blackbird's Song*

*The Burial Ground*

*House*

*Swimming from the Flames* (short fiction)

# the turning

A NOVEL BY

# PAULINE
# HOLDSTOCK

NEW STAR BOOKS

VANCOUVER

Published by New Star Books Ltd., 2504 York Avenue, Vancouver, B.C.
V6K 1E3. All rights reserved. No part of this work may be reproduced or
used in any form or by any means—graphic, electronic or mechanical—
without prior written permission of the publisher. Any request for
photocopying or other reprographic copying must be sent in writing
to the Canadian Copyright Licensing Agency (CANCOPY), 6 Adelaide
Street East, Suite 900, Toronto, Ontario M5C 1H6.

The publisher gratefully acknowledges financial assistance from the
Canada Council and the Cultural Services Branch, Province of British
Columbia.

Edited by Audrey McClellan
Text and cover design by Val Speidel
Cover photograph by Jamie Griffiths
Printed and bound in Canada by Best Book Manufacturers
1   2   3   4   5     00   99   98   97   96

While *The Turning* is set against historical events, it is nonetheless a work
of fiction and is peopled wholly by characters of the author's imagination.

CANADIAN CATALOGUING IN PUBLICATION DATA

Holdstock, Pauline, 1948–
  The turning

  ISBN 0-921586-53-1

  1. Title.
PS8565.O622T87  1996      C813´.54      C96-910621-1
PR9199.3.H548T87  1996

*In memory of the ones who give us our stories*


*For John*

 *One*

No one that night had seen or heard her strike, the fog had been so thick. Only later when it thinned, lifted by a light wind from the shore, had the lights of the English ship been seen in the clearing dark. All night she had stuck there, pinned to the rock, a wooden butterfly. The falling tide dragged her stern down so far the captain, all his passengers huddled and some bleating on the forecastle, had the boats made ready. But he was loath to give the order, the fog, as it was, a wall about them, the treacherous rocks. He had the bells rung. Some in the town said they had heard. In their sleep it must have been. They thought it was the steeple bell tolling from the drowned church. And then it had not come again.

When the tide was at its lowest the captain silenced the bells. Of its own accord the bleating stopped. The passengers looked into each other's eyes. Not a soul that was not listening to the creaking of the timbers, giving them room. At each new sound, men and women rummaged in each other's gaze, looking for fear, for the first sign, at which they must let go and scramble. Of use to one another while the danger was imminent, they were of no use at all, they knew, should it break upon them.

The sailors stood apart, kept their eyes towards the darkness at the stern and listened with their heads cocked to catch the faintest change, the smallest significance. Each one ready to be the first to shout. The captain held his repeater in his hand and slowly smiled. His ship, which had been a bow pulled tight, about to fling its freight of arrows into the dark and fog, was slowly, minutely easing. The captain's watch chimed one. The tide had been rising now for twenty minutes. His flock resumed their bleating. The captain went to his quarters and poured himself another drink. The first mate went over to the passengers who there, skewered to the coast of France in a blind fog, felt themselves saved and laughed. Though one sour fellow did think to ask what happened at *high* tide, nodding energetically as if he knew. No one answered except to joke. They were revellers all on the crest of a rising hysteria and they could take whatever fate would offer. The captain had his fifth drink while he considered what to do.

It was a little after two when the fog, at first without wind, began suddenly to lift, not lift but vanish like a miracle, and a yawning mother at a harbour window first caught sight of the lights where only one should be, in the blackness out towards the Dog's Teeth. Someone, wanting to be more safe than sorry—for what if they were Prussians—ran to the schoolhouse where the guard were stationed and hammered on the door. And so the day began noisily in that still night, in that other year.

But the men at the makeshift garrison were hard to wake, and before they had commandeered a vessel for themselves there were fishing boats already under way (for who knew how fast a ship like that might break apart, lose its riches to the deep?).

ELISA AND HER daughter, Janik, stood on the hill above the harbour to watch. A light breeze getting up from the land had driven off the last of the fog. The garrison boat cast off with a volley of gunfire. Out at sea, the drunken captain answered with the bell, but the wind carried the sound away. The black of the night was a clear black, clean, the sea rocking, gently yet, the stars glittering.

If a photographic camera could make a picture in the night,
thought Elisa. The lanterns of the fishing boats dipped and
bobbed towards the stricken ship until the voices of the men were
lost and the boats were nothing more than candles floating on a
black sea.

'The Angel of God keep him,' said Janik.

Elisa scanned the water. She could not tell one boat from the
other. She suspected that her husband was one of those the furthest out.

'He'll come back,' she said. And not with the help of any
angel, she might have added, except that it would rouse her
daughter to his defence, and that would only be tiresome here on
this hill, at this hour of the not-yet day with the wind beginning
to bite.


JANIK'S FATHER, PAUL Gagnon, was not a fisherman. He called
himself a boat builder and was the owner of a yard of some
repute. The world turned for him; things had a habit of coming
his way. To others it seemed (or did he have it seem?) he made
the world go round, and for this facility he was much admired.
There was about him such a sense of well-being that it was
difficult to begrudge him his luck. He had his father to thank.
Paul Gagnon's father, Matthew Kenyon, had come from Ireland
in the second decade of the century, stepped onto the quay on the
coast of northern France with little else but bluff and a readiness
to smile. He, this genial Irishman, took the name the Frenchmen
seemed to want to give him and got by with signs and smiles
while his ear absorbed the fancy tongue. He smiled himself a job
and eventually a wife from Paris (ready to retire from a lucrative
career of her own, but who was ever to know?). He lied
effusively, beguilingly, and discovered that he was indeed the
boat builder he declared himself to be.

He built boats of extraordinary sweetness of line and smiled
himself a partner and a small house. When his first child was born
he was generous, bestowing his straw-coloured hair, his blue eyes,

and naturally his smile. It was enough to make his wife run away. Matthew Gagnon, whose interest in her coarse appeal had waned, was too much used to good fortune to any longer be astonished. Without reflection he took himself a childless widow to care for the boy. She was conveniently barren, and had savings. And so, looking about himself and finding everything in its place and everything as it should be, Matthew Gagnon was well pleased.

The boy, Janik's father, grew. The world came his way, the house, the business when his father died (preoccupied and without a smile). The old partner sickened, sold him all his share, such a fine boy, Paul. Paul needed hardly to smile at all. But he did and, like his father, beamed a course through the accommodating world.

And just in the way that his hair was a little brighter, his eyes bluer, Paul Gagnon seemed always to know how to make the compliant world yield just a little more. He liked to say that his wife fell at his feet when she first set eyes on him and it was true, or almost, her foot catching on the end of a yardarm that lay ready for fitting and she collapsing in a blur of slubbed silk among the shavings. It was where he would want a wife to be. Quicker than his customer, her portly father, Paul Gagnon was there, helping her up. Even the old man felt the lightning pass between them. And both men thought: here now is a possibility.

For several years Paul Gagnon had thought about a wife. He could have chosen from any number with less to offer, except that he wanted more; even with a thriving business, smiles were not enough in a small town for a man with no family. Now here was this woman from Trouville, nowhere more remote—or more convenient—with the dark silk of her eyes and a father ready to oblige.

Paul Gagnon, who knew how to be patient when it was necessary, waited until a suitable sum had been named, and married Elisa Villeneuve.

By now well used to getting what he wanted, he felt considerable surprise to receive one year later, all unasked for, a red-haired, blue-eyed baby girl. The doctor was grinning with relief, but Paul Gagnon was furious. Eighteen hours. To think his wife had almost died for this, a daughter. It was as if he had been offered a rock to swallow, been told: Go on, everyone else does. His indignation was gigantic, nor could he voice it but must content himself with treating the doctor to a brutal lack of courtesy. Almost as if moved by revenge, the old doctor, as he was leaving, turned back and added that in his opinion it would not be far short of murder to let her have another. Paul Gagnon hid his displeasure well. Regrets and disappointments were not pieces with which he cared to play; they did not suit his style. He did after all love his wife. A son was not everything. He concentrated all his energies on satisfactions he could control, and of these money was the easiest. In the town he became known, not without admiration, as Le Gagnant, winning at cards, winning at business, and winning more than once or twice at the brothel, where a successful wager procured favours no decent man would care to ask of his wife.

As for his daughter, Janik, she continued to be not quite what he had hoped for, growing strange and difficult to love, a spiky kind of child; he bought her presents, toys, trinkets, ribbons, once a pony, and felt better.

THE BOATS WORKED fast. Some seemed to be coming back before all of them were out. The gas lamps on the quay had all been lighted and there was much activity in the harbour. Elisa and Janik walked down. People were saying it was an English packet, a barque out of Southampton, and ninety souls to bring ashore. The mayor was there, and Père Gaspé, half the town too, with lanterns and with torches, to welcome this event, almost as thrilling as the war with Prussia but not so dangerous, except perhaps for the boys who had left their beds to jostle on the very edge of the quay, cheering every boat as if this were a regatta, the passengers that climbed the slippery steps the victors.

And then above the confusion came a bang like a gun across the water, and out at the rock the ship's planking had suddenly parted, though no one knew it at that instant of the cracking air, only later they said, those who were near enough, those who saw, that it was like a bud bursting, a wing opening, and then, they said, there were people in the sea like insects flailing, calling, and some drowning before they could be reached. The echo of the splitting timber silenced all the crowd. Elisa waited, trying not to dread; there might be no need. Some of the passengers who were in the boats before it happened came ashore looking fearful, guilty to be alive, for what if fellow travellers should have died? No one wanted now to leave the scene, the promise of disaster. Someone brought blankets and those who had been rescued waited with the rest. A boat came in with a bedraggled company, haggard with cold and fear, their teeth showing clenched in the light of the lanterns, their eyes still watching their drowning selves, not yet believing they were saved until their feet slipped on the difficult stone. At that the boys began to cheer again and someone on the quay began to cry.

And then it was her husband's boat and there was Paul, his broad back, his quick, uncompromising movements. He was standing up, now bending, making ready a line, which was caught, made fast; he had come in against the iron ladder and quickly drew a crowd about him, the women he handed up scarcely able to move without help, their sodden skirts, the weight of the water.

What Elisa saw then she did not understand at once: the group with her husband moving as one then faltering, breaking apart, Paul energetic among the turning, the suspended figures, who attached themselves like drifting weed to bystanders and were carried away until only one man was left and came on with him, following as Paul spotted her in the crowd and made his way over.

'I'm going out again,' he said. 'Take this gentleman home.' This Englishman, Elisa heard at once as he spoke: '*Madame*,' holding his teeth together, making his lips work.

'It is not far,' Elisa said. He smiled for this irrelevance and put a damp arm briefly out to her.

'Go on ahead and make up the fire,' she said to Janik. 'Quickly.'

They did not speak on the way up from the harbour except once when Elisa asked if he was all right.

'Yes,' he said but was thinking how he ought to have stayed, tried to help, look for more, though it was not likely there were any more in the water, and the promise of dry clothes did attract.

THE GAGNON HOUSE was at the top of the hill on the road that led eastwards out of the harbour and past the boatyards. It turned abruptly to make the climb, for no other reason it seemed than to give Paul Gagnon and others like him a chance to live at height and look down on those for whom life seemed to be no end of trouble and care. The houses here had a big, square, solid look. They had gardens behind high grey walls, and courtyards, balconies, and even turrets if their owners had travelled and seen what could be done with blocks of granite. The turrets were a useful distraction for one's guests, who could entertain themselves for hours at the windows, or anyway for five minutes before dinner, if provided with a spy-glass. But turrets were beyond the pretensions of most of the inhabitants. Until the crest of the hill the street was lined all the way from the harbour with the tall slate-hung buildings of the town, crammed shoulder to shoulder. November winds sometimes ripped the slates from the houses and flung them to the cobbles, hitting pedestrians only sometimes, but always fatally.

The Englishman was coughing when he reached the house. Janik opened the door. She listened to his boots squelch as he followed Elisa past the closed rooms, past the staircase, and through to the kitchen at the back.

Here there was a large fireplace, that in a farmhouse would have been used for cooking, and a table with a long settle on either side. On the far side of the room, two steps down, was the kitchen proper with its new iron range, a sink, not in granite but brilliant porcelain, and a large copper. Paul Gagnon liked his money to make its mark.

The fire was made up but Elisa went at once to it and knelt

down to put on more wood. The Englishman's coat dropped to the hearth beside her and the fire hissed. When she looked up he was pulling his wet shirt over his head.

'Get a blanket, Janik,' she said.

He squatted down on his heels beside her and reached out to the fire as if he would crawl in. Elisa drew a low stool close to the hearth.

'There.'

He looked at her. The side of his face was twitching with cold.

'I'll see to the bed,' she said, 'and bring you something warm. Stay there.'

So that Janik did confront the man alone when she returned with the blanket. His long back. His spine. And he had taken his boots off and his stockings. She stood a little too far away and held the blanket out.

'*Meu-si*,' he said, this foreigner, getting up and taking it. '*Mademoiselle*,' giving the word more syllables than it had ever had. He shook out the blanket and wrapped it round himself. Then he turned his back to her and she saw with alarm that he was removing his breeches. It was a relief when he sat down again. Seeing him restored to this old woman's pose was a comfort and gave her courage.

'Would you like something to drink?'

The man said, but it took her some time to understand, that he did not want to be any trouble. She said it was no trouble.

Elisa was in the kitchen. She had set some water to heat on the range and had a bowl of brandy warming. She leaned towards Janik and whispered. 'Go and get in the bed.'

Janik did not answer. Such a lack of sound, like the silence that follows broken glass. So that Elisa must look up from the brandy and find herself at once annoyed—oh the horror on her daughter's face. To be so prudish yet to fly at once to the thought of it.

'Stupid child.' Something about the mistake made her want to hiss. Because now she must be seen to have shared the thought? 'To warm it while I make up the bottles.' The innocent earthen bed bottles in vindication beside the range. And it was in that moment, watching Janik stricken with her own imaginings, that Elisa knew what her husband had already seen, that her child was a woman. For more than a year now, Paul had been trying to marry his daughter off. But she, Elisa, had refused to believe, until now.

She ladled the brandy into a cup and took it in to the Englishman.

He was sitting on the stool, roughing the wetness out of his hair with the palm of his hand. He shook his head like a dog. His clothes in a pile dripped from the edge of the hearth. Elisa sat down while he drank.

'Do you think all were brought off?' she asked.

He held the cup between both hands. Without looking up, he shook his head.

'No,' he said. He was forced to use the simplest words and they were sufficient. 'The ship broke. There were people in the water. We tried. They went down so fast.'

She saw him in the water, in the darkness, casting about for a wife, a child.

'Were you alone?'

He said, 'Yes, thank God.' Which only prompted further questions in her mind. But she could not ask.

And he was saying the captain was at fault. It was poor sailing all the way but the captain would not have it. Thought he knew where he was going even in a blind fog. 'A man like that,' he said, and shook his head again.

'Well,' she said, 'but they are all the same.' And he was not sure she meant sea captains.

'I'll see if your bed is ready.' She carried the warmed bottles away, leaving him to finish his drink in front of the fire.


FOR THE SAKE of the Englishman, Janik lay on her back between the cold sheets of the spare bed with the coverlet up to her chin. She stared at the ceiling while her teeth performed a soft simian chatter in her head. Nor would her knees lie still.

*The faces of the nuns hovered and almost smiled.*

*'Are you feeling better, Janik Gagnon?'*

*'Yes, Sister.'*

*'Your Guardian Angel has been with you.'*

*How did she know?*

*'He has kept you from the Angel of Death. We must give thanks.'*

*But Janik could not be bothered. Besides he was waiting.*

*When she woke again the ceiling was empty for only a moment before Sister Aloycius hove into view again. The wings of her head-piece were uncelestial. No angel this but a seagull against the wind.*

*'You are thirsty.'*

*'No, Sister.'*

*'Let us give thanks. For the intercession of our Blessed Lady and all the holy saints in Heaven, Saint Michael the archangel, blessed John the Baptist, the Holy Apostles, Peter and Paul, our poor and blessed sister, Clare, Saint Francis the blessed . . .*

*Janik closed her eyes and he was there again, burning beside her, a towering of glory, making her dizzy with it, faint with it. He extended his hand to her and she held on. The giant wings opened with the crackling of a carriage hood unfolding above her head. She did not open her eyes again for a long time.*

*'You have been very ill. Our Lord was ready to receive you. Always remember that. By His grace you live. Your name may be called at any moment. Remember that.'*

*Sister Aloycius batted away. Janik lay listening, hoping to hear her name.*

JANIK GAGNON HAD not surprised her mother when she had announced five years earlier on her twelfth birthday that she wanted to enter the convent and join the sisters who had cared for her in her sickness. The presence of a feverish, delirious child in their school was not something the nuns cared to advertise, and so Elisa had never learned the extent or the severity of the sickness, had never guessed at any crisis. Nevertheless, when Janik made her announcement, Elisa accepted it. There had always been about her daughter a piety that alarmed. She had made an altar in her room and prayed there three times a day, sometimes more. The candles she lit were so many they were a danger. She said if she was to be poor she must use tallow. The room smelled like a butcher's shop. Her mother said it made her gag.

'Is that why you did not become a nun, Maman?'

At which Elisa Gagnon had to smile.

'Surely you wanted to.'

Her mother said that even had she wanted to they would not have had her.

Then the unspoken sins Janik imagined for her mother's ragged, crippled soul tapping at the gilded gates of heaven made her cry. Assiduous tears, as habitual as prayers. She burned even more candles.

At last, to demonstrate that the candles were not strictly necessary on her behalf, Elisa Gagnon revealed the nature of her sin, which could not, even by an overheated imagination, be called mortal. In the refectory, she said, of her own convent, the little girls floated crusts in the thin brown soup. Baking day was Monday. Every last piece of bread had to be finished on Sunday. Gums were pierced and milk teeth cracked like eggshells. Elisa Villeneuve was not hungry. She took a handful of crusts and tucked them up her skirt into her bloomers. When she left the refectory she walked as if she held a pillow stuffed with broken glass between her knees. Behind the loggia her companions watched. She had shaken out the crusts and wrapped them in her tucker and now she sat astride the wall and waved in lunatic encouragement at the sky. The first bird came silently; the others followed shrieking. She threw the bread straight up, and above her head the birds plummeted and tumbled in thin air. Juggling with seagulls. There was nothing finer. In the infinite blue.

Even Janik could feel relief at such a sin. And, yes, she could see that her mother could never have been a religious, her sins too mundane by far. She did not mind. It left her time to pray to God to strengthen her own vocation.

She was pleased at last to find her prayers answered and her way encouragingly beset with difficulties, the perverse proof that her calling was genuine.

There was a nun, Sister Bartholomeo, with the complexion of a fisherman, ruddy. She fished for souls.

'Any one of you could be called at any moment,' she said. 'Listen for the call, the voice of Our Lord, or perhaps the voice of the Holy Virgin His mother, calling you to give up your home and your family, your friends, your belongings, all that you own, yes, even your most private thoughts, your hopes and your dreams, your most precious visions that belong to you alone, everything, to lay down your life and become a Sister in Jesus. A Holy Sister of the order of Saint Ursula. There can be no higher crown.'

Janik was dismayed. She could not give up her angel. It was not possible.

'No higher crown. Those who do not heed the call to poverty, those who think that they can cling to any part of the riches God has bestowed on them, are deluding themselves. Theirs will be a crown of brass.'

'But a vision is a gift from God.' Janik could not keep silent.

Sister Bartholomeo was curious. And must find out more. She baited her words carefully and caught, as she suspected, not a wholesome soul but this rare and no doubt poisonous thing, this Janik with hair the colour of hell's flames and now visions loud with angels' wings. Or devils. And anyway it was nearly time for the Angelus and lunch and she had not finished the lesson.

'Sit down,' she said, 'Janik Gagnon. You are a fool.'

But Janik Gagnon would not sit down. The mouths of the other girls gaped.

' "He that calleth his brother a fool is in danger of hellfire." Sister.'

Now the girls were cheered and sputtered at the idea of danger, glad that it was Janik and not they who were in it.

Sister Bartholomeo's lips drew together to a tight beak. Janik felt nausea heaving with a sea swell and rising fast. But the par-quet at her feet shone. Not on me, it said. Not on me.

As she grew, Janik's vocation, far from abating, had become an obsession. When she was of an age to enter the novitiate, her father became concerned. A daughter was expensive, yes. There was no doubt about that. Which made it all the more important, especially where there were no sons, for her to bring in some return; but a daughter in a convent was an asset locked away without interest. Paul Gagnon had other ideas.

Before the close examination of intent, he asked for a word. Mother Marie-Joseph, the mother superior, came to the grille and inclined her head. When he had finished she said, 'I see,' and put away his words until she should have a use for them.

Janik Gagnon went in to her examination.

The three nuns sat behind a high table. Mother Marie-Joseph, pallid and still, presided, on her right the florid Bartholomeo, on her left Sister Marie-Justinian, who was held to be holy and looked most miserable to be present.

Mother Marie-Joseph's voice matched her thin body.

'Sister Bartholomeo tells me you say you see angels.'

'Only one, Mother.'

Yet one alone was altogether more disconcerting than a promiscuous host with trumpets.

'When do you see this angel?'

'When he wants to come and see me.'

Mother Marie-Joseph slowly closed her pale eyes for a moment.

'And do you bow down?'

Janik Gagnon seemed not to understand.

'Do you genuflect before him? Is he to be revered?'

'He is all glory.'

'So you genuflect.'

'No. He does not require it.'

'Then how do you comport yourself in his presence.'

'I stand with him. Sometimes I am lying down.'

Ah but they knew it. Here it was.

'What do you mean?'

'If I am in bed.'

'Why would you be in bed?'

Janik was surprised at this display of dullness in such a lofty being.

'To go to sleep, Mother.' Someone sighed impatiently. Janik was sorry; she appeared to have cut some thread that was necessary to the conversation. 'That is when he might come,' she said.

There! 'So not to go to sleep, but to wait for him.'

'Not exactly.'

'But you contradict yourself.'

'Well, yes then. I don't know, Mother.'

'Why do you wait for him?'

'Because he is all glory.'

But this the Mother Superior could not endure. A fantasy yes, that could be punished. But this, a vision when they had toiled thirty, forty years seeing nothing more than that the crucifix was dusty, the plaster peeling from the Holy Virgin. It was not right. She asked Janik to wait outside.

There was little discussion. Mother Marie-Joseph said simply that she had pertinent information to impart. Whatever Monsieur Gagnon had been suggesting had not itself been clear to her. Certain words, however, she knew instinctively were useful and these she fluted to the sisters in her reedy voice: unsuitable, unfit, not epileptic but . . . necessitating the care of a doctor, a certain predisposition, instability. Sister Marie-Justinian, never a nun more impolitic, said all the more reason. Sister Bartholomeo, not so simple, disagreed. To spend the rest of her days witnessing a rapture that was not her own . . . Like her pallid sister, she preferred the peeling virgin.

The girl was summoned.

'Tell your father he may take you home,' they said. 'We shall pray for you.'

Janik Gagnon began not to believe in the good sisters. In

doubting her they undermined their own validity. She took to her bed and waited. Bereft of angels, she was desolate. Expecting tears, her mother and father were perplexed. Elisa called the new doctor, Escher. He said it seemed to be an inversion of hysteria, she was so silent. He said her temperature was inexplicably low.

Elisa tried again to reach her daughter.

'Can it be so terrible,' she asked, 'to remain with us in the world?' And then, for no very good reason, but casting for consolation, 'Not all the saints were religious, you know.'

Janik, who had never said she wanted to be a saint, did, nevertheless, now begin to think. To go her own way, to be somehow above the law of the Church, it did appeal. A life of service did not have to be within walls, after all. And then, too, a visitation might be encouraged while the mind was elsewhere. She began with her father's boots. She polished them with all the care of an old nun polishing altar vessels and set them by the door each morning, praising God. So that her father began at that time to think that she might yet have the makings of a wife.


IT WAS IN October of her sixteenth year, the year before the English ship, that Janik was taken unaware as she had hoped. She was attending the annual feast day for the children of Saint Ursula. All the former pupils, women now with whalebone and bonnets, some with velvet whether they could afford it or not, came to be served luncheon by the biddable nuns. Sister Marie-Justinian looked across the heads of the guests when they were seated and thought of starlings gathering noisily, the common sheen of the feathers. She walked to the dais at the head of the refectory where she would read. Janik from among the bonnets watched with detachment as she went. It might have been her vocation walking away from her, but she was not sorry, all her desire laid to rest in favour of boot blacking and visits to the sick.

The voices subsided and the guests waited, as they waited every year, to be regaled with some ancient virginity. The old nun began to read from the life of Saint Catherine. The room was warm and Janik had to strain to hear the words but soon was lost, remembering a dream she could not remember dreaming, a sudden thing out of darkness, a release of glory that carried her a vast distance to a place she had always known. The sun through the refectory window struck fire from knives and rings, fell in bright embers on the plates, the linen cloth. And Janik burned with another, an other fire and listened to the wind it drew, the rushing.

*How the wings burned!*

Janik's head was filled with the echo of a sound she could not remember. The whiteness scalded her eyes. She opened them and focussed on the cool blue and white of the fireplace tiles. Something that had been spinning was slowing down. She had a sense of a presence she had missed. Her loneliness now was immense and she was cold.

'You can get up,' Elisa said. 'Is the bed warm?'

IT WAS BEGINNING to get light when Paul Gagnon came back. The old pointer that lay all day and all night outside the kitchen door woke with a racket of barking that stopped at once. Paul Gagnon kicked off his boots noisily. Elisa and Janik had fallen asleep by the fire. The Englishman, Alan Bridges was his name, had gone to the bed prepared for him. Elisa sat up.

'You're back. Safely.'

Her husband was warming his feet back to life in front of the fire.

'Of course. I wouldn't be risking my neck for the English.' His laughter muddled over his meaning; Elisa supposed it was a joke.

'And everyone else? The passengers?'

'No one knows yet. Some lost, that's certain. Over the side when she split apart.'

'Was there nothing to be done?'

He straightened up and looked at his wife, his eyes steady.
'Nothing.'

'And the survivors? Were there no more to bring back?'

'All accounted for.'

'Do they have somewhere to go? The ones you brought in, where are they?'

'They were a rough lot. Crew I think.'

'I should not have minded.'

'I would.'

He sat down next to his wife and pulled her to him. 'Now come to bed and warm me for an hour. My bones are as cold as the grave.'

Elisa put her blanket over Janik who did not wake.

In bed, Paul Gagnon was asleep in moments, huddling to his wife like a great child. She felt the cold from his bones seep into hers. In no time at all she was colder than he was. She thought of the Englishman as he had gone to bed. '*Je vous remercis, Madame.*' *Re-meu-si.* In his foreign voice. Saying her daugher's name. *Mademoiselle Jeanne-ique.* Getting it almost right. And then *Meu-si* again. His two hands round hers, the light strength of his grip. Something there not solid, as if the bones were hollow. The skin dry and cool. Her husband's hands, she thought, clutched. His flesh was heavy and solid, hot.

She thought of Janik curled on the settle. The shame of her daughter's thought, her own surprise. Then in the tentative light she thought of them; she thought of them, God forgive, together, her daughter beside the thin man and he rolling to her, on her. Until she was her own daughter beneath him, his hips bearing down on hers.

Paul was asleep.

Outside the gulls had begun.

IN AN HOUR or so Paul Gagnon was about again, down to the harbour to see, Elisa knew, if there was any salvaging to be had. Janik had woken and gone to her own bed. The Englishman did not appear. When the servant, Marguerite, arrived, Elisa sent her to see if he wanted anything.

She came back shaking her head. 'He says he will not eat. He looks strange.'

It was a cross to bear, a stupid servant. Elisa did not ask questions. She went up to see.

When she went in, the Englishman was sitting on the edge of the bed, shaking. He looked at her.

'I think I have a fever,' he said, apologizing, as if he could help it. She could see that his skin was slick. His eyes seemed to want to turn back in his head and he could not keep still. And suddenly this was no solitary stranger they had put up for the night. This man belonged to someone. She was afraid.

'Make a tisane,' she said to Marguerite who dithered at the door.

'Were you alone?' She had to ask again, though she had heard the answer. Yes, he was alone.

'Your family is in England?'

He nodded.

'Would you like me to write to them?'

'In my coat there is a letter with my address.'

She thought of the pool of water on the hearth where the coat dripped the night before.

'I will come up again with a pen and you can tell me what to put. Get back into bed.'

When Elisa returned, he was asleep. He sounded, she thought, as if on each breath he took he was about to speak.


JANIK REMEMBERED THE Englishman and the wreck and got up. She said her prayers and dressed quickly, the house around her new and different, advertising mutely the presence of a stranger, the knowledge of his presence itself a stranger seated at the table of her mind's house, palms down, waiting to be addressed, attended to. Leaving her room, she was on her guard, anxious not to be taken by surprise by the unfamiliar shape of the stranger's body occupying the known spaces of the stairs, the hall. He was not about.

Her mother was in the kitchen. Marguerite tissed and tussed. 'Mademoiselle Janik. How fresh you look. When all the world is sinking in the sea. Ah, to be young! And your chocolate waiting.'

Her mother was rubbing dry linden blossoms into a jug, crushing the flowers as if they were poison, dirt. As if she would rub them out.

Marguerite set down the cup of chocolate. 'There my lamb. Drink while it is hot,' though anyone could see it had a skin and had been standing.

'It is for the Englishman,' said Elisa, seeing her daughter watching her with the blossoms. 'He is sick.' Her own crossness compelled her to annoy. It did not matter whom. And so she said, 'We will send the angels,' and hoped that her daughter would hear her unbelief and be disturbed.

But Janik continued to sip before she answered. 'They were here this morning,' she said. Nor was it meant as a rejoinder. It was not possible, Elisa saw, to sip chocolate with more equanimity than this daughter of hers.

'Marguerite,' she said, 'You will take this up when it is ready. Don't forget. Janik and I shall walk down to the harbour.'

ALAN BRIDGES WAS not asleep, nor was he quite awake. The light hurt his eyes and he had turned over with his back to the window. He was aware of the inside of his body. The outside was fully occupied merely existing around it. Or perhaps it was keeping the inside in. In any event the fever did not allow the luxury of thought. There was only feeling, and all of it internal.

There was a sound at the door and a movement. He heard the swish of skirts as someone came in. But it was a serving woman. He closed his eyes while she recited her speech. 'Madame says it is necessary to take this while it is still hot. If you please, sir.' She went out, leaving the glass just out of reach on the night table. But it did not matter. Alan Bridges did not open his eyes again before it grew cold. Instead he lay down on the shingles of his sickness and let the tide of fever creep. It was the easiest thing in the world.

THEY COULD SEE the wreck, the *Lady Morgan*, when they walked out on the western side. She was stuck there still on the rock, the planking out like a broken wing. The water was alive with boats again, bringing off cargo and the rest of the baggage. The harbour master's boat was anchored near. Others were about, balancing like gulls on the waves, waiting for scraps. As if we are so poor, thought Elisa, that we must scavenge.

They went down to the quayside where all the talk was of the next tide and whether it would carry her off. There was a stack of trunks and boxes against the wall. Most of the cargo she was carrying, worsted and woollen yarn mainly, was already off.

'If she goes, she goes.' The old man lighting his pipe was not concerned. If you reached seventy-two and could still light your own pipe, the loss of a ship was neither here nor there. His friend nodded.

'We've done all we can.' Who had not moved from his observation post on the first bale that had been set down.

'All we can.'

'For whatever reason.' The seated man's voice carried its own freight of meaning but his friend only continued to puff at his pipe. 'I said no matter what the reasons. Done all we can, some of us. For whatever private reason.' Would his friend never be moved? Did he have to have everything spelled out? 'Good or bad.'

'What's that?' his friend biting, finally.

Elisa did not want to hear but knew she must.

'Well you do not think it is the same as it was in our day, do you?'

But the smoker did not make a habit of thinking. The silence was long.

'There are boats out there I'm telling you would have stayed in their mooring last night if it were not for one thing. Gain, my friend. Gain.'

Yet the first man was reluctant to believe and let his voice roll
in his mouth a while in wordless disparagement of such a
thought, though he did not have the words to deny it.

'I'm telling you. Gain. And I could name names.'

'Look.' Elisa drew Janik towards a fishing boat where some
men were working with block and tackle to bring ashore a mare
that lay hobbled on the deck. They had passed slings under the
animal's belly, but now, when they began hauling, Elisa saw that
it was dead. As the cradles took the weight, a brown fluid gushed
from the animal's mouth.

Janik turned away.

'What are they doing?'

'They're just bringing it ashore. I'm sorry, I didn't know.'

'Why are they? It's dead.'

Elisa shrugged.

'Why didn't they just leave it?'

'I expect they want the meat.'

Janik put her hand over her mouth.

'Come on. We don't want to stay here.'

One of the men began to kick repeatedly, rhythmically at the
horse's belly just behind the ribs. A live horse would be worth
more.


PAUL GAGNON WAS pleased with the way the morning was
turning out. What he had heard about the Englishman proved his
intuition sound; he congratulated himself on landing such a
well-to-do fish in the guest bed. And here at the harbour things
couldn't have arranged themselves with more ease. It had been
decided to bring off the English barque at the next high tide and
then try to tow her round to the dry dock. Right now they would
need to work fast to get rid of the ballast and patch her up as best
they could before the tide. Le Gagnant said splendid, splendid.
He could provide the men; he would do everything he could.
Which made everyone smile, the chief mate, the harbour master,
the pilots, everyone. And, he said, to the smiling faces, he would

not charge for the work. Not in full. So now how could a man argue without sounding churlish?

In an hour the work was under way. But the damage was extensive. Oh, beyond, far beyond, Le Gagnant said, what had at first been apparent. They would do what they could and continue in the morning. The carrying off would have to wait until the next day. In the meantime, the work of lightening continued so that when she left the rock the damaged section of her hull would be well above the water. The work was difficult, of that there was no question. They had to shift what was left of the ballast to her sound side. Then, when they brought her off with the the ground tackle, the holed planking could be patched. And then there were dangers. When she came off she would be as unpredictable as a wild mare. She could swing round smooth and easy and be led by the forelock or, as everyone knew, she could rear and buck away from the devastating rock and ultimately go down. And if that should happen and the boats working her had come in too close, then no amount of letting go would save them. As for Gagnon, the chief mate, and the men who, it was agreed by drawing lots, would stay aboard, they would take their chances. If they judged she was going to go, they would take to the boat that the bosun would have standing off and row for their lives. Paul Gagnon was not shy of danger—in certain circumstances. He knew too the men who would come aboard a listing ship and not think of risk but opportunity.


ELISA AND JANIK stopped at the church on their way back. The steps were strewn with boxes and trunks, some of them open, the lives of the passengers spilled on the grey stones. Elisa found a box with the Englishman's name.

'We'll find a carter,' she said, 'to bring it up to the house.'

Inside the church the chairs had been moved aside and mattresses laid down on the tiles. Some of the passengers were still sleeping. The others stepped over them. Elisa could not find the doctor anywhere. Someone said he had gone somewhere to sleep but not to his house, where he would only be disturbed.

'Then we should go home,' said Elisa.

But Janik had other plans. 'I am staying here,' she said.

'But there is nothing you can do.'

'I can pray.'

Elisa was thinking of the broken ship and the view from the point. She was thinking of the pale light on the water and the picture it would make. If Marguerite could be persuaded. Or the yard boy.

'All right,' she said, and it might have been the answer to almost anything.

Besides, there was the Englishman.


WHEN SHE GOT back, Marguerite was ironing sheets slowly, in the way she had, as if it were the only job she would ever do all day, all her life.

'All finished in the kitchen?' Elisa asked. Though she knew she wasn't.

'Yes, Madame.' Marguerite never made difficulties for herself.

'And the Englishman?'

'Yes, Madame.'

Useless to point out that this was not an answer. Still in her bonnet, Elisa went upstairs and opened the door quietly.

The Englishman lay on the pillows with his eyes closed and his neck stretched out as if reaching for air. His hair was dark with sweat and stuck across his temple. He had not touched the remedy she had prepared. A stink of vomit came from the pot under the bed. She pulled up the sheet and she could feel the heat from him though he shivered, making a complaining noise in his throat. His lips were crusted with yellow and there was a faint smell of bile. She went to the washstand and wrung out a cloth to sponge his face and neck. It caught on the stubble of his beard.

When she had finished she removed the chamber pot and went downstairs. She told Marguerite to go for the doctor.

The Englishman's coat hung by the hearth. It seemed important now to know to whom she should write, her guest so deathly, languishing and seeming to worsen. The coat had stopped dripping and had begun to dry in patches. From an inside pocket she drew out a pocket book and some papers. There were letters, their envelopes marbled with the wet ink from the addresses. The red ticket from the passenger service was there, thickened and softened with the water. She looked at the envelopes again and pulled out the letter from one; its ink, too, had bled. In another envelope was a cutting from a newspaper. It was printed in English but she could still recognize one or two words: INFORMATION . . . ENGLISH GENTLEMEN . . . SIEGE OF PARIS . . . and further on APARTMENTS. There were several more lines of text before the notice ended with the address of a Paris estate agent. It might be useful. She took the cutting and laid the other items to dry on the mantle. She was alone now with the stranger upstairs suddenly a corpse if she did not go up at once. As if by her not looking he would die. She hung up her bonnet and shawl and went up again to sit beside the bed.

It seemed like hours before Marguerite returned, and not with any doctor. She had looked everywhere, she said, and then she had met Monsieur again and he had sent her home. Marguerite, though she might not be credited with any brain, nevertheless knew enough not to repeat Monsieur's words about rubbish, and the man not needing any doctor, and it was just a chill, and go along, Madame is a good nurse.

AND SO ELISA sat for hours more, reading and sometimes slipping into sleep, to wake from time to time with a start to a death rattle she had heard in her head: Marguerite at the grate downstairs, the door opening when Janik returned. A candle, said Janik. That was the answer.

And then in the evening the man's fever took hold and he began to burn with it, a dark patch on the sheet spreading out from under his shoulders. For an hour Elisa sponged the long, thin limbs with vinegar, wondering how she came to be disposed in this unlikely pietà but knowing that the rite was hers alone, and her daughter, though she might make a better Virgin, could not do this thing, let her hands travel this man's skin. And then she saw him dead and there was her daughter, in the veil of the convent, sponging the cold flesh, and both of them beyond her. She began to pray with words more panic-stricken than eloquent. Don't let him die, don't. Though she had more faith in vinegar. Nevertheless, when the fever did finally break she thanked God, glad to see the man frown slightly and begin to shiver. At last he asked in a voice that seemed like his own for more blankets.

PAUL GAGNON CAME home with Doctor Escher. They had met at the harbour; the doctor said he had heard he was needed at the house. Gagnon did his best to convey a certain lack of urgency but the men were friends. 'Well,' said the doctor, 'I will come all the same, why not?' and Gagnon, knowing he was thinking of a glass or two, could hardly tell him no.

'The man's asleep,' said Elisa. 'Don't wake him.' But the doctor felt compelled to earn his reward and did just that, though he was tired and would have preferred not to. He applied a plaster, which was quicker than a bleeding, and went in search of Gagnon, who had already poured the drinks. The Englishman lay awake in some discomfort but plainly was not about to die. Madame Gagnon was told to go to bed. But still she had to look in once, twice in the night, just to be sure.

THE SUN HAD been up for some time when Elisa woke the next morning. She went straight to the Englishman's room and looked in. The air was very close. She went to the window and opened it, keeping the shutter closed. He slept on. At the bedside she put a hand on his forehead. It was cool and dry. She left her hand there a moment, not wanting to disturb, but not minding all the same if his eyes should slide open, take her in. But his eyes remained closed. He was somewhere else. England perhaps.

Downstairs she found that her husband had already left. Janik,

Marguerite said, had gone to pray. There had been people at the harbour early. Come to watch the ship being brought off. The whole town would be there, she said, hoping.

'And I think we should be there too,' replied Elisa. 'With the camera.'

Which did make the buoyed heart sink, when a person knew the heft of it all, and that a person would be doing most of the carrying.

'Are you sure, Madame? There will be a great crush.'

'Not where we are going. Is that boy around?'

Marguerite had to admit that he was.

'Then tell him to get the gig ready while we get the things together.'

Elisa had had the camera since Janik was small. Paul had bought it, one of his surprises, and set it on the table in front of them. 'Handsome isn't it?' he had said and patted it; for him it was a thing achieved. Elisa was not so sure. She said, 'How does it work?' 'Simple,' said Paul. This was a wife who complicated everything. 'It's all here. Any more coffee?'

The pamphlet was entitled 'Drawing From Life: The Art of Making Portraits With The Sun.' Elisa took it away and learned its impossible secrets, the two sliding boxes on the desk next to her, the brass-bound lens. These at least were not trinkets. To conjure even the image of life from such inert material; it was an unlikely thing, improbable. Who would not want to try?

'I shall make a picture of Janik for you,' she had said to Paul, 'and it shall hang in the office at the yard and watch over you while you are away from us.'

'Perhaps it will charm all our customers,' he replied.

She had made lists. She went to the glazier to have plates cut. She went to the chemist for pyrogallic acid and potassium iodide. At silver salts he began to pick at a boil on his chin and at potassium cyanide said he would have to make up an order. He didn't know. And so she began again. She took the ferry to Le Havre and found a photographic studio. Now it was easy. She returned with a parcel of brown bottles, no less than eight. There were only the printing frames to make, the paper to buy, and she was ready. If she could start with some experiments.

Marguerite, full of anxiety, had stood rigid against the wall of the house, an insurgent before the firing squad, the legs of the tripod fixed now finally and steadier than her own, her mistress no help at all under the black cloth, even her voice disguised. Elisa took her first picture—and Marguerite breathed again.

Conspirators, they had hurried to the cellar to develop it, the plate a secret document in its wooden sheath, the light encoded there, in darkness. In the cellar there was much fumbling and indecision, a certain amount of 'Open the door,' as well as 'Shut the door,' while Elisa, inarticulate in her excitement, tilted the fluid across the glass.

'Just a crack. Ah. Oh, look. No. Stay there. It's coming.' But she put down the beaker and slid the glass into the pan of hyposulphite, afraid of losing the image that had begun to creep of its own accord in every direction at once across the plate. And even then not believing it would be bound in the magic liquid.

'Open the door. Quick, come here.' The two women had stared at the white-haired, black-faced Marguerite staring back in diabolic reversal from her unearthly bath. Nor was she about to disappear. Like witches they had cackled.

They took the plate to the scullery, poured nine cans of water carefully over, bathing their newborn. Their creation which they hid. It had not been perfect after all, only a ghostly success, faint, and the terrified Marguerite frozen there was not Paul Gagnon's daughter; but it was success of a sort and they must make more, practice, taking more care, more time, to get them right. They made two others, each better than the last, and set them in frames with the coated paper out in the sun on the grass to print. And Marguerite, between looking, did find time to wonder who would shell the beans and make the cream for the dry chicken she had roasted too long while her mistress got up to these tricks.

Elisa at dinner that first night had smiled to remember the three Marguerites curling in the cellar, the last with a repressed smile of her own, the experienced sitter.

'I think,' she had said to Paul, 'I shall make your picture of Janik tomorrow. Everything is ready.'

'I have to say,' said the notary's wife that night at dinner, 'as the child's godmother, I have to say you sow the seed of vanity. The hobby of photography leads to dubious destinations.' Madame Crécy found something new to say each Thursday and never criticized the same thing twice. It made Paul Gagnon wonder that his oldest friend had managed to live with his unfathomable choice of wife.

'Nonsense,' said Elisa. 'It shall be an offering, a prayer.' And began to have ideas.

The next day, Marguerite, wringing the neck of the Peking duck, had wondered at the limitless nature of the demands her mistress could make. And rebelled.

'There,' she said and dumped the duck. 'I do not do the other part.'

The picture took nearly all day to make but was at last printed onto paper and inscribed.

'You give it to him,' Elisa said the next evening when Paul Gagnon took his coffee. Janik handed him the portrait. His daughter, with tousled hair as if she had just got up and looking wan and somewhat abandoned, had sprouted angel wings and leaned with naked arms and shoulders over something he presumed to be a cloud but which he recognised to be the greasy fleece that had for some time lain in the shed. For once his easy charming tongue deserted him; it was not what he had imagined and he said so.

When she looked again, Elisa had to admit, though only to herself, that it was not what she had imagined either. What she had thought to reproduce was not there at all.

The setback was temporary. From that day Elisa set about increasing her knowledge and refining her skill, and increasing, her husband noticed, the paraphernalia she required for the practice of her art.

Outside, she created a studio, converting the glasshouse to her purposes with a bench for working on and blinds to control the light. Nearby was the coalshed she used now for her darkroom. To make photographs away from the house, however, required a good deal of preparation. She had bought herself a portable darkroom, a small upright tent with a folding table to stand inside. For the developing materials, Felix in the boatyard had made an ingenious box that, upended, opened out to form a small cupboard with the bottles and funnels on their racks inside. It, too, could stand inside the tent.

This was the equipment, along with the camera and a great quantity of water carried in several carboys, that had now to be loaded onto the gig for the excursion to the harbour.

It was at times like this that Marguerite was beset with doubts about her mistress's activities. Carrying the developing box between them to the gig, she could not help thinking how like it was to a child's coffin.

When it was all loaded up they wrapped themselves against what weather they might meet on the cliff top.

'Have you seen?' Marguerite was holding out a pair of binoculars. She laughed guiltily. The leather case was saturated. It smelled of dog. Elisa took out the binoculars. The brass was tarnished. She took them to the window and looked out. The suddenness of the material world astonished. 'You've been prying,' she said. 'But I won't tell. Here.' She handed them back to Marguerite. 'Bring them. He won't be needing them today.' And something she had said made her think of the papers drying on the mantle. She thought she could guess the meaning of the newspaper notice.

Wrapped in their scarves and heavy cloaks, they set out. But it was not cold. The sun had driven off the mist and the air was sbright. Elisa drove the gig past the crowds on the quay and out along the western cliff road that led to the beacon. They stopped and teth-ered the horse, carrying the equipment between them out to the scrubby grass that thatched the cliff. From this small promontory they had a clear view back towards the rocks and the barque.

JANIK, TOO, HAD taken the western road. But she had walked out past the beacon to where the road became a track and then a path, which led to a chapel on the cliff. This chapel, the chapel of Saint-Christophe, was built from the timbers of a wreck. A section of the ribs and keel had been carried up the cliff to be overturned there and set in place to form a nave of seven arches. The whole then had been covered over in weatherboard so that the result was something like a roof that reached, like the shell of a tortoise, to the ground. The altar's position, beyond the furthest arch, gave it a low and secret look. Here might sit the thing that dwelt inside the shell. It was all the more difficult to approach in its terrible intimacy. Janik knelt at the back. Sometimes in this place the wind stroked the planking like a hand over dry grass. But this October day was as still as it had dawned. The feet of gulls smacked cleverly on the roof. Janik could hear them as they landed and took off, the rush of air like flames fanned. Her angel had wings of flame. Creature of wonderful reversal, its flames fanned air with fire, beat it to life, lit it. When he appeared she shook. She burned her face with looking at the glory, with longing. 'For my father,' she began, 'to keep him safe this day I pray . . .' But the radiance of the angel faded, his light diminished and was replaced by a phosphorescent gleam and there, dripping from the sea, lank and dank and with his head bowed, stood the lean Englishman, a puddle forming at his feet.

Janik was undaunted. While she had never been moved to wrestle like Jacob with her angel she did not flinch now from this waterlogged stranger. Who might well douse the fire. All morning under the shell of the hull she wrestled, exorcising him slowly but surely from her vision.

The gulls had gone. The chapel was very quiet.


*Janik saw her father astride an upturned boat that crawled the waves like a turtle. His teeth crammed with nails, he bent forward to hammer at the planking when from beside the boat there came hands reaching. She saw the face of the man in the water and might have known it, she could not tell. His finger ends hooked on a plank. He was not in distress this man, only intent as her father turned and hammered at the hooked fingers. The stranger, concentrating on his fate, slid under the waves.*

JANIK CLOSED HER eyes and shuddered, then without warning she felt her stomach heave so that she had to rush from the chapel. Outside, she vomited on the grass.

When it was over she was cold. She wrapped her shawl more tightly round her and went to shut the door. It made a hollow sound that terrified. She turned to go. As she started back along the path, she heard the gulls again behind her. She knew what they were fighting over.

WHEN PAUL GAGNON returned home that night, he did not receive the welcome he expected. The work had been difficult and dangerous; there had been an accident, a life lost, but they had done it nevertheless and everything had turned out as he had hoped. The weather had been with them. It looked as if in the calm they would be able to haul the ship off and, if the first mate was worth his salt, she would come away clean. The captain had no hand in it at all, being then in the grip of the sickness which had stricken more than half of the survivors and which was held by many to be owing to the foul water carried on board for drinking—a view that almost as many liked to contradict, observing that the captain never touched the stuff. In any event, with or without the captain, the first mate did know his business. Judging how much ballast to give the starboard side, away from the rock, was a delicate matter: any more and the hull on the port side would be driven up and under the rock with the effect of crushing it further; not enough and the ship would be lost. Pulling her away would be like pulling a jar away from its stopper.

With the captain incapacitated and the first mate shifting life and death out of sight in the dank holds, the stage was clear. Le

Gagnant was the showman. He strode. He sucked in the early morning air. He beamed encouragement. French, English, it was all the same. Were this the *Great Western* herself he would get her off. From the stern he had a kedge anchor laid out to seaward, using a fishing boat to carry it out and put it down a distance off. He stationed men at the capstan. At the same time, two more boats, with towing lines secured to the bitts and standing off a short distance, had their own anchors laid out in the same manner.

When it was certain that all three anchors would hold, and with only an hour before the tide, Le Gagnant gave the order to take the strain. At the signal, the men in the fishing boats began to take up the slack. The men on the English ship worked the capstan; the cables, against the grinding and the shouting, began to lift, dripping, from the water. Gagnon watched the slow progress of the arcs flattening and creeping out towards the anchors. As each line came taut he gave the signal for the men to stop. They waited, resting on the bars, catching their breath.

After a while the boards of the English ship began to creak. The stern began to lift. The men at the capstan took up their positions again and the signal was sent to the boats to seaward. The cable was coaxed in and the *Lady Morgan* began miraculously to shift, began to move and seemed about to slip effortlessly into the water—but stuck. Le Gagnant gave the order to surge the capstan and the men, on a command, sprang away while the bars flew round, unravelling their effort. And no one saw, they said, until later, that a man who had been near the port bulwark had gone. It had all been so quick. The order was to surge and for that every man needed all his wits. The pawls raised, the flying bars that could break a back. The cable whiptailing across the deck. And in a moment they had laid hold again and were taking up the slack. No one, they said, had noticed a man missing. And did believe it to be true. And the ship came away clean, leaning away like an affronted woman.

They made her secure at once and got to work on the damage. It took all day, but they did it. She was out there now, strung out,

an unlikely acrobat upon the water, balancing sink and swim on
the knife edge of her keel in defiance of all the laws of physics,
making the long cables shiver each time she lifted on the swell.
Everything had turned out as he had hoped.


JANIK, ASLEEP IN her room, dreamed of a spider in a web of
light. Had she been awake she would have kissed her father,
grateful for his rough bulk that went into the world and performed important feats.


DOWNSTAIRS, PAUL GAGNON rubbed his mouth with the back
of his hand. He had been thirsty.

'You would not believe the ease of it. She floated like a dream.'

'I saw.'

'I said we could do it and we did. We did it.'

'I saw.'

'Beautiful.'

'Who was it?'

He waited too long, Elisa thought, before he answered.

'The man who went over?'

Elisa would not answer at all, would not play this game.

'He was one of the crew,' said Paul Gagnon and shook his
head. 'Ah, yes. It was too bad, that.'

'Was the boat worth it?'

And now he glanced at her sharply and frowned. He began to
sense an implication, not to say an accusation, and he said slowly,
to make sure, 'Worth what?'

'A man's life.'

How he disliked the self-righteous tilt of her chin.

'What do you mean, "worth it"? It wasn't a transaction. It
wasn't part of any plan. It was an accident.'

She raised her head as if she were to say, Ah, I see. But she said
nothing, only got up and went out. For which he clenched his fist.

THE NEXT DAY dawned palely beautiful and no good at all for drawing boats to dock without steam. But Paul Gagnon had thought of that. He had a friend in Le Havre who owed him a favour and the tugs arrived just after first light. Gagnon was already on the quay. In the absence of the grey-faced captain, the first mate was to conduct the boat's passage to the dock, with Gagnon to remain stationed on shore to supervise the docking, the harbour master said, if he would not mind. Le Gagnant minded not at all, was more than happy. It was a good arrangement. The harbour master had the pilot boat made ready and the ground tackle was taken up as the sunight slid across the river's mouth under the remnants of the night's fog.

Janik, watching from her window, saw the tugs begin to draw away. It might have been an insect on the water, the boats and the hawsers making awkward legs, the foremost probing, finding the way, the others dragging, resisting, extended on the skin of the sea. She dressed as quickly as she could and hurried out. In search of catastrophe (Elisa shook her head), a slingful of prayers at her back.

And who was praying for the drowned man? Elisa went to work in the glasshouse.


JANIK JOINED THE small crowd that had already gathered at the dry dock beside the harbour. She was just in time to see the pilot and the first tug come into view and then the ship itself at a disgraceful angle rounding the end of the quay. A cheer went up. And there was her father, legs astride, proprietorial.

'Good man. You did it.' For who else was there to congratulate? Onlookers clapped him on the back, the shoulders, shook his hand. Hadn't they heard him themselves, with the harbour master, describe in detail how she should come in, how lie?

'Good man.'

And Le Gagnant smiled as Le Gagnant could, though the stricken ship was not yet in and the most ticklish part was yet to come.

Slowly a boat moved in with a slack cable. Another was taken
to a winch on the other side.

Paul Gagnon and the harbour master conferred, concocting a
science all their own where none had existed. In a little while they
were ready and Gagnon gave the signal. A tug moved away
across the mouth of the dock. The men on the dockside began to
work the windlass. The cable came in slowly, the shouts of the
men rhythmic, at intervals, like knots marking its length. And
minutely, preposterously, she righted and swung at the same time
slowly into the dock.

But the cheering was too soon for she continued her long slow
roll and would not stop, so that one of the winches on the far side
that should have held her was screaming to give way and did, its
handle breaking the skull of the youth who had been nearest in
his eagerness to help.

Janik watched the ship hanging between the ropes, the
wounded side rotating with perfect certainty towards the water.

On the dock the young man wriggled like a worm in a puddle.

Gagnon saw with horror how the ship would end.

'Let her go! Let her go!'

The men at the windlass could barely pay out fast enough.
And then a great shout went up as the patching on the damaged
side gave way under pressure from water that had come in, no
one knew from where, and travelled, no one knew how, with the
roll to find its way out at the weakest spot, gushing through the
reopened hole.

And so the roll was arrested and Le Gagnant had the gates
closed, the dock drained, and the ship secured without any further trouble.

Yes, he said later, his reputation ballooning, illuminated with
the day's events, it all went according to plan. Of course one
could never be sure with these things, but there. Luck had been
with him.

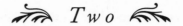 *Two*

ELISA HAD NOT heard the footstep behind her when Bridges spoke.

'I should like . . .'

The solution she had been carefully funnelling was flung in a reckless snake across the bench.

'I'm sorry.'

'No, no. It was not your fault.'

Nor could he help her as she wiped it up but must stand foolish in his blanket, garb for an idiot.

'I should like to ask where my clothes are?' He had to laugh to confirm again his foolishness. And she now, clothed in her own blanket of shame, was saved only by the presence of the uncomplicated servant.

'Marguerite. Find Mr. Bridges his clothes at once.'

And Bridges barefoot followed her.

ALAN BRIDGES, DRESSED in his shirt and breeches and standing in front of the glass, tied his white stock at the neck and was a man again. He put on his yellow waistcoat, sorry for the streak of something that might have been tar on the front. His boots, too, he noticed, would not be the same again but drew up at the toe where the fire had dried the sole too fast. He would have liked not to put on his frockcoat. It smelled of smoke from its drying at the hearth and there were water marks patterning the cloth. But it would not do to leave it off. He went to the window. The women were still in the glasshouse.

'MADAME.' EVEN WATER-STAINED clothes restored confidence, a little. God, the woman was nice looking. She was pushing back her hair using her wrist and the back of her hand. Her hands were stained with black. Her eyes were black. He took in everything now. There was something Spanish about her, or lighter. He looked around and saw that the glasshouse was a studio. There were photographic plates stacked against the sides. There were blinds covering part of the roof and the sides, and the bench was full of bottles and papers and card.

She smiled at him, waiting. And then she picked up a print and handed it to him. The image was pale but he saw the ship then as he had not seen it before, stuck there on the rock, ridiculous in its distress.

'Keep it,' she said. 'I am making some small ones, like post-cards. This is not a good one. But it is something.'

'Thank you,' said Bridges, his self-possession, like his shoes, curling now at the edges. There was a certain lack of regard here for convention. It did disarm. 'Madame . . .' he realized that he did not know her name, 'Madame, I have to thank you for your generous hospitality. You have been most kind . . .'

'You are not leaving?'

'I had intended, yes . . .'

'Like that?' She glanced over his clothes. 'I don't think so.' Her amusement was direct, not to say unfair: her fallen hair, the stained apron. The conversation was more difficult than Bridges had anticipated.

'I shall find my baggage at the harbour, I expect?'

'I have asked for it to be sent up.'

'That is most kind. I shall be able to leave at once.'

'And then?'

'I beg your pardon?'

'And then what? What will you do?'

'My plans, Madame . . .'

'Madame Gagnon.'

'My plans, Madame, have not been affected.'

'And they are?'

He was defensive now, telling her she had overstepped the mark, his mark. 'I shall collect my things and proceed as planned to the Hôtel Cherbourg.'

'Then you would be some distance.'

'In the town?'

'Not in this town. Nor in Le Havre.'

She saw now that he had no idea how far off course the ship had been.

'You were going to Paris?'

He answered stiffly, 'I had thought of it,' not prepared to admit that he had determined on it, planned it, like scores of other British and Americans with a taste for the unusual. For them the prospect of Paris getting ready for a siege was a promise of spectacle: the city a fortress and half a million men-at-arms manoeuvring within; barricades erected, buildings demolished; sheep and oxen in the city parks, caged beasts in the squares and encampments on the Champs-Elysées. It would be a show worth watching.

'There cannot be many people who would think of it at such a time.'

'I do not think I should like to do what many people think of.' Although the syntax proved almost too much for Bridges' French, the simplicity of the thought did convince. And amuse. Elisa watched him for a moment or two.

'You shall stay here,' she said. And it was as if she had crumpled the newspaper cutting with the Paris address in her palm and thrown it away. 'For a few more days at least.'

At which Bridges might have balked, the strings of his life

being snatched so, this way and that. But she smiled still and in a moment undid all the damage. 'No, I am serious. *Je vous prie,*' she said, her lips most slow and careful. And she began to wipe her hands on her apron. 'We shall like it very much,' her eyes cast down against all resistance. Which in any case he did not wish to make.

'Thank you,' said Bridges, but did not say how much relieved he was, having no money about him, not even a note from his banker; he had it still but it was nothing more than a limp scrap scribbled over with indecipherable blue-black runes. To say nothing of the note from his brother, which must have been loose in his pocket at the moment of his thirty-foot plunge into the Channel and had vanished altogether. It would give him time to write to his banker, his wretched brother, too, though he hated to do it, to give him the satisfaction of reiterating his stinking terms—*with the sole proviso that said funds be for exclusive use without the confines of the British Isles.* But it would have to be done. Meanwhile he could get himself some clothes if this burgher's name was good for credit. A yellow waistcoat seemed suddenly essential. Then, too, he could make some plans—which this woman assumed he had already—perhaps there might be introductions, contacts in Paris. Then, too, he could look at this woman. Again.

'You are most kind.' But she would not look up.


IN THE AFTERNOON, Elisa went back to her glasshouse to make another print of the wreck. She went to prepare the paper with a conscious effort not to think, not to articulate to herself what she was doing. She might have thought to inspect the glass again that held the negative, but she did not do it. It was when she took the paper to the shed to sensitise it, when she was standing there in the dark, that she knew what she was preparing to expose, what the man Bridges had perhaps already found on the faint original somewhere in his room. She set the paper in the frame behind the plate and took it outside, propping it up with bricks for the best angle. She was a music hall artist setting up her props, a parlour illusionist about to raise a spirit. And then what? She did not want to know what happened next. She trimmed her lamp behind the curtain in the coalshed and set the pan of hyposulphite ready to receive the image, then went inside to speak to Marguerite. They drew all the water she needed for rinsing and still it was not time to take the frame in. She passed the rest of the time setting her glasshouse in order and at last, when she looked again, she judged the image to be right. She carried the print to the shed to fix it, then took it outside again to rinse, knowing she was rushing the process because she had seen already, but would not admit to herself that she had. In her glasshouse when it was all finished she let her eyes look and look. Here was her husband and here was the man who fell. The man who was falling. He was suspended here, caught in the act. It was the last photograph she had taken, just before the ship began to respond. A few moments later the vessel was off the rock and floating again. From her position on the promontory that day she had been able to take in the whole ship from a three-quarter view. The cables to the tugs were taut. There was Paul, standing aft with his back to the sea but looking away from her, and further to the right of the picture, in the direction he was looking, was something else: a dark blur and in the centre a whiteness. There was no mistaking it. It was a human face and it was turned towards her husband.

'IT IS NOT one of your best,' said Paul Gagnon when she showed him that night.

He reached across and picked it up. 'You should take one now while she's in dry dock,' he said, and tossed it back down on the table.

'Have another look,' she said. 'There is something I don't understand.'

Paul Gagnon sighed. 'I'm tired,' he said. 'I have to go up.'

'But there is something you need to explain.'

'What?'

If only he had said, I can't. But 'What?' 'What?' was misplaced. It was the hammer that hits the thumb. She was incensed. 'You know what.' Her finger was insistent, pointing. 'You are looking right at him. The man, this man. This man is looking at you. The man who drowned.'

Paul Gagnon snatched the photograph from under the jabbing finger, his lips set tight, damming up words. After what may have been a minute, he said, 'There is no man there.' He was already getting up from his chair. 'I said it wasn't one of your best.'

FOR A FEW days the harbour continued to draw the people and then there was nothing more to watch or to watch for, nothing to surpass the pathos of the infant wrapped in kelp or the ghastly drama of the bodies of the lovers still clutching each other. The dead had almost all washed ashore in the first thirty-six hours, except for the man who fell and a young girl. The girl had been found on the beach west of the Pointe du Chèvre on the morning that the other victims were to be buried, the morning her parents had said that they would not leave until her body was found, making it seem that she rose from the deep, the dutiful daughter, to be buried with her hair still wet. The harbour was quiet again. The travellers who were determined to see out their passage on the *Lady Morgan* had taken themselves to Le Havre, where the English among them hoped to make their needs more readily understood.

Tonight Gagnon was looking forward to his dinner. He dressed quickly. He had been all day at the dry dock. The contract for repairs was sealed, the work had begun, and Marguerite, he knew, had bought two ducks to roast.

The table in the dark dining room was laid for seven. The doctor, when he had attended Bridges, had put up his hand in a dismissive gesture at the mention of a bill, and Gagnon—more readily than the doctor would have liked—had said, 'Well then, thank you. But you shall not escape dinner. When your patient is up. I'll send you a note.'

The Gagnon dinners were becoming well known. They had doubled in frequency since the feast of Saint Ursula, the day when Paul Gagnon's most private insinuations had crowded in a carriage and come home to haunt him: his own daughter, Janik, accompanied home by a sister from the convent, stupid with visions. All his whispered innuendo come to life. In so public a place. Instability . . . unpredictability . . . words that could scuttle all his efforts.

'Elisa.' he had said, thinking how wise now to engage the local families in a brassy circle of goodwill, 'I think a dinner each week is not too many.' And he doubled the number of invitations he extended, though the number of families with money were few and some guests were forced to come twice.

He had been hopeful that one or more of the young men he encouraged might begin to take his daughter seriously. To show she was not moonstruck, he insisted that she dine with them, these young men, these gauche lads in their disguise of manhood, strutting the cut of their coats, the colour. But then, seeing she was no help, the way she stared, lifted her chin sometimes as if she had heard something, or failed to, he did not encourage her; he concentrated instead on dazzling the youths himself, singly of course, confidentially, by the chimney corner, with the prospect of the wealth and prestige which would accrue to any partner— should he ever wish to take one.

But the months went by. Le Gagnant was not used to such a lack of response. It was as if these youths were afraid. Or that they sensed the pale figure burning in her room above them. His wife was not a help at all, spending her days, as only now he began to notice, out in her glasshouse (how he regretted the camera, never a gift more abused) like a mad alchemist, making pictures, and arriving at the table with blackened hands. Some of the young men, he noticed, too, were even diverted from the business in hand to dally momentarily with the technical difficulties of wet collodion.

Then he would say, 'Ah,' and fill their glasses. 'But enough of pastimes. They eat both time and money. To return to business.'

And he would outline his plans to expand the boatyard. And they did love to come, the young men. Le Gagnant fed them well, his wine was excellent, and his wife. His daughter, well one had to be careful but she showed little interest and expected (hoped for, if they only knew) none at all in return. The dinners were always a success, for the guests at least. But then the Prussian king had arranged his own diversion for the young men, and it was more than interesting to them—almost as if it was devised so that the parents could be thankful: There. Now our sons have other distractons.

In the drawing room, Alan Bridges replaced the picture in his pocket and went over to the window, trying to take his mind off the conversation that threatened to turn the sweet smell of roasting meat. Inspired by the photograph of the wreck, the doctor was telling Madame Crécy about the accident with the winch. The handle, he said, had embedded itself in the lad's skull just above the ear. Bridges, who had earlier taken a shaky walk to the quay, had already heard several accounts, with varying quantities of gore supplied to suit the listener. Madame Crécy, who seemed to have some importance within this family, seemed also to have quite an appetite in that direction.

'Someone is always hurt,' said Madame Gagnon, perhaps to diminish the drama, for hadn't there been enough? But it was all the invitation Madame Crécy needed. She knew the doctor could supply a fund of details concerning the bodies washed ashore. She was particularly interested in the lovers, the newlyweds, she called them, found in each other's arms.

'Ah,' said Escher. 'Sometimes you have to look more closely. You did not hear, I take it, that the fingers of the girl were found in the young man's mouth. Bitten off. She was, it seems, drowning him. He had been fighting for his life.'

'May I?' said Bridges and opened the glass doors onto the narrow balcony. He stepped outside. The air was cold and smelled wetly of fog coming in, but he could still see the lights down at the harbour and the erratic lamps of two carriages making their way up the hill on the other side. Like the white faces in the water that appeared and disappeared and then did not appear again. He was lucky to be alive. The woman in the great cloak had almost taken him down. But then he had grabbed a line and somehow they had reached a boat, though how they had got in he could not remember. More cooking smells wafted up to him from the street. He was decidedly, extraordinarily hungry.

'In cases like those—' the doctor was saying as Bridges came back in, and stopped, seeing the Englishman smile across the room. He turned round.

Janik Gagnon was in the doorway. She had lifted her head slightly as if to take a deep breath. The room might have been a pool of deep water.

She greeted each in turn.

The daughter, Bridges noticed, smiled less than the mother. She looked from one guest to the other as if in the presence of dangerous, unpredictable creatures.

'Mademoiselle Janik.' Doctor Escher drew up a chair for her.

'You were talking about the accident,' she said.

'Yes. All very sad.' The doctor, quite prepared to put aside discretion with the mother, judged it proper to protect the daughter and added, 'But he will be all right.'

'He's going to die.' The engulfing silences that followed her most simple remarks were always a surprise to Janik. 'God keep his soul,' she added, hoping to amend.

Elisa tonight was stirred to generosity, of a kind, towards her daughter. To be Janik in society, she thought, must be like going about with a clubbed foot. She put down the subject with more grace than she was used to showing.

'No one can know, Janik, what God has in store. Ah, there is your father.'

Who came now into his own room to his own guests with an expansive air and a clap of palms, dismissing social cripples, knocking the halt aside.

'Well. My dears.' And kissed the women, expert and unthinking: possession, fondness in the proper order. 'Madame Crécy, Frédéric, my friend. My dear doctor.' He shook his hand. 'And

my guest, *Mister* Bridges—eh? You meet the doctor under happier circumstances, I think. In fact the last time he was here I don't
believe you could be said to have "met" the doctor at all.' At which
Bridges showed his good nature and laughed obligingly.

'Well, we're ready, I think, to go in.'

Bridges, made ravenous by his long fast and the scent of the
cooking, was glad of the lack of formality as they took their
seats. But dinner proceeded at a snail's pace, helped not at all by
Marguerite's errors and spills.

'To our visitor from the sea!' They raised their glasses.

'Tell me,' said Doctor Escher, 'were you coming to France for
business or for pleasure?'

'I had hoped for both.' But Bridges could see that this was not
enough.

'You were on your way to Paris, were you not?' Elisa tried to
help him out. And satisfy her curiosity.

'Ah!' said the notary, Crécy, making some discovery of his
own. 'But only Prussians, surely, are on their way to Paris?'
Somehow smug now, as if he were making the man stumble.

'I hope not only Prussians. For the sake of Paris.'

'Of course not.' Gagnon was quick to intervene. There was the
matter of a country's honour. France knew how to conduct a war.
And besides, aligning his guest with the Prussians seemed somehow to be a slur on his own honour—or anyway his perspicacity in
bringing the foreigner into his home. Paris was in trouble, no one
could deny it. But weren't his own countrymen marching to her
relief? 'You forget General d'Aurelle,' he said. 'And what about
the *mobiles*. Look how many Bretons are marching.' Not that he
knew. 'Anyway,' as the soup arrived, 'Paris can look after herself
tonight.' For which Bridges was relieved. And not only Bridges.
Paris was getting tedious; since the Prussians had begun to close
on Paris, they talked of nothing else. There were, after all, subjects
closer to home. The leisurely pace of the meal served Le Gagnant
perfectly for the telling of his tale. How he did like to elaborate the
workings of the cables and the beams and the tackle, dragging
the ship across the Turkish carpet, balancing her, dripping, on the

buffet for all to see the angle, and setting her down, after moving the fruit, in dry triumph in the middle of the table. His ship. For by now he was the owner and the agent and the captain all at once and his manner did convince and the story engross.

Janik did not take her eyes from her father.

But the meat in Elisa's mouth was made sour by what she knew he kept back from the telling. And the man? She could not swallow her food for the words. And the man who was lost? He surfaced and surfaced again between them. And he might have been pointing.

Until at last Madame Crécy sighted him. 'But wasn't there another accident?' she said. 'A life lost?'

'Certainly there was—' Gagnon found himself interrupting his own bluff confirmation to glance involuntarily at Elisa. And she met his eye, so that his gaze was caught there, meeting hers, and it required an effort of will to free it and move on.

Still the eyes of both of them were not too quick for Bridges who saw something slip between them but could not grasp it, their mouths betraying nothing, this private wire they had between them not for strangers.

'A sorry business.' Gagnon recovered his drift. 'But these things . . .'

'And of course he may never be found,' said Doctor Escher.

Which, the notary's wife seemed to think, brought them back again to the boy, who might never recover and so was still able to provide some gratification. 'But you were there most of the day, Janik? You saw this other accident?'

'Yes, I saw. I did not stay after.'

'Janik likes to pray,' said Elisa, whose generosity had left her.

Gagnon would have liked at times to smother his wife. 'Janik retired at that time,' he said, 'as was proper.' And he might have been hastily covering an exposed limb of his daughter's, Elisa thought, the clubbed foot perhaps nosing out from under silk. But it was no use.

'I went to the church,' she said. 'But not to pray for the boy, There would have been no point.'

'It was so bad?' Madame Crécy might have slavered in her pursuit of detail.

But Bridges was after something more. It intrigued. He leaned forward. 'You said the boy would die?'

It was an indiscretion. He knew that. His hostess had quashed the subject once. But he was a foreigner. Surely he was not expected to understand everything?

The doctor, too, leaned forward; he, too, would like to know.

'Yes,' said Janik.

'You must have your reasons for saying such a thing.'

'Yes.'

'Marguerite,' Elisa Gagnon raised her voice against these guests, going further now than she would ever care to risk. 'Marguerite bring the cheese, if you will.'

But all now waited to hear.

'Yes. I heard the rush of wings. It is always a sign. And there was a shadow across the sun.'

'Auspicy,' said Crécy.

'I beg your pardon?'

'Auspicy. It is the classical art of prognostication by means of observing the flight of birds. Practised by the Romans you know.' Or was it Greeks? But anyway he was glad to show that his knowledge, like the doctor's, could soar from time to time. 'A soothsayer would survey the sky from some vantage point and watch for omens.'

Bridges sat back and ditched the vision of shock-haired ancients on promontories for one of Janik Gagnon at the cliff's edge, unearthly enough to be carried away by the wings of her own streaming hair.

'A seagull. Wouldn't that be right, doctor?' Gagnon the practical reached to fill his friend's glass, but the doctor was not so sure, sharing, as he did, the girl's prognosis.

ELISA AND JANIK retired when Monsieur and Madame Crécy left. Bridges would have liked to go to his bed, but Gagnon and the doctor wanted to hear what England thought about the war and whether England planned to toady to the Germans still and pretend to be neutral, and how long was it going to take for England to come out on the side of France and Justice? And so Bridges was compelled to turn some phrases that managed to fall short of disloyalty while still pleasing his host. But it was not easy. He used his poor French to excuse his lack of knowledge, for Bridges' interest in the subject was far from political, was, to say the least, detached. He found it interesting in the way the behaviour of animals is interesting. These French, these Germans. They would blow each other to bits. Any dunce could see it a mile away. The prospect of Paris under siege had been to Alan Bridges every bit as promising as the Great Exhibition, though he was not fool enough to say so. Instead, while Gagnon held forth on honour, he nodded sagely—and accepted all the wine that was poured for him.

UPSTAIRS, JANIK COULD not wait to ask.

'Maman? You believe me, don't you?'

She made Elisa feel tired. It seemed it was not enough for her daughter to leave the common path, to plunge off into untrodden and dangerous parts, but she must have the rest of them along with her. To tear our hands on the brambles, thought Elisa, knock our feet on the roots. To come with no warning to the edge of the precipice.

' "Believe." I don't see that it matters if I believe or anyone else. It is you who saw the angel.'

'Heard.'

'Heard, then. You know what you heard. It is not a question for me.'

'But do you believe?'

'Is it important?'

'You do, don't you? Believe me?'

'Yes. I believe what you say is as you saw, heard it. I know you don't lie to me.'

'But no one takes any notice. The doctor, if he believed me, would be with the boy now.'

'Perhaps you see too many angels.'

'I cannot believe you have never seen one.'

Janik had taken everything off. She was lifting her nightshift above her head, letting it fall. Elisa saw her own body then, as it had been. He had come up to her just there as she stood, just then, had caught it before it fell and thrown it aside. And he had stood before her in his nakedness. They had stood without touching. We are in Eden, she had said and he had stepped forward. Then, yes, Elisa thought, then I heard wings. A rush of feathers that grew louder as we fell, until it was a roar of angels calling but we fell, in a steep tunnel of wind we fell from Eden and I did not want to stop.

'Yes,' she said. 'Once. It was a long time ago.' She said good night.

In her own room she stood a long time remembering. It had never been the same. Whatever refinements or elaborations her husband invented, no wings beat about her ears again, ever. Was it necessary then to retrace a path to Eden? Do as the priests say, repent and mortify the flesh. Climb all the way up—in order to fall again magnificently into the dark?

And if Janik saw angels now, what would she see when her time came? Perhaps heaven itself would split apart. Or Janik, she had made herself so precious. No, her daughter would not marry. Elisa could see that, though her husband, she knew, was determined to make her. Paul Gagnon, boat builder, would have a son, yes. In a suit of English wool by now, and a cravat of Chinese silk, to walk with him through the yard, to stand back and take in the sheer of that one or the draught of this. To garner all the tricks and turns of making deals. To observe unobserved how to manage men and to learn through his fingers and his nose as well as his eye how to judge the trueness of the timber. Oh yes, she knew how it broke his heart to have only his shadow follow him through the yellow dust. And so he must wait for a grandchild. And meanwhile a son-in-law would do. Therefore must Janik take a husband. Janik who is keeping herself for Christ. Who has been to the door of heaven and left her name, who cries when she prays for the beggars outside the cathedral, who walks with downcast eyes because she walks in the company of angels; Janik who sleeps each night with her eyes open watching for light; Janik who bleeds each month for the sin of Eve and suffers even toothache for the pain of the world. Janik whose joy it is to pray for us sinners, now and forever.

But still he would have her married. He was determined, casting about the way he did, playing the good neighbour here, the firm friend there, to any worthy with a son on two good legs. The sons, however, were skittish as colts and would shy away. They want a wife, thought Elisa, who at the blessing on Sunday would rise and leave with dignity with all the other wives, not kneel oblivious, a soft moan on her lips. Desire and ecstasy they reserved for themselves, and kept it out of the marriage bed. No, these young men, she knew, would be happy to have to do with Janik only when she was insulated by the grey habit and the white wimple; then they could have their safe, perfumed wives take along their podgy daughters to be taught how to pray. In moderation.

And Janik? What did she want, apart from angels? How appalled the girl had been, on the night of the wreck, at her own misconstruction: to put herself to bed with a stranger. But that in itself, that shock was a signal, for the thought would not have appalled a child. Oh yes, she was awake. And yet the Englishman did not in himself seem to unsettle her daughter. She ate and drank in his presence, Elisa noticed, as if his lean face belonged on the body of just another family friend, old and affable across the table. His lean face. Elisa closed her eyes. She did not care what her daughter thought, what her daughter felt. He is beautiful, she thought. Allowed herself to think. And my body whispers to me. Sins. Which I would not wait to commit. If I were Janik.

IT WAS TWO in the morning when Tor outside began to bark at the boy who had come for the doctor.

'He's dying!' the boy said. And tried again, 'He's dying,' sounding this time less triumphant, for the men were already grave, had had time to put on gravity, having heard his steps across the yard, running, dodging the dog, his frantic breath on the other side of the door before they opened. So they looked down solemnly, and while they did not thrill to the news as the boy did, they did nevertheless feel a certain satisfaction, a certain not-unpleasant rightness in the way things behaved. It was fitting that they in their position should be thus called upon to save ships, save lives. And dinner was finished. It was a proper conclusion to an evening's talk of salvage and value and risk and commitment. It lent weight to their affairs and proved their worth in the world, and saved the dinner—that, too—from insignificance. And above all, it was not their own deaths that he came to tell.

The doctor put out his pipe, put on his heroic greatcoat, and plunged into the fog after the boy, to go and draw blood from his patient, and thereby cause his heart to stop for good.

'Well,' said Gagnon, closing the door, 'Poor lad.' And now smiling, 'We should talk again tomorrow, my friend. I think I can be of some help to you. I hope I can.' For Alan Bridges had at half past one, and after the fifth bottle of claret, revealed just how large were the funds at his disposal.

They said good night and Bridges went up to his room. Elisa heard his hollow cough and the door close behind him. Her husband, noisier, followed. She thought now, although she had been waiting for him, that she would like to be asleep. But he came over and sat down on the edge of the bed beside her to take off his boots.

'Didn't you hear all the noise?' He pushed at her shoulder.

'Yes. I heard. Is everything all right?' She turned on her back.

'Yes. Some poor wretch for Escher.' But poor wretches now could drown in pools of their own blood. When Le Gagnant had a skinful of wine inside him, a rich stranger in the next room, and a sleepy wife on her back. He pulled down the covers and touched her on the neck, one hand heavy on her breast. She closed her eyes and his mouth opened on hers. He stank of wine and smoke. She pushed him away. Although she did want.

'Come to bed,' she said, whispering because of what she meant.

He undressed and was clumsy. She did not like to look. Then, in the cold room, he pulled the covers down to her feet and got up on the bed. Like a child, she thought, to his favourite toy. He knelt astride her and she had to turn away from the pleased look he wore, obscenely pleased, surveying every line and shadow, telling her worth, his fortune, so that she had to reach up to his neck and pull him down, pressing his face into the crook of her shoulder. For still her body did long for him. But he would not be held. He was an artisan, fashioning his desire, working it. She clenched her teeth. Even in drink his hands did not forget, were making of her what he wanted, a barque for his desire, were poking and squeezing. She was being fashioned and there was no stopping it. In his throat and in his nose he expressed his satisfaction with his work. He was heavy. If she could move herself. She was stifling in flesh. She was drowning. If she could stop her eyes, her mind, from watching, her ears from listening.

In the next room, Bridges put out the lamp.

THE WORK ON the *Lady Morgan* was almost complete. Gagnon had only two men left on the job to caulk and pitch. The ship's owner, who turned out to be a Dutchman called Greev, had seen the work and was pleased.

'It should be your business, salvage,' he said. He knew best; his foreign lilt declared it.

'It may well be,' said Gagnon. 'If I can find a partner, eh?'

Bridges smiled, no longer sure of the ground on which he stood. Two weeks ago he was not much more than a waterlogged piece of jetsam without a banker's note to his name; this week, his host's prospective partner. A man of business. It did not do to pretend too much self-determination here, not at least until the ground settled. Things seemed to progress best for him when he took no hand in them at all. And so he merely smiled and inclined his head a little.

The three men took a stroll along the harbour wall. The nuggety details of remuneration, of hours and men and materials and compensation and dues, had been pursed up neatly, but not without difficulty, in the harbour master's office. Now Le Gagnant and the Dutchman could indulge themselves a little with puffy talk of net worth and steam and operations grand in scale. Bridges listened to see how it was done.

At the last turn, by the harbour office again, they stopped and inhaled noisily to indicate that matters were concluding.

'Well.'

'Well.'

'I thank you, Monsieur Gagnon, once again.'

'Not at all. I'm glad I could be of service to you. Let us hope you won't need my services again, eh?'

They shook hands. A laugh, a smile from the man who had just paid a small fortune to have his own ship back and who waved now as he left them. The Englishman could not help but admire.

'Now you and I, we have to talk some more, I think.'

For they had talked. They had walked in the boatyard and watched while Felix, the master builder, worked. Felix could not speak but coaxed seabirds out of trees. While Gagnon had expounded on the principles of displacement, somewhere in among the spicy wood, among the knees and beams and frames and posts, they had exchanged the pieces of information that mattered. They were passed between them, cold and heavy and useful as iron tools, as indisputable. You pass me that adze and here's the chisel. Paul Gagnon was looking for a partner. Alan Bridges was looking for an investment, abroad. And much more was said besides—while Felix worked in silence—as they ducked beneath a keel here, a sternpost there. Times were no longer certain, Gagnon made no secret. Who could say how long a builder of wooden ships would last? There were iron ships over in Le

Havre every day. It was time to open doors, to look to new horizons. Over the yellow planking, between the lines of measured hemp, they embroidered their theme. Such an age of opportunity, yes, for those with courage, vision. One would not want to be left standing, no, though many would be; and here they could not quite decide on the worse fate for laggards—to be left standing or to go under. Both would do, yes, a fate worse than death in this age of commercial enterprise. Oh, one could not afford to be slow, no. And they even approached the shape of the thing, treading lightly, coming in at an angle: the nature of the partnership that might be considered, the availability of the funds.

And yet. Under the piles of sawdust, behind the leaning timbers, there were things left unsaid, particular questions that Gagnon did not care to ask. For in the end these were men who were not fools, who knew that it did not always do to fill in all the gaps with details, the burrs, the hooks, that snagged things. So Bridges found he did not need to talk at all about his elder brother, about his control of the estate, about his volcanic temper and what had caused the last eruption. Certainly the word 'remittance' was never put upon the air. Nor did there seem to be a point in examining particulars such as the fact that Bridges' banker received instructions only from this human volcano, his brother.

Nor did either man at that time reveal all that was on his mind concerning matters other than the enterprise in hand.

And so the letter to the banker was sent (and another to Alfred Bridges), asking for the funds to be made ready for imminent withdrawal, all of them.

Life as far as Alan Bridges could see was, and always had been, pleasantly uncomplicated. Here was a man with a business and no money; he, on the other hand, was—or would be—a man with money and no business. It was only people like his brother who fouled the lines.

The reply came on a sailing from Portsmouth five days later. The money could be made available for immediate investment— at no less than four percent. Bridges, forced to appear hardheaded, named the figure as if it were his own.

This was enough for another walk through the wood shavings.
At which Gagnon could scuff. With his head on one side and his
eyebrows raised a little too apologetically, his clever lips pressed
together a little too regretfully. As if it were not he who had first
broached the subject of a partnership, not he who had dreamed up
the scheme out of pure cigar smoke, but Bridges; and as much as
he would have liked to accommodate him, well, he knew how
things lay. So that subtly, oh so finely, the balance between them
was adjusted and even Bridges, late of Flotsam and Jetsam with
not a serious proposal in his head, even Bridges did begin to
believe that this proposition, a proposition worth the saving and
a crime to let go, was the one thing in the world he would like to
see come off, if it were possible, and that the one thing in the world
he did not want to be was a laggard. Going under.

Gagnon stopped, flicked the edges of his jacket back, and
thrust his hands into his trouser pockets. 'I shall have to think,' he
said. Then he took Bridges by the shoulder in a gesture that
implied both comradeship and control.

'Shall we walk?'

'Why not? It's a fine morning.'

They walked out of the yard and up out of the harbour onto
the western cliffs.

'Come on,' said Gagnon. 'We'll go a little further. I'll show
you a curiosity.'

From a distance the chapel looked as if a giant wave had
hurled it to the cliff top.

'Remarkable, isn't it? Built by a fisherman's widow just before
the Revolution. It's the chapel of Saint-Christophe.'

They walked round to the lee side. 'We shall enjoy a cigar,'
said Gagnon. 'Then we shall talk.'

His cigar lit, Bridges walked to the end of the upturned boat,
found a purchase and swung onto the roof of the chapel, reaching down to help Gagnon after him.

The two men sat for a moment, inhaling. Bridges ran his hand
along the planking.

'Could be our first salvage operation,' he said. Then, blowing his smoke out sharply, 'Think what that would do for our reputation.'

Gagnon roared his approval of the vision: the two of them with donkeys and tackle, hauling the chapel downhill and into the town. He shook his head.

'Alain, my friend,' he said. 'Alain, my friend.'

And Bridges could not help but bask a little. Who had thought to be friendless for a day or two at least.

'So my friend. We make a beginning. Your banker is an agreeable man. Let us assume you, too, are open to suggestion. If you agree to the terms I shall outline, you will need a day or two more perhaps to arrange your affairs and then, if all is in order we shall draw up a contract.'

'That is reasonable. Admirable,' added Bridges, who could see that he was about to relinquish all control in the affair.

'Good then. Now I put to you my suggestion. And I put it to you, Monsieur Bridges, in my own way. I shall not attempt to be delicate, although it is a matter of some delicacy. You and I, however, are men of experience. You will not be offended. My daughter, Monsieur Bridges, Alain, as you have already observed, is of a marriageable age.'

The stirrings of panic began in Bridges' chest. Had the man been in contact with England after all? What did he know? But it was ridiculous. He lifted his hand in protest, ash blowing back into his eyes and mouth.

He spat a little. 'Monsieur Gagnon, forgive me. Far be it from me—'

But it was not what Gagnon wanted, this protestation, this disclaimer, this denial of all interest. It was precisely what he did not want and would scupper all his plans. He interrupted, laying his hand on Bridges' arm.

'Not necessary, Monsieur Bridges. One can dispense with speeches. You are, let us be frank, a man of substance. Now, while my daughter's dowry may not be large, it must, viewed as a return on your investment, awaken considerably more interest than four percent. She is, as I said, of marriageable age.' (Bridges shook his

head.) 'You are a bachelor. Nothing could be more natural . . .'
But the Englishman, he could see, was not attending, was still
brushing ash from his clothes, brushing away the possibility of
any liaison, licit or otherwise.

'Monsieur Bridges,' did he have to squawk it, like a seagull? 'I
give you my daughter.'

Bridges stopped. He made to speak and it was as if the breeze
snatched the first word from his open mouth. He turned his head
to see where it had gone. The man's daughter in lieu of interest.

'Monsieur Gagnon,' he looked down at his new French boots.
'I don't know what to say.'

Bridges jumped down and ground out his cigar with the sole
of his boot.

'Monsieur Gagnon,' he said, grinding, 'without wishing to
sound ungracious, and while I am not blind to your daughter's not
inconsiderable—' grinding on, but the phrases did begin to come,
'—charms, I can only say, presented, with so sudden a prospect,
that—' there was nothing left to grind, '—I shall have to think.'

Paul Gagnon, clambering down, thought of tennis. Phpp!
Phpp! And smiled. 'Of course, but of course you must think
about it. You must take time. I shall leave you now. I have to get
back to the yard. We shall talk some more tonight. Eh, Alain?'

And Alan Bridges, not yet recovered, nodded vigorously, raising his hand as Gagnon turned and set off towards the town.

Time. And not only to think. For Alan Bridges, if the prospect
pleased him, would have to write again to England, not, as
Gagnon might assume, to give fresh instructions to his banker,
but humbly to petition his own brother. He began to realize how
important it was that he keep certain particulars to himself. It was
clear that his host had not after all been disabused; it would be as
well for now to let matters stand as they were.

And there was the prospect itself, at which Bridges could not
help but laugh, imagining Alfred reading the letter, replacing
his teacup in the saucer to read again. Alice listening as he read
aloud. Their faces. Oh, it was rich. There was no doubt that the
carrying off of such a thing would be a rare enjoyment. But the

thing itself? The *jolie* Janik? No. In England he could have had any number as young, as pretty. They did not interest him. Life held enough pleasures without them. Besides, the *jolie* Janik was only moderately *jolie* to him. He did not like the way she moved, as if her body were in the way. When she reached for something, her arm was like a strange animal, let out of its cage for a moment. It moved as if it were not used to freedom, wobbling in the unfamiliar air. Though she did intrigue. She held her head a certain way as if she were listening, tilted back. And her eyes in their outrageous modesty provoked. Blue eyes, with long, pale lashes. Like Alice. But nevertheless. To ally oneself with a stranger's house, by means of a stranger's child. It was to lose one's independence in no uncertain manner. There would be responsibilities. A man in such a position was never free. He had seen it. And yet. And yet.

WHEN HE GOT back, Marguerite let him in. She giggled nervously and bobbed, while from upstairs came the sound of an argument. The voices of the two women were raised like hackles on the air.

'Madame!' Marguerite screeched in her eagerness to serve.

Bridges put out his hand. 'No,' he said. 'I'm going to my room.'

She opened her mouth to call again.

'No, please,' he said. 'It is not necessary.'

He tried not to listen as he went upstairs. It was Janik's voice, defiant but threatened, petulant: 'I still do not believe.'

And how cold the mother, how bleak: 'Then you must live with your nightmare. If you prefer it.'

He closed his door.

A moment later he was at the window to see which one of the women had gone out with a swish of skirts and a slamming of the front door.

Then Bridges knew certain things. He knew he was glad that it was Elisa Gagnon who remained behind. He knew he would leave his room when he heard her go down. And he would watch her eyes again when she spoke. He knew all of these things but

acknowledged none. Instead he set himself to consider Gagnon's
proposition.


ELISA BEGAN HERSELF to doubt the picture. She was sorry she
had shown the photograph to Janik. Such a small act to be so
irreversible. But she had shown it and now there was no unshow-
ing it. Only denial. And Janik all in pieces.

She was not sure why she had done it, except that the truth
might have the power to destroy some devil, and Janik had a
devil to destroy. Janik beside her, her eyes red and swollen: 'It is
this dream. I have it always. Always the same one since the wreck,
and not always at night. It comes to me when I try to pray.' And
Janik telling her the uncanny dream of her father on the upturned
boat, her father hammering at the hands of a drowning man. Elisa
had listened with the hairs rising on the back of her neck. Paul on
board the English ship, she had thought. Paul turning away.

'Why does it keep coming back?'

How like her husband, Elisa thought, to shift even his con-
science and not have to suffer. She would have turned on him if
he had been there. But still she had to hurt somebody, and said,
'Because it is true.' The brutality in her voice. She did not like it,
so that next she must offer mangled explanations—an accident,
my sweet, a drowning—that did more harm than good.

'Yes but that was an accident! An accident, Maman! It is not
the same.'

It was dangerous to go on. She had not gone so far with Paul.
But the red-eyed child was vulnerable and made it easy.

'No,' she said. 'But he might have been saved.' As if the truth
were a lion and she must throw her daughter to it, see her torn
apart. She looked. But Janik was unharmed, was waiting for more,
might have had her hand on the lion's very neck. Or might have
been challenging Elisa to join her. She was, it occurred to Elisa,
exacting some pound of flesh of her own.

And so she said it in the silence, even though she did not want
it to be true, would have preferred still to honour her husband.

'Your father saw. He might have saved him.' Thinking: There you are, Janik, my last pretensions of loyalty, if that is your price, if that is the price of truth.

But the sacrifice was for nothing. Janik did not flinch. She was invulnerable.

'No,' she said. 'I do not believe it.'

Elisa went then in search of proof and returned from the glass-house with the photograph, the irrefutable in her hand. Or perhaps it was the evidence she hoped her daughter might demolish.

Janik looked at it and looked away.

'I shall show Father,' she had said.

'I have shown him,' Elisa said.

'He will explain it.'

'He has nothing to say.'

'I don't believe it.'

'Nothing new to say. He simply says it is not true. It is a fault.' Which was almost like prompting. Perhaps she hoped that her daughter would see something she had missed, would show her no, look, he can't have seen, it wasn't possible; for of course she wanted her husband not to have seen. She, too, wanted to disbe-lieve with the conviction of faith and so exorcise the falling man, falling from the boat, from her picture, falling from his life, dis-solving in the inexorable current of time. But it was not possible; the man, the face, had leaked into her consciousness until she saw it more clearly than she had in its own moment. She saw it in every detail that was not there on the plate, the face terrorized with the certain knowledge, the eyes imploring. She looked and looked again, hoping to see her husband's head turned, his face averted, unconscious of the quick drama at the port bulwark, the disappearing act. But always his face was turned towards the falling man, even though at that instant—she knew exactly when because as she had let the shutter fall, a great shout had gone up as if in response—he gave the order to take the strain again.

How she would wrench the head around, away. Her wrists ached with the longing.

'Some kind of flaw,' she went on. But Janik was looking too closely and now Elisa was overcome with terror. 'Or a movement,' she said, but it was no use. The truth could not bear such exposure. 'A shadow, or a mark,' but every suggestion sounded weaker than the last until, 'No,' Janik had shouted, 'no,' and let the street door slam behind her.

The damage she had done, and not only to Janik. It did not matter, she realized, whether the man was there or not; she had raised a spirit of another kind and nothing now could be the same.

But perhaps that was what she had wanted. For wasn't it in the nature of truth to devastate, and hadn't she known that all along? And now Janik knew it too. And would not be able to forgive.

She picked up the photograph and went downstairs to take it back to her glasshouse.

BRIDGES EXAMINED THE wallpaper. He waited. He let his eye follow the rhythm of the pattern while his mind reproduced the sound of Elisa opening the door, closing it, going down. After what he considered a decent interval, he followed.

The drawing room was empty, the dining room too. Bridges heard a sound and went through to the kitchen. He looked into the scullery but it was only Marguerite wrestling with sheets at the mangle.

'Madame is not here,' she said.

'No,' said Bridges and wondered why she did not irritate him more. He went outside. The tripod was leaning against the wall next to the open gate. Elisa came out of her glasshouse carrying a heavy brass-bound box. Bridges met her.

'Here, let me help.'

'No. I have it, thank you.' She set the box down beside the tripod.

'You need an assistant.'

'You'll do,' she said, and went back inside the glasshouse. 'There's one more box.'

He helped her carry the developing tent out to the road and load it onto the gig.

She told him she was going to the harbour to experiment. She wanted to get it right, she said. There was a problem that she hadn't solved.

Bridges lifted the camera slowly. He watched her swing the tripod up and onto the seat. She was all movement, all purpose, making him want to slow her down. Or stop her.

'Look.' She came to help him, who was not helping her fast enough. 'There. Thank you, Monsieur Bridges.' And already she was climbing up into the gig, but she remembered suddenly and looked at him. 'But I'm sorry. You were looking for me.'

'Oh, yes. It was nothing. The, er, the inkwell is dry—' He was moving his finger in a circular sign over the palm of his hand and having to use English as well as French. 'I have to write a letter,' he said. He did not like to say it. It seemed suddenly underhand.

'Ah, yes. Marguerite.' She urged the horse forward. 'She knows where the ink is. Now I have to go. Thank you, Monsieur Bridges, for your help.' How the man strolling into her garden, handing up the boxes with his bony hands, had changed the complexion of the moment. She was no longer hurrying out but hurrying away. She snapped the reins.

'No trouble at all,' said Bridges to the crunching wheels.


WHEN ELISA REACHED the bluff overlooking the harbour, she did not unpack the camera and the boxes but sat in the gig for a long time and looked at the glitter of the sea. It did not really matter whether Paul had seen, whether Paul had turned away or not. What mattered was only that he was capable.


AN HOUR LATER Alan Bridges had written his letter and posted it. It was only asking for approval after all. The thing itself was not done, not even decided. There was room to turn round. Anything could happen.

'AH, BEFORE YOU go, Madame. Monsieur A.F. Bridges of England. Something for him. From his father.'

'I doubt it. Unless it's from the grave.'

The postmaster was never sure when Madame Gagnon was being facetious. He was conscientious in his work, pigeonholing this correspondent and that, moving them from one to the other, sometimes trading places. It was important for him to know the affairs of each—and duly to report to the others. He had heard the banter about Le Gagnant's English spy and took it seriously. Marguerite Cochard had seen the binoculars.

'Yes, look. On the back. You will find I am not in error.'

Elisa looked. Like most tedious people, the postmaster was usually right.

'I beg your pardon,' she said. She hoped Mister A.F. Bridges of England would be pleased with the resurrection, a thought she judged too taxing for the postmaster and kept to herself.

On the way home, she made excuses for Bridges; he need not have been lying. She had spoken to him at some length the day after the dinner. His father had died two years previously, he had told her. He had been a man of some means, he said, and it had left him, Bridges, in an undeniably enviable position. She had dispensed with tact. If she was in law, suddenly and without consultation, to become something—how could she say 'a mother'?—to this man, as it seemed her husband would have it (and to which possibility the man himself might even lean), then she would ask what she wished, say what she wanted. 'And you have no other family?' Though she did not mean family but wife; one had heard of stranger things. But the Englishman had laughed his easy laugh and had not been put out. 'None to speak of,' he had answered.

She went in through the side gate in the wall. Bridges was lying on his back under the apple tree as if it were summer, with his knees bent and his arms outstretched.

'Are you sleeping?'

He got up to greet her, brushing himself off.

'Resting,' he said.

She saw the basket of apples behind him, and the bits of grey-green lichen in his hair.

'After your hard labour.' She looked at the basket of apples again and thanked him.

'Oh, I have a concealed interest, Madame. Marguerite's tarts are very good.'

But this was too much like dalliance, she knew. Perhaps they both knew.

'Monsieur Bridges, I have a letter for you.' And this desire to play games.

'From England? Thank you.'

Yet she did not offer it.

'One would think you had sent it to yourself.'

He did not answer.

'It bears the same name. "Mister A.F. Bridges" from and to.' She could not without appearing rude withhold it any longer, preferring as she did, but only just, to deal with this man within the bounds of convention, on solid ground. But he smiled as he took it and did not say thank you, and the smile was not altogether appropriate, might not have been entirely out of place on the lips of a gambler clasping aces. It did provoke, so that she, since he seemed to want to loiter where the footing was uncertain, stepped resolutely closer.

'I thought you said your father was dead.'

He raised his eyebrows at this directness and nodded, still smiling, tolerating, but waiting just long enough.

'My brother,' he said at last. 'Alfred.'

'Your younger brother?'

More a conjuror than a fabricator in matters concerning the truth, Bridges was not fond of lies, preferring to let implication or omission do their work, fascinated by the way people created what suited them out of their own inferences. The result, he felt, was more illusion than falsehood, and the creators had only themselves to blame. Such a lie, however, as this question demanded was not, he had always thought, quite sporting. And so, yes, older, he had to admit and hope at the same time that her position as his hostess would restrain her from raising the next question—which was surely by now on her mind—concerning his estate. He could think of no reason why she should not raise it with her husband.

But, 'Ah,' was all she said. She said it without judgment or surprise, only a suggestion of sadness (or was that an illusion of his own?), and prepared herself to listen. Then he had no choice but to begin, though he had not known he would, not planned it, to have her standing there, patient, like that, her head slightly to one side looking, waiting, as one waits for another to remove a splinter from a finger (only a small hurt to come, surely), looking, waiting, perhaps hoping to hear something that would not disappoint.

'I'm sorry.' It did not seem quite enough. 'I did not think you needed to know. But of course you must. I'm sorry. I apply to Alfred for all my needs. It is a private arrangement and has worked well enough—though I realize your husband may not welcome it. But that is all there is to it. It is not a remittance. I merely apply to Alfred, obtain his approval, and he sends me my requirements.'

'And there are no terms?' Now, leaving all politeness, she was at the dangerous brink.

'Not as such. No.' It would have been nothing to leave the matter there and yet he wanted to go on. She still waiting, her head still tilted. 'I shall be honest with you,' knowing where his confession might lead, knowing that she might ask every question and the risk would be as deep as water and he would answer with the truth; but if she did not ask, if she proved bound by convention, then there was no risk at all, for then he would not want her.

'He does not make terms for any one request. The money is mine as soon as he approves it. But yes, there is one condition overriding all.' And now he had lost his footing altogether. 'A single stipulation.'

She waited for him to be engulfed.

'He has asked me to stay away.'

'From England? Then Monsieur Bridges you are, I think, what you say you are not.'

'No. There is no legal bond on me. Nothing. It is, as I implied, a domestic affair.' He knew what he was about to do, knew too the risk. 'I was very foolish at the time, very selfish. I had been living in the house.'

She waited.

'He thinks that I seduced his wife.'

So that now it was for her to step from the rocks and slide among the risky weed. She spoke quietly.

'And did you?' But she knew before she asked that he would say yes.

WHEN JANIK CRIED or prayed, she did not bow her head, prayer being, for her, something of a meteorological event, tears too. She did not bow down but, rather, offered herself, always in the anticipation of wings. Which now beat the air. A wind pulsed against her face. She turned her face to catch it, the sweeping of a cosmic eyelash on skin. Her own eyes closed against it. When she opened them the air was empty again, the angel had gone, but a little distance off, momentarily, was the Englishman. He was squatting in front of her on some rocks near the water's edge, his arms resting on his knees, his hands slack. And he was watching her. Then he too was gone. She rubbed her face.

'WELL!'

How Gagnon loved to rub his hands together. This was not greed, no. This was satisfaction with life all round and how it managed to his advantage. Oh, but it gave him pleasure. It was like a good line between his fingers. He could do anything with it.

'Well!' He surveyed his table and his waiting guests. 'What are we waiting for? Sit down, sit down!'

Which was easier said than done, for Gagnon was placing his daughter on his right and the English visitor on the right hand of his wife and the architecture of society was beginning to crumble.

To begin with, here was the old and venerable Clothilde Villeneuve, but she fortunately minded not at all where she sat as long as the food was plentiful and hot and the conversation loud. Since Elisa's father had died, his sister Clothilde had, with some of his estate, discovered the world, and approved. She wanted to see and, although she was almost completely deaf, hear everything. She especially liked to travel, putting up with untold discomforts in cold coaches and soot-black trains for the sake of meeting new people and seeing new sights. Gagnon drew out the chair on his left for her. Then Madame Crécy, wife of his oldest friend, was forced to fill her lungs with a large amount of air to buffer the affront. But Gagnon was quick and before the air could escape placed her farther down, on Bridges' right, where he hoped that with the attention the Englishman was about to receive she would consider it an honour. Marèchal, taking the place between Madame Crécy and Tante Clothilde, completed this side of the table. Marèchal the unfortunate, Marèchal the long-suffering, of the long jaw and lacklustre eyes who, but for his lack of substance, might just a year before have found himself in Bridges' place. Marèchal who was destined to go through life on the back of might-haves and almosts. Marèchal worked in the harbour master's office and was almost useful—or might be.

On Janik's side of the table sat the doctor on her right, and Gabrielle Girondal. Gabrielle had attended the convent with Janik. She was somewhat earnest, this girl, solid, everything about her large, capable, pleasant. She had been the darling of the nuns and liked now to go to Le Havre to work at the Seaman's Trust where her mother raised funds for distressed families. A more lively model for Janik would have been preferable. But there, her father was the harbour master and there were some significances that could not be overlooked. Frédéric Crécy, last on this side, took the place on Madame Gagnon's left.

The guests sat down, Tante Clothilde making little warbling notes of pleasure and anticipation.

'Well,' said Paul Gagnon again, glad to see the edifice still standing. 'My friends.' Such moments were almost the only sustenance one needed. He was satisfied before he began. 'I expect you have guessed the reason for this little celebration.'

And the doctor, who always found himself manipulated by this man and never knew how, and Madame Crécy and Marèchal and Tante Clothilde, who had not quite caught it but could tell when he had stopped speaking, all made their inarticulate expressions of pleasure—trusting they would like the announcement whatever it was—a noise high in the throat that was supposed to show surprise and an anticipation of delight. They were good guests, pliable, like good rope, like life.

'You will have noticed certainly that our friend the young Englishman—'

Marèchal looked down the table and thought him not so young at all, not nearly as young as he certainly.

'—is still with us.'

'Like a rain cloud,' Bridges assured, smiling.

He was relaxed, this Englishman, had no nervous edge to him at all.

'And,' Gagnon continued, 'if you look here beside me you will see the reason in the flesh.'

But Janik, intractable, would not look up, preferring to meditate privately on her father's gross insensitivity, drawing attention to her with such an expression, on such an occasion. *En chair et en os.* It was not right.

But the guests looked and dared to smile and make their knowing noises, hoping to God they had not got it wrong.

'Yes, from today, the betrothal of my daughter, my dear one, and our familiar stranger, *Mister* Bridges, is official.'

In their relief they applauded and shook hands and kissed if they were entitled. Nor was Bridges slow to take his hostess's hand and put his mouth upon the back, though he had to bend low to do it, she realizing his intent and holding back; so that Crécy, whom, it appeared, no one was moved to kiss, saw and had to question (to himself and later to his wife) the propriety, not of the kiss, which was of course in order, but of the holding back, which signalled, together with a certain inappropriate aversion of the eyes on the part of Madame Gagnon, some other not altogether felicitous thing—in the circumstances. Crécy raised his glass and proposed a toast and subtly readjusted his long-held opinion of his host's astuteness.

Now Bridges, who had finished misbehaving, could look with convincing longing on his fiancée. Yes, the wedding was set for Christmas. No, his brother could not travel, would sadly not be able to attend. Faulty French excused him lengthy explanations; he had only to enjoy the good wishes of the company, and by the time the pork arrived he was ready to propose a toast of his own.

'*À la barque noble, la Lady Morgan, et à la malchance le plus excellent, qui l'a conduit ici pour s'enfoncer sur ce qui doît être la roche la plus propice de toute France.*'

'*Bravo!*' Gagnon was charmed. '*Bien dit, Alain.*' And yet his daughter would not be moved to smile. He could tell she was about to speak. She looked regrettably sheep-like in her discomfort.

'And let us not forget the dead.'

'Amen,' said Gabrielle.

In the astonished silence Elisa took pity. Her daughter a freak. She did her best to explain.

'Yes. After all, it was not so propitious for everyone. And for those we offer our prayers, of course. And now—'

But her husband in his impatience snatched her words, '—let us enjoy this excellent roast.'

Then Elisa saw him biting at the meat, which was most tender, as if to kill it a second time and knew that he felt himself accused. And Marèchal must choose this moment to ask about her photographs.

'Yes. I made a photograph of the wreck. It was most interesting.' She almost whispered. Everything she said seemed now an insinuation. But the accusation that hovered was as much against herself and her disloyalty as against her husband.

And now Clothilde must bray. 'What is this that you are saying?'

So that she had to repeat it. 'We were talking about the wreck.'

'She has made some photographs.' Marèchal said. The stupid Marèchal who could not keep quiet.

'I beg your pardon?'

'I have made some photographs, Tante. Of the wreck.'

'Of the wreck?'

The conversation of her neighbours could not compete, and Bridges had to wonder at the sudden malignancy in the eye of his host, who stared now at his wife as at an adversary or an animal that might move at any moment against him.

'In fact,' Bridges began to say, already reaching to his inside pocket, 'I have —' when suddenly, inexplicably, Janik was up and round the table and standing by him.

'Monsieur Bridges? Alain?' Her voice was playful, was not Janik's. On an instant she was the daughter her father had wanted for years. 'Let us go and help Marguerite.'

So the photographs were forgotten by the guests at least, who laughed now, remembering love, and said *ah* and *là*, and conjured flighty noises from their throats. While Bridges wondered at the abrupt onset of affection on the part of his betrothed, and felt foolish.

He excused himself and went out with Janik. In the kitchen they passed Marguerite, who might indeed have thanked them for their help, had it been offered, struggling as she was with a heavy pan from which the hot fat streamed dangerously.

In the dining room the guests moved easily from courtship to adultery and had stories by the handful to tell. Clothilde entertained with the tale of a *charivari*, how the whole village just outside Trouville gave a farmer's widow her just deserts, seeing her courted too soon, too indecently, she still all in mourning, by a young impoverished tanner. Madame Crécy tutted but would not interrupt, waiting for the details. Clothilde happy enough to comply. How the villagers yoked the two back to back, conducted a mock marriage, the whole service backwards. How they tied the two on a mule, still back to back, drove it through the streets, the mule stopping to bray then to piss and then at last to rile and kick until they fell off in the mud. Crécy dribbled a little when he laughed.

Outside, it was cold. Janik smiled and breathed as if she had been deprived of air in the house. Bridges was waiting but she had nothing to say. All that mattered was that she was away from her father and the look in his eye that convicted him. At the mention of the photograph she had turned instinctively towards him as if to protect him from the blows her mother might be about to inflict. The expression she had seen then on his face drove her from her chair and round to Bridges. She did not want to see more. But it was too late. In the garden, in the cool air, she knew that there were no more certainties.

'You must not mind their fun.' Though he knew that that was not it.

She smiled unhappily.

'They will be sorry you left the table. They love to celebrate.' And Bridges too, who would have loved to continue drinking his wine in the warm, and had been looking forward to the roast. 'We shall have all our lives——' But he could not say it. The thought chilled. 'Come. We have not sealed the thing.' He caught her hand and pulled. Her face was turned away awkwardly. His kiss connected with her temple. It was less than satisfactory. Now she turned her face up and waited. She was as chaste as his grandmother in her coffin waiting to be pecked by all the dutiful living, and it was only her slight, almost imperceptible, shivering that did excite and save his own kiss from perfect chastity.

'I think it is not warm enough to stay,' he said. 'Let us walk after lunch. We'll leave the others and walk out towards the cliffs.'

'Yes, I'd like that.'

Though she did not say how she would like now to walk away for good and leave her parents to perish on their own particular rock.


THE PORK LOIN was succulent and there was a fine fresh cream for the compote. Marguerite was rosy with compliments, the guests were warmed with memories of courtship, and, for the moment, Madame and Monsieur had pushed the drowning man back down. Prussians were safer at table and the talk now was happily all of war. Bridges and Janik had left for their walk, taking Gabrielle since she had work to do, and so one could be frank, brutal if one pleased, though not perhaps about the English, in the circumstances.

'Well, Marèchal. It's more than a month now. What do you say? Would you care to revise your prediction?'

'A little more time that's all . . .'

'You said a month,' the doctor reminded him. ' "The siege can't last more than a month," you said, "just give them time to get organized".'

So now Marèchal was forced to suffer not only the English, who came and stole young girls from out of one's grasp, but also the stupidity of the posturing Parisiens who could not even break out of their own city. His irritation was so great that he could barely answer, but Gagnon was already holding forth.

'So what do they do? They fight instead among themselves. The Government of National Defence sits idle while its own people pelt it with abuse. Its own National Guard. It will be bullets next. No, no amount of time will save them from the Prussians,' he said, who knew everything with certainty. 'It's too late now. If there was to be a sortie, Trochu should have ordered it at once, in the first week. The whole city to pour out en masse. The Prussian line would never have held.'

The doctor agreed. 'Exactly,' he said. 'And now who has to pay the price? Who is it who has to get them out of the hole now? It's always the same. It's the Frenchman that pays for the mistakes of the Parisien. It's you and I, my friend.' Which earned him another glass of wine.

Marèchal, who had had time to recover, coughed and said, 'One could always leave them, and their precious National Guard, to stew. Who, after all, needs Paris?' and found himself suddenly clever. But not for long.

'I should say King Wilhelm,' said Elisa. 'He seems to need it quite badly.'

'I should like to say,' said Madame Crécy, 'That you are all

forgetting your own countrymen. Despatched to the defence of
the city and now themselves shut up inside to starve. Would you
abandon them, too?'

'The *mobiles*?' said Marèchal. Who would as soon forget
them, having already struggled with and defeated the idea of
risking life and limb to save such a motley collection of men, set-
tling instead—and quite comfortably until now—for the purchase of a substitute to perform his own service in the regular
army. But Crécy, in the security of his years, had no trouble at all
with the idea.

'The blood of France,' he proclaimed. 'The very lifeblood of
our country, who give of their own precious blood in her
defence. Who would not rush to their assistance?'

Elisa looked at him and wondered.

'Did you say the English?' said Tante Clothilde.

And this was even more preposterous. The languid Bridges.
Who might have leaned interested and not unsympathetic from
an upper window in a Paris street while the urchins broke the last
of the bread below. Or leaned against railings to see how
Parisiens defended themselves against the German army. She
had never mentioned his ostensible purpose in coming to
France—the advertisement for the apartment—and the outrageous admission that she had afterwards drawn from him. Nor
did she think she would.

The doctor made a small sound from his nose that might have
been contempt, but he was on his best behaviour and Gagnon
was by now well beyond observing such minutiae.

'Oh, the English! Yes!' he said. 'Let them come too! But no,
Tante Villeneuve, that is not what he said, no. Let France go to
the aid of Paris.'

'But let us finish our wine first,' said Elisa, who had not
expected to provoke such bombast. But it was too late. Before the
betrothed returned, the cups and the plates had been nosed aside
by gunboats in the Seine, Rouen had closed her gates but would
never fall, the cheeses and the pears had been stockpiled in Le
Havre—one never knew—while the sound of sabres had

replaced the spoons, and Prussian helmets had been seen to fly from heads outside the window.

Almost everyone agreed that the meal was a great success and that the pork was tender and that war was glorious. And something that Elisa said and soon forgot, something about an Englishman in Paris and the *ambulances*, the field hospitals, he was providing, stuck in the mind of at least one of the diners, who felt himself judged and saw a way to end the dismal daily round of gout and goitres.


OUTSIDE, ALAN BRIDGES was holding Janik's hand on his arm as they came back up the hill. Marriage, Janik was saying, was a state of high self-sacrifice. Bridges said he could not quite agree and stopped listening while she expounded.

'Ah! They return,' said Madame Crécy, who, looking perhaps for Prussian helmets, had caught sight of the pair.

'What wouldn't I give to hear.' Clothilde was warbling her naughty delight as heads turned to watch the pair pass by the window.

'Ah, but the secrets of lovers . . .' said the doctor.

'. . . are holier than the Temple,' said Elisa.

Though Marèchal, sour and out of temper, looked far from awed.

ICE

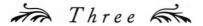 *Three*

THE WINTER OF 1870 was bitter. The cold came on as hard and unforgiving as the Prussian army. There were ice floes at the mouth of the river. The old men down at the harbour said, as they said every year, there had not been a year like it, not as long as they could remember, a cold to break stones. But this year it was true. Friends when they met would only nod, not wanting to remove the hand from the coat or open the mouth to the freezing air. There had not been such a time, they said, since '48, though perhaps they were thinking of gunfire. The rattle of guns could be heard now, coming sometimes from the other side of the river, sometimes south from the direction of Pont-Audemar. There were shortages of food, the *charcuterie* a place to bicker when you could not buy, and travel was a hazardous undertaking and sometimes not possible at all. Deep ruts from the rains had frozen solid, and carts were ships impaled on waves of ice. Still the soldiers moved, one way or another, shunting back and forth in a landscape the colour of hooves.

At first, with the Prussians closing on Paris, the war had seemed remote, someone else's business. All the reports had said Paris, like a scrawny animal in a trap, was holding on, holding out, and not about to breathe her last; the plight of Paris—endlessly fascinating considered with a glass of cider by the fire in Le Coq d'Or—was only momentarily engaging outside in the wind. But then the Prussian army, not content with Paris, had begun to press towards the coast and the people felt themselves ready. Weren't there reports of German setbacks all over France? The outcome of the war was surely in their own hands.

Gagnon gave over the administration of what little business remained at the yard to Bridges. He had seen the wretched state of the soldiers' boots and had determined that the day would go to the men who knew where the supplies were and how to move them. He was everywhere at once. Already he had made himself too useful to be put to work on the defences. Contracts with the regular army, he found, could be secured at the drop of a hat by anyone who claimed to know the port, the estuary, the tides, the seaworthiness of old cargo boats, the Seine at night, the quickest way to scuttle a barge, the easiest way to block a channel. Le Gagnant knew it all. And how it suited him to say a thing must be done or undone and to observe whole squads of men move to do it. It was more than worth his while to travel to Le Havre, where siege works continued and where, with one or two imaginative suggestions concerning bridges on an approach road, he built himself a reputation as something of a wizard in the business of sabotage. Nor did he forget certain names he collected and tucked away for future exploitation; the war after all would one day end (however many boots it took). For every act of destruction there would be rebuilding.

As for Bridges, he would have liked simply to keep his head down and look as much as possible like a Frenchman. There were those who would have him cast in the role of a Prussian spy. The idea had lately been revived—and with considerably less humour than before. Paul Gagnon was all for proving them wrong. He looked for the first opportunity and found it in a stalled shipment of what, in such crates, could only be arms. Why or how the boat had found its way to their port no one knew, but there to meet it was a Government agent who must have known in advance. He was trying without much luck to stop the captain unloading the shipment. It was bound for Le Mans but would never get through either by road or rail. The captain, he insisted, was to continue round to St. Malo, from which point the journey south would be safer. But the captain had the flexibility of mind of a British bulldog and was holding firm to his orders. Who better than Bridges to act as intermediary between this ship's captain, unable to speak a word of French, and this man of Gambetta's, a measly-looking bureaucrat disabled by what seemed like a less than rudimentary grasp of any language at all? The compliant Bridges reluctantly obliged—and damaged his reputation further. Neutrality, it seemed, was not a simple business. There were international regulations, and if this was a British boat and if Britain was neutral, then the contents of these unmarked crates were contraband; no one in the port knew exactly where they were bound; no one knew exactly what Bridges was arranging with the captain. Who knew where the crates might finally be broken open? In the end, Bridges aroused more suspicions than he allayed, suspicions that, being more specific, were this time less freely aired.

Gagnon, unaware, considered the intervention a success. He was ready for more, might command commissions now that he knew the ropes. But for Bridges, ropes of any kind were mere entanglement. He pointed out that although he had never been one for allegiances, in this instance allegiance to neutrality seemed like a perfectly good idea and he was not about to contribute to the hostilities with another boatload of guns that might or might not ever reach its proper destination (thinking, what difference did it make, they were mad these warring sides both, with their mustered spikes and spurs). His strength of expression, even without his private observations, surprised. Gagnon looked at him a second time. Well. It was not amiss. And besides, a new idea occurred. Though Bridges might balk at the idea of illicit traffic in guns, he surely could not object to shipments of food. Paris eventually, whatever the outcome of the war, must be fed. Bridges could make the necessary connections. When the time was right it would be nothing to charter the boats. They would bring shipments across from England when the siege was lifted, have them in Paris in thirty-six hours. They might do it all on a government contract if they were lucky.

Bridges let him talk. Schemes were fine if a person had the energy, though on the whole life was more peaceful without them. He preferred it when Gagnon was away.

The house was sometimes very quiet. Janik had taken to going each day to the convent where beds had been set up for the wounded. She had sat one evening at home and talked to Bridges long and seriously about her duties as a Frenchwoman. Bridges, in the face of her fire, had not been able to say that it was mad and unneccessary and anyway she was just a child, but instead had risen at five each morning to walk her to the gates. Day after colder day all through late November. To sweep around the iron feet of the empty beds and to pray. Bridges began to wonder whether they prayed there that the beds would not be filled or that they would. There was plenty of time for wondering. He and Elisa with the house to themselves, Marguerite somewhere down at the harbour, standing in a huddle of wives and daughters waiting for fish or paraffin or sausage. He liked it when they sat down to eat together, the two of them, he and Elisa. He liked it that lately they seemed to have forgotten how to make conversation, would look up from their bowls at the same time, have to smile, look away, look back the very next second, know the other would be looking. Elisa said once, laughing, we are like an old couple, you and I. And all afternoon he had wondered if her words had conjured in her head the vision they had in his: not an old couple at all.

But the Prussian army could be counted on to put paid to wondering. By December, enemy troops were at the gates of Rouen. Rouen had to be saved. She was all that stood between the advancing Prussians and their own bedroom windows. Rouen was the last bastion before the coast, and the people of the coast were the last hope for the Seine and all that part of France. They were ready, more than ready; they were straining for the

chance to march to the relief of their countrymen, nor would
they stop at Rouen.

Orders came for all detachments of the guard and every vol-
unteer contingent to mobilize at once. The army and navy gave
one another orders, sent supplies here, men there, and at last sent
ships up the river carrying heavy artillery to the beleaguered city.
Gagnon in a bar in Le Havre drank to victory. Janik in the convent stayed up all night to pray.

BRIDGES IN THE freezing dark, chopping wood for the French
soldiers inside the house, thought he had never been so cold in
his life. The ice of the last week had turned to gelid puddles and
then to ice again in the same time it had taken the French troops
to reach Rouen—and find themselves outmatched. The battle,
some said, was nothing more than covering fire for the turning
men. In a matter of days Rouen had given the order to spike the
very guns that had been brought to her relief, and the troops that
had been sent to her defence came scrambling back in a jumble of
iron and steel, broken leather and sodden canvas. Sixty-three
miles they covered in three days. Some could have said running.

As they poured through the fishing port late that afternoon on
their way back to Le Havre, staggering a little, some stumbling,
Bridges observed to himself that he was having, after all, a ring-
side seat, which was ironic considering how quickly on his
arrival he had lost interest in the war and taken instead to the
prospect of marriage. Here now was what he had come to see, the
world gone mad and the possibility of battle daily approaching
the doorstep. Now, in this freezing dark, his hands too cold
to grip the axe, Bridges had to wonder if he too was mad. Opening the door to fifteen stinking soldiers. Taking orders without
argument, they looked so wretched, from the young adjutant
who counted them off, just a lad, fifteen men to be billeted until
morning. He had stood with Elisa and watched as they disposed

themselves where they could around the fire like dogs, the lucky ones stretched stiff on beds, oblivious to the grime they left upon the bolsters. Too tired to wait for the soup that Marguerite was making. Gagnon would no doubt have procured himself an officer or two to entertain for the night, but Gagnon was still away somewhere blowing up bridges—French bridges! And Janik, in her way equally driven. His fiancée! More faithful to the convent than to him. Elisa Gagnon might be the only sane one among them, waiting for the sickness to pass. He hoped this brush with war would be enough for Janik at least. He had had enough of fervour, had been almost arrested yesterday by the fanatics down at the bar because of Janik. Demanding to know his business, more than sceptical when he said he had come from the convent. He cursed Janik then for not being there to extricate him. He had left her at the gate. She had said she would not come back as long as she was needed. And Bridges was no one to her, no one, to say no. Bridges then might not have existed. Well he existed now. Here he was chopping wood. For France. He just hoped God had given Janik some soldiers of her own to attend to. Because God knew what she would do if not.

IN THE MORNING Elisa could not bring herself to shake awake the corpses assigned her. They slept on the settle and the floor in front of the kitchen fire with their limbs all awry. They stank. They looked, she thought, as men must look after a battle, discomposed, at odds with their bodies. She had pictures of soldiers but they bore no relation to these men in the kitchen. They were portraits, taken in the summer most of them, when the first wave of young men had caught the smell of saltpetre. They were upright, their limbs aligned by expectation, every nerve awake, their eyes ready to receive the future. These men lay about with their numb bodies at impossible angles. They filled her kitchen with intimations of death. She was glad they snored. She told Marguerite to warm the soup for breakfast and went outside. It was even colder than the day before. Bridges was out at the woodpile already, collecting an armful of the wood he had split.

'You're up early,' she said. He smiled.

'*Le Monsieur* is always up early isn't he?'

'You don't have to be *le Monsieur* for me. They're all right.' She nodded towards the house.

'They look a bit rough to me.'

'No. They just stink.'

'Well. Perhaps I like being *le Monsieur*.' Though both might know *le Monsieur* would have been back inside by now with twice the amount of wood, not standing, hugging half an armful to his chest.

In the house the men were beginning to rouse. One of them came outside and made water splashily into the frozen leaves of laurel. They waited until he had finished and then went in, Elisa guilty suddenly that these were other mothers' sons and she was not there for them.


THAT MORNING THE soldiers continued on to Le Havre. Marguerite went down to the harbour to see what food she might find. The afternoon was very quiet. Elisa found the photographs and took the album with a lamp into the dining room. She was at once dissatisfied with the posed pictures. There was her picture of Émile Harmon, the bailiff's son. One of the first to enlist, he had come to her in his uniform, silly with pride and trying not to show it. He stood erect, unsmiling, wearing his soldier's tunic as if it were cloth of gold hanging from his shoulders. She had made a print for his parents and mounted it in a frame. And there was the boy Martin, Émile's cousin, for all the world as if he were in a tailor's shop for a fitting. He stood uncertainly in his brand new uniform, holding the *chassepot* out to the side like a ceremonial staff—keeping it at a distance?— and he had his head lowered and slightly forward, looking at the camera from under his eyebrows, a question in his eyes. Is this it? Is this how a soldier stands?

If she had been able to make a picture now of the men in the kitchen . . . But who would want it? Or if she could have found Émile Harmon, his body dislocated (by sleep if he was lucky) and his pride dissolved, and if she had been able to make a photograph of him so or, better, at the moment of waking, which picture would show Émile? That, or the one she had in front of her? She thought she would try to reprint the pictures in a special way. Perhaps if they were pale, like lost children, like the ghosts of memory?

She wrapped herself up in a cape and went out to the glasshouse to see if she had any albumen paper.

It unnerved her, this inkling that there might be no essence at all, only Émile at this moment, Émile at that. That the two were not the same somehow denied Harmon the boy his status as subject; it made of him merely an object played upon by circumstance. It was unnerving, to think of existing only in relation to a moment. A person could not touch, or anyway hold, another. A person could go mad thinking about it.

Only the picture of Felix was satisfactory. She had taken it later than the rest. Felix ignored the chair turned slightly sideways under him and sat instead square to the camera, upright, his legs wide apart and his feet planted firmly on the ground, his hands resting on his thighs, almost on his hips, thumbs to the outside, fingers pointing in. Elisa wanted a warrior at rest. But this warrior's eyebrows were raised slightly in amusement and his mute lips were trying not to form their unsoldierly smile beneath the thick beard.

One day in October, without any warning, he had simply hung up his apron and left the boatyard to enlist with a contingent of *franc-tireurs* making their way east into the occupied regions. At first, because he could not speak, they had not wanted him. Then he had written on a piece of paper: 'I cannot be questioned.' They gave him a *chassepot* and asked to see him shoot. He fired one shot to get the feel of the thing and then turned away from their target and severed the bowline of a boat across the harbour.

Felix who always wore rope-soled canvas slippers he made
himself had tucked his trousers into brown leather boots and had
a rifle across his back when he came to say goodbye to Elisa that
day. She had seen too that he had a knife stuck through the sash
that was his only mark of uniform. 'I could make your portrait,'
she had said, 'if you like.' And Felix, because he knew she wanted
to, had agreed, going with his good nature meekly to sit before
the camera in the glasshouse.

Elisa had fretted. Once or twice she had looked up from the
ground glass where she viewed the composition of her picture
and in desperation straightened her own shoulders, tossed her
own head the way she willed Felix to. Felix the *franc-tireur*. But
when she looked back he was still Felix, resolutely mild and
patient.

And then he had shifted his pose uneasily and put his hand on
the hilt of the knife, and Elisa thought of him in the icy wind at
night, cutting wires, cutting other people's tongues.

*Janik woke. The sound of lapping was at her door sill. She got out of
bed to go and see, but when she opened the door the sound came from
down in the street. In her bare feet she went down, carrying no lamp.
She could see. She could feel the breath of the nuns and the soldiers in
the air around her head, all the separate breaths like creatures, not
quite birds, not quite insects, entering the air, hanging there, vanish-
ing when others took their place. She reached the great doors to the
street and opened them, knowing already that the street would be
empty, the sound of water more distant.*

*Outside, it was wet and muddy. She could see where the sea had
retreated. Soon there were others with her, soldiers going the same
way. They were filthy and bedraggled, some of them were maimed
and disfigured. There was a great silence on all the crowd. They came
to a beach where their leader stood with his back to the sea, except that
there was no water. The tide was a great distance out. Behind the man*

*there was only sand—or was it mud?—as far as the eye could see. He begin an oration, a lament for the day that his country was bathed in red. They all knew they must walk out to where the sea had gone and would have but, when they stepped down from the shingle where they stood, their feet resisted. This was not sand under their feet, or if it was it was saturated with something slick, thicker than water and dark. Janik turned, saw herself turn. The sound was louder now, the sound of lapping. She saw Janik lift her nightdress. She saw herself open, flooding with blood, spilling it on the sand, emptying, the soldiers silent, watching, their wounds leaking. They would drown, all of them, in this blood. Until a man without legs dragged himself forward, to her, as she watched herself, came forward and put out his tongue to where the blood issued and began to lap.*

JANIK HAD A taste of war and it was like lamb in her mouth. With human bodies to spill their fluids and dirty the starched linens, her work at the convent descended to the most demeaning of chores. Still it was a holy duty; she might have been an acolyte preparing altar vessels, her unobtrusive gestures, her devout attention to the stinking pans.

But the injured soldiers were at the convent not much longer than the men who had passed through, and it was only two days before they were transferred to the hospital in Le Havre. Janik was desolate, infected with longing like a lover deserted. She was asked to return home until she was needed again.

Bridges said it was where she should be. He was sitting by the fire with one leg over the arm of his chair. Janik sat across from him on the settle, still in her travelling clothes. She was irritated by him, by almost everything about him, his complacency, his imperfect speech. And really he had nothing to say, seemed only to want to look, as if they could communicate like animals. It made her feel indecent. It was not civilized. More than anything she was irritated by his inaction. But then this man was English, would never be anything else. Even his hair, the way it fell without purpose over one eye, irritated her. She drank her warm brandy and left him sitting by the fire.

She lay awake at night and did not know why.

The angels stayed away. She had no visions. At the convent she had dreamed them. She had dreamed of angels struggling out of the mud at the mouth of the river, their wings dragged down with the weight of the water, mud smearing their bodies, their legs. She had dreamed an angel impossibly dead. She had tried to lick it alive.

Elisa, seeing her lamp still burning, came in to her.

'You will feel better,' Elisa said to her, 'when you are married and the waiting is over.' Thinking, what does that have to do with it, with this panic-eyed daughter awake in her bed at two in the morning with a nameless malaise? But she said it anyway, having nothing else to offer.

'I cannot.'

For a second or two Elisa took her daughter's meaning as absolute. It was an open window in a high room. Only the dizzying air outside. But she was mistaken.

'I cannot think of a wedding at this time. With this war.'

'Life must go on.'

'But not a wedding. Not at this time.'

'The banns have been read, Janik.'

'That makes no difference. It is not what I am called to do at this moment.'

Elisa looked at her daughter for a long time. How she had been shaped by the sisters, taken their words to heart where others brushed them off like dangerous sparks. She remembered a conversation they had had. Janik repeating an old nun's words, saying once in the life of every soul a challenge would come and a choice would have to be made. Saying only if the path the soul chose was the one it least wanted would that soul be true. Dangerous.

'Your head must ache with listening,' she said.

'What do you mean?'

'Are you saying you are changing your mind?'

'I don't know. But we cannot marry at Christmas, I know that.'

'We may have peace by Christmas.'

'It is not what they are saying.'

'Well then you must talk to Alain.'

'Will you? Please?'

Elisa's hands at the lamp could not release darkness quickly enough.

'No,' she said, her anger at herself so fierce now it might have been visible even in the utter dark. She squeezed her eyes shut as if that could hide it from herself: And risk losing him? And the rest of it so despicable: For me.

'No, Janik. I will not. That you have to do yourself.'


BRIDGES THE NEXT morning could not have been more sober as he listened.

'I cannot,' Janik said. 'I cannot. Not while France is suffering.'

What did she want to do? Lie down and get trampled with the rest of France? Go and fight? He could hear the sour note in his own voice but she did not even hear the words.

'Listen,' he said to her, 'if the worse comes to the worst, your safest place is at my side, as my wife.' He did not like to be brutal. Surely she understood. But she shook her head.

'There is work to be done,' she said. She might have been in the grip of a dream, or a fever. Clearly one had to be patient, repeat words gently. 'My love, there is nothing you can do.' Which seemed only to rouse her. She got hold of his hands.

'There is everything,' she said. And she did mean it. 'Everything. It would be a kind of treachery to sit by, no, not to sit by, to go about my life, our lives, as if nothing were happening.' And as if only then remembering persuasion: 'I could not devote myself to you as I should. It would not be right.' So that then he had to wonder if this was just a first convenient step on a path that led away from their marriage. This woman, this child, lived in unknown country, had a map of her own to follow and he could not read it. Perhaps she never did mean to marry. Which made her for the first time truly desirable, not for her blazing hair and pale skin that aroused in him a less than pure curiosity to see the rest of her, but because, more than anything, she might not after all be his.

When she took her hands away, the marks of her nails were still in his palms.

Drinking at Le Coq d'Or, Vavin and Courtebois had their own ideas about Bridges. Everyone when Rouen fell had expected the British to enter the war on the side, of course, of justice. But the British did not bat a supercilious eyelid; the British were unmoved—and Gladstone reaffirmed neutrality. Was that possible? Neutrality? No country could remain truly neutral, they said, in the face of such a conflict. They helped each other to another drink, they were so much in agreement. If one was not for, one was against. Wasn't that so? Certainly they had hit upon the kernel, the nut of the matter. And Courtebois, two days later, cracked it. Look, he said. No need to wonder any more why France was crawling with Englishmen. English so-called gentlemen. He unfolded a copy of *Le Havre*, and spread it on the table. ENGLISH SPIES the article was entitled, *Worms at Work on the Foundations of Civilization*. Vavin began to read. The drinkers at the next table listened. What was the meaning, the writer demanded, of the estimated eight hundred English who had entered France since war was declared? And what was the supposed intention of these eight hundred persons? To view the siege of Paris at close quarters? And here the paper reproduced an advertisement which had appeared in an August edition of *The Times* of London. The translation was printed underneath:

*Notice for the benefit of English gentlemen*
*wishing to attend the Siege of Paris.*

*Comfortable apartments, completely shell-proof;*
*rooms in the basement for impressionable persons.*

Was one, the writer asked, expected seriously to believe in the innocence of such activities? Might there not be some connection between these 'tourists' and the unnatural speed and ease of the Prussian investment last September? Had anyone, for instance, verified the credentials of the supposed estate agent? A question as academic as all the rest, since clearly verification was impossible, there being no passage in or out of Paris unless by balloon and no communication except by carrier pigeon. Vavin nevertheless paused to raise his eyebrows at its significance. The article went on to list the damning evidence of espionage: forty landmines found to be laid without firing devices, no less than thirty-four arrests of suspicious personages in the vicinity of the north-eastern semaphore station alone, three consignments of arms unaccounted for, a despatch case of maps found by *franc-tireurs* on the approach road to Versailles, headquarters of the Prussian High Command.

Vavin finished reading and pursed his lips a little. Courtebois refolded the paper, not needing, now that he had branded all itinerant Englishmen spies, to make any comment at all.

PAUL GAGNON HAD been away for several days. When he returned he found the envelope on his desk at the yard. It was marked, 'Personal and Private.'

'Look at this.' He dropped it on the table in front of Elisa. 'Left in my office. Someone without the courage to make insinuations to my face.'

Elisa opened the envelope and unfolded the page torn from *Le Havre*.

'Insinuations about British travellers.' He snatched it up again

so that he could smack at it to show his disgust. 'Saying he's a
Prussian agent. There's been talk. Harmon told me. Look!' He
spread it in front of her again. She had been sitting at the table,
comparing her prints with the ones she had made earlier in the
year. Gagnon in his indignation closed the album with a bang.

'He said he didn't know who. Scared to say who.'

Elisa read in silence.

'God knows. If I knew who it was Alain would have to challenge him, clear his name. This sort of thing going round. Dragging us all in the mud.'

Elisa felt as if a wave were approaching from a great distance.
She was going to begin to shake. She wanted to speak while her
voice could be trusted. 'It's pure malice. We know he is not a spy.
Janik knows.'

'That is not enough. You don't know the world.' He was pac-
ing now. How much easier for him if the rumour-monger could
have materialized, presented chin or nose for his fists. He shoved
one of the chairs violently into place at the table. 'And that's part
of it. You. There are ladies engaged in more productive work
than this in support of the war. You know what you said the other
day in front of Crécy? "I don't support the war".'

'I don't.' She was getting up and gathering her things from the
table, about to leave. Why stay out in a storm? He blocked her
way and got hold of her by the shoulders.

'Don't say that again. Not to me and not to anyone. Young
men out there fighting to defend you, to save you, to save Janik
from German soldiers.'

'I was only saying we could call for an armistice, before any
more suffering is caused.'

He let go of her arm but he was not listening. 'Think about
that. Do you want us to defend you or not?' And he would be out
of the room himself now. She would not have an answer worth
listening to.

'Us?'

She said it to his back. It was provocation, but didn't he

deserve it? Hadn't he known all along what she had meant about the war? She looked at him. So angry now he could be in danger of gibbering.

'You want me to pick up a rifle and go and fight?'

'Why not?'

'Because no one else is doing the work I am doing. They cannot. Go down there to headquarters and ask them who they need when it comes to moving men and arms. If they want to move one squadron even.'

Never had he felt so unjustly accused. Every time he reached the door to leave in disgust he was compelled to return on a new thought.

'Perhaps you would like the doctor too to take up a rifle?' And all this talk of guns not amiss at this particular moment when he would willingly have put his wife against a wall and pointed one at her. Now see if you can be quiet. Though she was in fact, and wisely, not saying a word.

He had his hand on the door knob again. 'Some ladies,' he said, 'accompany the troops with provisions.'

It was a terrible irrelevance and perhaps he knew it because this time he went out and closed the door.


WHEN HE HAD gone the shaking started. She opened the photograph album again and stared at the pages and tried not to think. Her eyes returned to the newspaper page. She did not have to read it again. The way the words lay in the advertisement—it was the same. She could recall the original. She did not have to go to the English paper again to try and decipher or compare. And so why then should she be unable to stop her hands from shaking? As if the envelope contained gunpowder and she held the lighted match. Or it were evidence of some outrageous crime, hers to destroy. The advertisement itself as she had first seen it on the damp newspaper cutting was no damnation. What had it become in its new context? The implication of the unknown sender had changed it utterly. Now it was without doubt, as indeed she had always suspected it would be, something to be kept hidden. Alain had never mentioned it. So now did they share a secret? It seemed to her murky as any water waiting to receive a falling man. She did not want it. She made herself look back at the photographs but did not see them. She was picturing instead a portrait of Bridges. If he were here in this collection? He would be outside, his back against a tree. It would be spring, his arms would be folded. But if she were to confront him now, or if she were to tell her husband what she knew, then everything would change, the tree lose its blossom, Bridges turn away, and this would happen for certain and all because of the words, whether or not the suspicions they aroused proved true.

The next morning, when Gagnon had left the house, Elisa took the small rectangle of the newspaper advertisement from the back of her drawer and put it in the pocket of her dress. Later, when she passed the fire, she threw it in.

IT WAS THAT same day in December when Gagnon came in with news of the smallpox in Le Havre. Terrible, he said, terrible, tearing bread and mopping up the juices from the stew. They would not believe how crowded. Half the countryside had come in. And fifty thousand troops already inside. So the thing was spreading like fire. They couldn't take over the emergency hospitals, the *ambulances*, at this stage. The Prussians were less than eight miles away. The city, he said, had taken over the whole of the old Hôtel Lion d'Or and all of the outbuildings. But there were not nearly enough beds. They didn't know what they were doing. And who was going to help?

It might have been an invitation, an exhortation. The next morning at breakfast, sitting in the brilliant light from the reflected snow outside, Janik announced her intention to go to Le Havre.

The silence that followed was not for what she was about to do but for what her parents and Bridges knew, by whatever reasoning, sound or unsound, they would not.

Bridges put down his napkin and put his hand out to hers on

the white cloth. She was quite still. You do this with the deranged, he thought, tread with care, speak softly, though Gagnon already had begun to bluster and fume, his daughter sweetly deaf.

'My darling,' Bridges said. 'You can't. You mustn't.'

'It is what I have to do.'

She was exasperating, this girl, to everyone. Her mother knew she would not be countered. She reached and brushed her daughter's face lightly with the back of her hand, and everyone knew what it meant, thinking of the skin riddled, the lips blistered. Then Bridges was driven to look inward and ask himself how he would conduct himself . . . in the event . . . It did not do to think of how the ships would sail again, after the war, of how mistakes, unlike a pock-marked skin, can so easily be shed, left on the dock side, and a person go all new to another place. Of how, in such a circumstance, even the pain of parting can be avoided. Better to think of how such an act would only be to his credit, saving Janik from finding herself unloved. Better, yes, to think of going now, before the event.

'I THINK WE should talk,' said her father afterwards in her room. It was not a conversation but a speech. Something admonitory, mainly about duty. She hardly listened, knowing, as she believed she did, where her duty lay. He spoke for a long time this man of the world, her father, who knew the lay of the land, knew the rules, the way. He spoke about reasonable expectations on a suitor's part, about fair dealings—what would be construed as such, or not, and rightly so, by the world at large—and in the same connection, almost in the same breath, he spoke about reasonable grounds for breaking a contract. Of all of which Janik understood not a word.

She got up early next morning to **prepare** herself with prayer. She would stay, she had agreed, for a few days more and leave the day after Christmas. Though anyone could see she had left already.

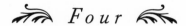 *Four*

YOU WOULD NOT think there was a war, said Marguerite, the kitchen a vision of plenty. Gagnon had seen to that.

They had walked back up the hill from Mass at Sainte-Catherine. It had not seemed safe this Christmas Eve to take the gig, the road down so steep. The cobbles were polished with ice and they had to help each other, laughing on the way back because it did not seem so dangerous going up, and perhaps because their duty was done and there was the thought of the meal, like fragrant smoke on the clear air. Elisa was careful not to slip. Bridges was careful to concern himself with Janik. When they reached the house, he held her back as Gagnon and Elisa went in. 'Don't go,' he said. 'Don't.' She drew back from him and saw the need in his eyes. It gave her a most private pleasure. This was power, this reining in of the happiness of another. This power and this pleasure could only be wrong. Without wanting to, she smiled, making Bridges think she did after all know how to play the coquette.

'No, I must,' she said. 'I have to. We talked about it,' and made to go past him in the doorway.

'Please,' he said, and held her, tired now of everything, all this pretence, wanting only to stop her and lay his mouth on hers, make her be his. She stopped, but only for a moment.

The kitchen was filled with the sweetness of apples and butter, the warm smell of chestnut soup. One had to take a breath, hanging up one's coat and wrap, one had to sigh with the foretaste of pleasure. Marguerite set to work straight away. After the soup, and while the pheasant was still cooking in the big earthen pot, she would make them an omelette with little pieces of kidney she had saved, just a taste. Then she would present her *galantine*, magnificent in its blue dish and prepared with fresh pork Monsieur had acquired she did not know where when she herself had seen none, not a scrap, for more than three weeks. He had seen that she had everything she needed. For the pheasant there was the celery ready to braise in butter, the little beetroots that she had cooked to make a salad, and afterwards there was the great stone-coloured bowl of snowy *fromage blanc* and the pears, the wonderful pears that had poached all afternoon in red wine. Who would not want to work for Madame with such a husband as she had?

Janik's eyes took it all in. As her mouth would not. Janik would have preferred to fast. But here were her parents and their mortal appetites, the table too soon a wreckage of crumbs and scrapings from the first courses. But still they were hungry for more, and her father could not wait with decency but would have them all off into the drawing room.

'Play something,' Elisa said. 'Play your father's favourite.' She took his hand. 'We will dance while Paris starves.' It was a mistake. And kick the shins, she might have said, of those who care and those who pretend to.

Janik turned round from the piano. 'I shall not,' she said.

'Then just play. Play.'

Gagnon scowled but Elisa would not be put off and he, after all, did love to dance.

And so Janik played and Paul and Elisa danced, in tune, in step, finishing in a climax of tight revolutions because the furniture was in the way. They pushed it back.

A polka next, that for Bridges could only disappoint. He took Elisa anyway, like mad galumphing peasants the two of them round the room. And then Janik played another waltz and Gagnon took back his wife, pulling her close: Look my friend, this is how true lovers dance, those who have lain together.

'Enough,' said Elisa. 'Janik must dance now. I insist. Come on. Here is Alain all ready,' she said. 'It is not sociable.' And so Janik got up and Elisa played, a tune so similar it seemed to slide into the last.

Gagnon poured more wine for everyone, pleased now, glowing.

When all the glasses were poured he turned, raising his own to drink.

'Ah, come, Alain, my friend,' he said, 'you can hold her tighter than that. She is as good as yours.' And Elisa, who had not looked, knew how they were dancing, holding close but awkward. She slipped into another waltz, simpler still. Three-quarter time. The measure that swells, fills, but never quite. The missing beat. Its possibility staving off the sorrow of the world.

Everyone was glad of Marguerite who came to say that the pheasant would be dry if they did not come.

And so they returned to the dining room and continued their meal.

Their feast. At which Janik only picked. She was tired, she said, not liking to say that her body craved nothing. Paul Gagnon, it was obvious, craved everything. He pushed the food into his mouth, his head wagging rhythmically to say it was good, yes it was very good. He opened two more bottles of wine, keeping one by him, liberal with the other, over liberal. Bridges, hungering no less perhaps, found satisfaction in a different manner, eating slowly, savouring, considering small ballets of flavour and texture on the tongue. Elisa, waiting for the next course, sat back and watched, taking pleasure in his pleasure. The mother with the hungry son?

Marguerite joined them. 'By me,' Gagnon said. 'Come here my good mistress who feeds us so well.' And she came to sit, happy, a little cowed but up to it, smiling, the master by this time jovial and loud.

'And I shall serve you.' Elisa stood up. She took the food round to their plates, serving, leaning, intimate with their needs and, losing her balance a little, sat down again to eat with them.

'No,' she said when they were finished, 'it is my duty tonight and my pleasure.' Which made Janik frown, who would have served as happily but seriously, without this hint of foolery and mockery her mother brought. Now here she was with the cheese, coming to each of them, elaborate in her solicitation, leaning, laughing and, no, it was too frivolous.

Bridges sat back in his chair and savoured her attention. But how serious his Janik. 'Here, Janik,' he said. 'I shall cut for you the finest slivers, the most delicate morsels.'

'If you were in Paris,' said Janik, 'you would only have a sliver to start with. It would be a gift.'

'Gifts! I am forgetting.' Gagnon got up clumsily, going over to the dresser and reaching up to bring down three packages.

'For you, Elisa my dear. And for my good friend and partner, my future son-in-law.' Bestowing was such pleasure. 'And for Marguerite who gives to us all year her good service. Janik, my angel, I must bring yours in.'

He stood by while they unwrapped their packages.

'You see, Alain? For when the trials of marriage are too much, eh?' And Bridges, who smoked cigars and only sometimes, obligingly put the porcelain pipe between his teeth and said, 'The true path to happiness.'

Marguerite began to make noises of her own happiness, 'Oh, Monsieur. Monsieur. Oh, I cannot. You are too generous. Oh!' With the new shawl already round her, her neck reaching for its softness.

'Paul, thank you,' said Elisa, and got up to kiss her husband for the photograph album he had given her, every page already filled: *The Seine and its Wonders*.

'You can see,' he said, turning as he went to the door, holding

out his arm with the back of his impatient hand towards the
book, 'how it should be done,' his fingers flicking.

He returned in a moment with a bulkier parcel. 'Clear this, clear this.' He waved at the clutter on the table, making Marguerite and Janik move. They snatched at the dishes, the table cloth, and in a moment the table was clear. Gagnon banged the parcel down. He cut the string with his pocket knife, pulled off the brown paper with a flourish, and yanked the end of the stuff so that the bulk of it, the whole bolt of it, the white silk, the astonishing pronouncement, rolled to the table edge. The blinding whiteness.

'For your wedding.' He kissed his daughter on the forehead. He would, he said, have bought a dress from Rouen, from Paris, if not for the war. But here was the next best thing, the best he could find. And find was the word for they had hidden this bolt in the back of the draper's. (Who would want to see it go for bandages or bed linen?) Could you blame them for jumping at his offer?

'White,' said Elisa. And it did have all the surprise of a new idea. No one knew quite what to say, how to take it. 'It will be different.'


THE SILK SEEMED to emit its own cool light. When she had thanked her father, Janik was glad to hide it away again in the brown paper and set it aside on a chair. A wedding dress in white. Her father had said it was the stylish thing in Paris. But there was something vulgar and immodest. She was to be dressed the way her mother might dress a sitter for the camera. It was not what she would have wanted. White for a novice, yes, a bride of Christ. But for a mortal marriage? To walk out in public in white, asking everyone to think of linen stained?

Gagnon, anyway, was happy, and Bridges too, who had indeed been prompted to think of linen stained.

Elisa had not tired of her game. She came in with a bottle of chartreuse, which she would not serve until the men were ready, made ready, she said. She sat them in front of the fire and drew up a small table with the glasses and the bottle. Then she knelt to take off their shoes.

'There,' she said, and was about to pour; then, 'Ah, no. But you will be too hot here by the fire. Your jackets, messieurs,' and helped them off with those too. Gagnon's eyelids were heavy. He did not look up but Bridges did and saw. Elisa was playing more than the servant. And she would not turn her gaze away from his. Janik was putting the last dishes on a tray.

'Come here,' he said, looking at Elisa, talking to Janik, 'my love. Come and sit by me.'

Janik came obediently and sat at his feet.

'Now, if everyone is settled.' Elisa filled the glasses. 'And for me,' she said, coming to the last glass. 'Just enough for a toast. To Peace. And to the wedding it will bring.'

They touched their glasses and exchanged kisses. Bridges could not make out the small noise he heard from Elisa's throat as she touched her lips to his cheek.

'I am going to bed now.' She put her glass down. And Janik, as if she knew that somehow she had been arranged, positioned like a stage prop for some obscure purpose, said, 'And I am coming.'

Bridges felt cheated. Elisa had set him up for a fall, but he was not sure at which point he had tripped.

He sat for a while longer with Gagnon who, coming out of something of a stupor, began to tell him bawdy tales but got little in return.

'Well?' said Gagnon. 'Well?'

Bridges laughed. 'You forget, sir, I do not have your status. Only a husband can frequent bordellos without damage to his reputation. You will have to wait.'

Gagnon grinned and shook his head.

'I have no tales to shock you. Yet,' said Bridges.


UPSTAIRS, JANIK WENT to her mother's room. Elisa was brushing her hair. She smiled and went on brushing.

'The white silk,' Janik said after a while, 'do you think it is proper?' Elisa did not like to say what she thought, which had to do with sacrificial virgins.

'I think it is beautiful.'

'The dark silk that you wore, your mother's own dress, that is beautiful.'

'And the white, too.'

'But not proper.'

Elisa sighed very quietly and continued to brush, wishing she could brush away this persistent daughter with her relentless worrying. 'Are you intent,' she said, 'on offending your father?'

Janik sighed and said goodnight.


AT SIX IN the morning, two days later, Janik's bag was already packed and placed by the front door. There had been fresh snow. The last flakes were still in the air. Bridges went with Janik on the ferry, a small steamer that made the run between their own port and Le Havre. For most of the crossing he stood with the other passengers crowding near the companionway where the heat from the engines beat out, carrying with it the smell of oil and brass. Janik stood apart up at the bow, her face unprotected against the cold. It might have been summer.

It did not begin to get light until they were almost across. The sky was heavy with more snow. When they disembarked at Le Havre there were no cabs. Every wheeled vehicle had been put into service one way or another. The streets were thronged. Bridges and Janik made their way on foot in the direction of the Lion d'Or, where the Poor Clares had set up the hospital. There were more soldiers in the streets than there were townspeople. The crowds were greatest wherever the streets converged, and Bridges and Janik found themselves repeatedly stepping back into the shovelled slush to keep from the wheels of the carts. The streets were awash with icy water fouled with the dung of the horses.

'You will not survive here. It's going to spread like wildfire.'

Bridges turned aside off the main thoroughfare they had been following. 'Janik. You don't have to do this. We can go back. Let me take you back.'

'As if I would.' Her face all smiling, glowing, but not with cold.

'Well at least let me find us some breakfast and we can talk about it.'

The café was noisy. They had run out of bread and were serving only chicken broth. The icy mud melting from boots was forming brown puddles under the tables and the oil heater was singeing gloves and mufflers. Janik would not talk. She only said, 'You know me better. You do,' and continued to look around.

She was a child at a party.

When Bridges had finished his soup, he folded his arms and watched her. She was listening to a conversation about engagements that were underway to the north. Hoping for battle wounds as well as pox to dress, he thought. It is like a bloodlust.

'I should like to see you safely in the hospital,' he said. 'Come on.' He had got colder sitting still, despite the number of people in the room. He wound his scarf round his neck several times.

But Janik went bare-throated in the cold, fearless, to serve, trusting perhaps in the fire of devotion to protect her body as it did her soul.

Bridges at the gate watching her go felt peculiarly unloved. She did not look back. Well, he said to himself, if this is what she must do. He was not her keeper, yet. And his resignation was useful. He had never looked again at his response to his own question: But what if . . . ? What if she contracted the disease? What if she came back disfigured? And now was not the time. It would do nothing to dispel this feeling of dishonour that had hold of him. Well.

He spent the day in cafés and in bars in the town and learned easily enough where the sailors and the militia went at nights and, more usefully, where they could not afford to go, and then as soon as it was dark he made his way there and spent the night with a woman from Marseilles.

THE FRESH SNOW disturbed again the solidity of that formidable winter. It made the icy landscape new again, laying down a thick covering of frozen light, turning everything that could still be seen and was not snow to black. Edges vanished with the redrawing of roofs and walls, and all at once permanence was undermined. Light from the ground. It was a novelty each time. Elisa, in boots and gaiters below and an indeterminate number of layers of clothing above, stood in the yard and tried to take a photograph of the plum tree, the continuity of its branches now broken with snow. But the collodion congealed in the cold and would not run off and when she tried to sight the image her own breath clouded the ground glass. Finally, when the cold in her fingers made her pinch her lips against her teeth, she gave up. Marguerite, in the glasshouse warming cans of water on the smoking stove, thanked God when she heard the clank of the tripod being folded.

'For what, Marguerite?'

'Ah, Monsieur!' She held her hand flat against her chest. 'It is not the first time. You creep like a cat.'

Bridges smiled. He stood in the doorway, his hands jammed into the deep pockets of his topcoat. He had come in through the gate that opened from the street at the back. And he had seen Elisa and her equipment up near the house. 'For what must we thank God?'

'Oh, for our good health, for the fine day. It is well always to thank God, eh? You should know. Thank God for life, no?'

Bridges went over to the stove.

'Madame is busy, then?'

'Mademoiselle Janik is safely delivered?' Marguerite was moved to ask.

Cheeky hussy were the words that sprang to Bridges mind, though he lacked the French to get them further.

And here was Elisa, carrying the camera and the tripod. She banged the snow from her boots as best she could and came inside, greeting Bridges.

'That's better.' She put down the equipment and pulled off the woollen mittens that were supposed to keep her hands warm while allowing her fingers to work. 'Feel!' Wishing she had not said it. Her hands now inside Bridges'. The servant watching. The silence. Like snow. Vast.

'You're like ice.'

She stepped away and held out her hands to the stove. Could have stuck them to the hot iron.

Marguerite asked if she might get on with her work.

'Of course,' said Elisa. 'You may as well empty the water. Perhaps when the weather is warmer we'll try again.

'I had to give in,' she said to Bridges. 'It's too cold for anything to work properly.'

'Including you.'

'I suppose. Is Janik settled?'

'I suppose.' Bridges gave a small laugh. How would he know, who had seen only the red hair melting the dark of the doorway as she disappeared inside? 'She was happy to be there, I know that.'

'Close the damper, will you?' said Elisa. 'I'm going to clear up these things and go in.'

'Where do you keep all your photographs?' said Bridges.

'In the house.'

'Would you show some more to me?'

'Oh, they are not special. But yes. If you like.' And she saw at once the picture of the man falling. If Bridges now should look and see it too? What then? At the beginning of winter the unresolved question had been a presence, a sheet of thin ice between her husband and herself, but with each day that they did not talk about it it thickened and grew cloudy. Neither of them any longer knew its depth though they could and did stand upon it in wordless confrontation and with the solid cold of it under their feet and the echoes of its creaking in their ears. Like cold through leather, the guilt of it seeped into her until it seemed that by her husband's act, or his failure to act, she was condemned, her sentence to lie beside—beneath—the guilty man, her mouth stopped by matrimony, her own inaction compounding his. For could she really bring the matter out and make it public? Her word against his? Who would take the word of a treacherous wife? Or, worse, what if they did? And anyway, did she really know?

That afternoon she sat with Bridges in the kitchen, where the light was best, with the folders and albums spread out on the table in front of them. Here were points of time illuminated, moments of experience frozen; and though she did know where she was going, Elisa put off looking at the picture of the wreck and for a while took pleasure in roaming the past, idly wandering and coming by chance on new perspectives. Bridges was more greedy. There was something tantalizing here. He could not get enough.

'No, I think these you cannot see.' She was slipping one or two back into a folder, but Bridges had seen. It was a door ajar on another life. A child sleeping, its fat limbs dimpled and braceleted, its cheek pressed against the mattress so that its lips parted. He did not have to be told that it was his future wife.

'Nor these, can he, Marguerite?' She was smiling, remembering.

Marguerite, who for some time had been standing in the doorway with her hands on her hips, waiting for her disapproval to be noted, lost patience and said, 'They're your photographs. Me, I'm going out to the butcher's.' And thought flesh.

Then all the rest of the photographs were for Bridges a blur. Who wanted only to see what was not permitted.

'And this one,' said Elisa. She was pushing a picture towards him, but he had seen it many times.

'Ah yes, the wreck.'

'It is the one you have, I believe.' She retrieved the picture from where he had pushed it slightly to one side, ready for the next, and slid it back under his hands again. 'It is not one of the best,' she said. Then, prompting, 'There are certain flaws.' How dogged, how relentless. It was not like her.

'Not to my eye,' said Bridges. 'But I wouldn't know. I didn't know much about it at the time either.' He smiled and was rueful.

So she remembered him, his hair stuck down, darkened with sweat, his throat wet, drowning in his fever, overtaken by events and washed away.

'No. It is all here, however.' In a last attempt to make him scrutinize the picture. 'Only marred in places, you see?'

But Bridges was seeing his own pictures and was not looking. He had not told and no one had asked about the things he had seen on the night the ship struck. He glanced at Elisa and in that space became for her the drowning man.

She gathered up the photographs and put them away, abandoning the idea of proof.

'So that is all,' she said. And now, because he looked vulnerable, she felt compelled to prise his fingers from the lifeline that they had found between them. 'For now. You know what my next commission will be.' And smiled, looking at him directly. 'As soon as we have peace. It cannot be far away.'

But Bridges was not about to let go. He met her gaze as steadily and would not answer, daring her to do it, to raise the subject, if that was what she really wanted.

So she was forced to persist in the heartless act, or seem foolish. Or acknowledge. She chose in her most polite language to be brutal.

'Janik has asked me, providing you have no objections, to make a wedding portrait. When the time comes.' Watching him slip from the line. He was gone.

'You would honour us,' he said.

THE GIRL HAD been very quiet in her work. Mother Marie-Leopold had at first been pleased with her. The victims had been coming daily in greater numbers; the sisters had had to lay down extra pallets in the hallways. There were more sick than they could ever attend without help. Some of the Ursulines had come over, but it was not enough. The Prussian sub-prefect had given permission for two sisters from Rouen to travel down, but there had been a delay and it was assumed they were held up somewhere along the way. At the convent of Mount Calvary in Le Havre, the sisters added them to their growing list of intentions at daily Mass and got on as best they could. And meanwhile the girl had arrived. What was one to do? If someone came knocking, who was Mother Marie-Leopold to turn her away? She had only done what she thought was right. And it had been right. The girl had worked hard. She was committed, not afraid of dirtying her hands. There were some in their own community who were more scared. It was shameful to see. There was Sister Thérèse, always at the sink, scrubbing and scrubbing at her hands and her nails, as if that could make any difference. If the Lord wanted to touch her with the sickness, it was in His power, as it was to heal. Who were they to try and alter the course of His will? Better to help these poor souls in their agony. And how they cried out! Dear God! It was as well to sleep with batting in your ears, or be prepared to get no sleep at all. But this strong carrot-haired girl, she had seemed able to take anything. She had seen her herself, sitting up with the dying, holding their blistered hands, her lips moving in prayer. Or at least she had thought it was prayer until Sister Bartholomeo had told her. The girl wasn't praying at all, she was upsetting the patients. It was hard to believe. The girl was devoted to her work. Sister Bartholomeo said the girl was preaching sedition, but what sense did that make? To dying men? To women and children? (And besides, how could she care when the bedpans were overflowing and all the linen dirty?) But then yesterday, just as she, Mother Marie-Leopold, was on her way through the refectory where more beds had been set up, a woman, one of the worst of the cases, clutched at her habit as she went by the bed. 'Don't let that red one sit with me,' the woman said. Her eyes intense under the swollen lids. And so last night she had decided to see for herself, had waited until the girl's soft steps had passed her door.

*They were the same soldiers who had walked out towards the sea. They held their arms slackly at their sides, the palms turned up in a gesture of helplessness. They were milling, lost. A voice was saying, 'If you are sick, if you are hungry . . .' There appeared the great doors of a palace and they were opened by footmen. 'If you are tired . . .' Janik at the top of the steps knelt with a basin in her hands. She washed the feet of the soldiers as they went in. They smiled down at her. Their spittle fell on her hands.*

*Inside was a great hall with long tables on each side forming a rectangle. There was a throne at the head table. The men came in and went to the empty chairs. They stood behind their places like children. Some of them were shaking. A figure in purple vestments came to sit at the throne. The footmen appeared bearing silver trays with covers. The throned figure held up a medal like a host and the footmen said 'Lamb of God. We are the lambs of God.' The men sat down. The footmen removed the covers and the bones clattered onto the plates. They were the bones of human hands and feet. The men picked them up and began to gnaw.*

JANIK GOT UP and did not put on her wrap. She walked quietly down the passage past the doors of the sleeping nuns. She went to the refectory. Sister Bartholomeo was asleep in her chair by the door, too exhausted to wake for the man who was calling out to her. Janik walked by her and went to the first bed. She knelt down.

'These are the sins of the kings and queens,' she began, 'of emperors and conquerors,' touching each sore, each blister. She moved on, uncovered a face so that her fingers could find all the eruptions, 'the sins of the generals and the bishops and the prefects. The sins of the deputies and the priests. The sins of your fathers. You suffer for them that they may be untouched.'

All the way down the ward she moved, ignoring the pleas for water or for help, reciting her litany of unrest. Mother Marie-Leopold stood and waited at the foot of the last bed. She said her name. The girl looked through her. She might have been blind.

IT WAS A pity. It was a great pity to lose such a good worker. But really she had no choice. She called the girl to her office. Janik came, dishevelled, drying her hands on her apron.

'Thank you, Mademoiselle,' said Mother Marie-Leopold. 'Your services have been warmly appreciated. May God reward you in His kingdom.' It was the best way, she thought, not to enter debate. Though the girl thought otherwise. But there were several phrases she could use yet: May God go with you; Let us accept His will; Your valise is at the door. But the protests and the questions were relentless. And it looked as if tears were threatening. Mother Marie-Leopold began to clean the nib of her pen.

Janik left with two of the sisters accompanying her to the ferry. She could not imagine what she had or had not done.

BRIDGES HAD BEEN very peaceful in La Madonne. It was steamy and noisy and he felt pleasantly anonymous. It was almost the end of January. The fierce cold had returned but without the menace of the earlier winter; it had thawed once and would again. Gagnon had gone up to Rouen and would not be back for two days. Nothing seemed so urgent any more. There was a sense of possibility, of space. The armistice had been signed. Janik would return from Le Havre in due course. But meanwhile. From his seat by the window he could see where the road from the harbour climbed the cliff on the western side. Where Elisa would walk. Every morning she walked to get warm, first putting on her wraps, a bonnet, a scarf, a hooded cloak.

'I have to,' she had said to him that morning. 'Even a fire is no use until I have walked.' She had looked straight at him. 'Sometimes,' she said, 'I walk as far as the sailor's chapel. Saint-Christophe.' Her gaze unwavering. 'I shall walk there today.'

There was plenty of time to decide if he would follow. He picked up his newspaper, a copy of *The Times*, given to him by the captain of a small English steamer that had brought over a consignment of food destined for Paris. Gagnon had now more than he could handle in the way of contracts and consignments, and Bridges had been left to conclude the business, getting the shipment unloaded and sent on its way. As always, Gagnon was one step ahead of everyone else. Small prepaid consignments in small chartered boats were the thing, he had said, even as early as Christmas. The war could not go on. Paris would have to be fed. The difficulty, Bridges had suggested, might come with the collection of monies at the other end but Gagnon, shrewd as ever, had made allowances. Who would have ready cash, he reasoned, at such a time? Those who demanded it were going to be disappointed. All Le Gagnant asked in return for his part in the revictualling was a promissory note—at small interest, to be redeemed in six months time. Bridges was more than happy to have Gagnon in hot pursuit of more.

He shook out the paper. It was several days old and the news was stale. The main French news was all of General Trochu's failed sortie the week before. According to *The Times*, the carnage at Buzenval had been beyond anything portrayed in the French newspapers. It had been a kind of massacre, brought about by disorderly, blundering ineptitude and even drunkenness. The Paris National Guard, it said, had been in disarray from the start; should not, the correspondent implied, have been deployed at all, poorly trained and suffering as the guardsmen were from all the strictures of the siege. The account was followed by a report from a correspondent with one of the American *ambulances* in the field. The descriptions left little to the imagination. Bridges was not as hungry as he might have been and ordered coffee. He turned his attention to other news, stepping word by strange-familiar word back towards England, across the news of suspicious dentists and arguments about the cost of new canals and on into the list of guests at a Gloucestershire hunt ball.

And suddenly there were foreign voices round him, a throaty, burred language knocking at his ears as if an invading army had

surged up the gravel drive in Cheltenham and into the blue and
white ballroom.

He looked up from his paper and saw two *mobiles*, Bretons by
their uniform, trying to make themselves understood by the
*patron*. An older man got up and went over, greeted them as if
they were old friends, clasped, kissed, and began to act as their
interpreter. He sat down at their table and began to talk with
them in their own language. In a little while he was summoning a
bottle of calvados and calling his friend over from the other table.
Soon there were others.

The regular, who had assumed the role of host to them,
relayed their story in bits and pieces to his friend, and before long
to the room.

They were in Paris on the twenty-second, he said. They were
right there in the thick of it, detailed to guard the Hôtel de Ville
when the trouble began. They knew it was coming. Something
had to snap after Buzenval. The signs had been there for days
before: the trouble in the streets, the National Guard acting like
thugs, setting on anyone dressed more than half-decently, drinking, too, more than they could handle, marching on government
buildings, demanding this, demanding that. When the sortie came
they weren't fit, half of them, to go out. But then the worst thing.
The quiet when they came back. A quiet like the grave, terrible.
Like dead men marching. The *mobile*, who might have made a living on the stage if he had been inclined, paused and took a long
drink while they waited for the outcome. He said everyone in his
detachment at the Hôtel de Ville was expecting trouble. Two men
were detailed for every window on every side. Two dozen men
were in the entrance hall alone. When the mob finally came, they
were ready. He refilled his glass, drank half and filled it again, fired
with the remembered glory. They had not been defending the
Hôtel de Ville. They had not been defending the Government,
nor Paris. They had been defending France. It was a vast mob,
armed. The leaders wore red sashes. 'Traitors,' he said. 'It was
disgusting, a whole battalion of the Guard turning their weapons
on us. There were women mixed up in it too. They were the worst,

got up in men's uniforms, one of them with a red sash, yelling at the others to shoot to kill. No negotiating with armed lunatics like that.' He shook his head and drank again. 'No question about it—You could see them taking aim. They were after blood, especially the mad woman. Got it, too. One of our men was still outside and they cut him down, right there against the wall. That was it. Every man fired at once. You'd think the building had exploded. You could look down on the square and it was like watching a pot of porridge boiling over.'

But though this audience was well-primed with his portraits of semi-lunatics and armed barbarians, it seemed to the speaker that they might need a few more prompts towards a more positive response, for they were uncomfortably quiet. Thinking of their fellow countrymen both firing and fired upon: his companion sensed it.

'Reds,' he said. 'The whole damned lot of them. It won't be the Prussians who bring the country down. It will be these damned communisticals. So we fired on them. Well, long live France.'

And he was effective, because now the embarrassed silence broke into murmurs of approval. Certainly. These men were heroes in this war that had not supplied enough. To put down a Red revolution. It was not nothing. Yes, and the threat was real, constant. It was men like these the country needed, and would that all men were as courageous.

So that now these young men, looking more like Basques than Frenchmen, felt themselves fearsome, and the first began to tell the thing (and the whole room listened) that until that moment had only shaken him, sliding into a corner of his mind where he did not want to look at it again but did, constantly: how he had seen one of the leaders kneeling, how he had aimed straight for the centre of his chest and would have shot him dead through the heart, but how the man at that instant had settled lower so that the bullet took off his *képi* and with it half his skull and something bubbled out as the man, on his back now, hit the stones.

Bridges got up and picked up his paper. He could hear them laughing behind him.

'He says,' the translator was also laughing, 'it looked like what he said before: "Porridge".'

Elisa was lighting the last row of candles when the chapel door opened and Bridges came in. 'Ah,' she said. Bridges said nothing but came to stand by her. She finished lighting the candles.

'What are you doing?' said Bridges.

'The pictures are interesting. Have you seen?' There were the Stations of the Cross, primitive, like a child's representation. She took a candle and led him over to the sixth: Christ turning his face to Veronica. 'They give me ideas for portraits. But some of them,' she said, 'are not well executed.' She crossed the church again and stood in front of another. 'In the twelfth, for instance, the agony is not achieved. It might be ecstasy.' She looked at Bridges then back at the painting and then at Bridges again. Both of them wishing they could take their eyes from the other.

'The armistice is signed,' Bridges said.

'Then the candles are for thanks.'

'That?'

'That the war is ending. That Janik and Paul will be home again.' She looked back at the painting. 'That we shall be saved.'

'You told me to come here.'

She walked away towards the door. 'I wanted to see. I had to know.'

'You knew already.'

She shook her head.

'Yes you knew.' Making her turn round, making her look at him.

She leaned back against the door and closed her eyes. Bridges held her wrists.

'It is a crucifixion,' she said.

They made their ways back separately, Bridges waiting, smoking, with his back against the hull of the chapel and then taking the road back down to the harbour, Elisa cutting across the top of the cliff to meet the road that came down through the valley.

She was barely in the house, her face still burning with the cold when Janik arrived at the door.

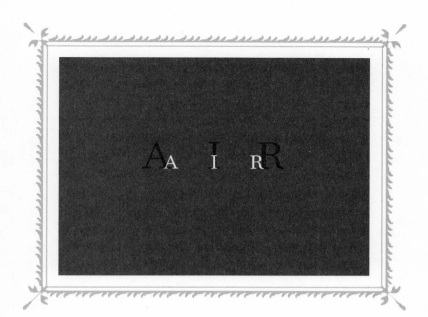

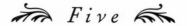 *Five*

THE WHITE SILK billowed above the reaching arms of the women. Janik stood, patient, as it bloomed about her head and fell.

'Ah, Madame, Madame,' said Marguerite.

But Elisa would not be drawn. 'Do it up,' she said, and Janik the obedient turned for Marguerite's thick fingers to push the tight buds of satin through the long line of buttonholes.

'Monsieur will fall in love a second time.' Though it was Paul Gagnon she meant. It was Paul Gagnon who had decreed this whiteness. 'A bride becomes an angel in such a dress.'

'The bodice is too tight,' Elisa said. 'Here.' She pinched at it. 'You will have to let it out. And here.' She had difficulty reconciling angels with brides. Her own wedding so much a matter of earth and blood, the clumsy slide from the foot of the bed to the floor, flowers and coloured ribbons, the wedding gown, her mother's, crumpled beneath them, the black silk always afterwards showing a mark like rust on the sleeve. She had worn a red Kashmir shawl with a pattern of green and gold. Paul approving her as if she had been a suit to be tried on. You are a fine woman, Elisa. I knew you would be. He covered her with the shawl when he got up. The flowers sticky in her hair.

They slid the silk from Janik's back, Janik bowing and bending to ease herself out, and Marguerite lifted the dress once to toss out the wrinkles so that it billowed again briefly before it settled on the carpet beside the scissors.

Janik submitted to the attentions and took the fittings with patience, tolerating even the clumsy innuendo when Marguerite reached the waist and could not resist. Or perhaps she did not notice. Maternity was furthest from her thoughts. The matter of begetting was an abstract, a distant thing (and so, it must be said, was Bridges) that had little to do with the sacrament of marriage. She was about to enter the sanctified state of Matrimony. Was there a hierarchy of sacraments? She would not believe it. If she could not enter Holy Orders she would enter Holy Matrimony with equal devotion. Nothing could keep her from Christ. He was leading her, she could see now, not where she wished to go but where she must. It was part of the plan. Even her father's fall from grace was part of it, teaching her the unconditional nature of obedience, that she must obey him now as before, accept his will now just as before, love him even, and she would, she would love him and she would love this gift of his, this husband pulled from the sea, this waterlogged and, she did suspect, godless man. Her sacrifice could only heighten the workings of Grace. In the evenings she prepared herself with prayer, scouring her soul. It was the alchemist's flask. It would, she felt sure, convert lust to grace at the first breath of desire and reveal the true holiness of Matrimony—to both of them, she hoped.

Bridges, on the other hand, was not in the habit of praying. In his room at night he clipped his nails and considered how he had allowed first Alfred and now this stranger, this father-in-law-to-be, to tie his hands. And he considered if he even minded. The loss of his freedom was a fact and must eventually be faced. But not now. He was a cat shut in the dairy and would take with pleasure from all the pans upon the shelf.

COURTEBOIS SAT BACK while Gagnon and Crécy talked. Crécy's office was slowly filling with cigar smoke.

'Armistice,' Crécy was saying, 'is merely the honourable name for it.'

'Come on, man. Be practical. If you had been shut in Paris these last few months losing business, if you had property there and had to sit in the cellar while Prussian shells broke your walls overhead, what would you want?'

'Oh, I'm only saying there is another word for it.'

'Capitulation. That's what you're saying. Well you know who else is using the word? The mob in the street, that's who, the riff-raff that brought us to it.'

'I'm not saying—'

'Yes you are. You're saying the Government has capitulated, when in fact it had no choice, when in fact the job was done for it by the National Guard when they got themselves defeated at Buzenval. The National Guard! The same whose no-good friends were out in the streets afterwards calling it capitulation. You want someone to blame, you look at the streets of Paris. You look at the streets of Belleville if you want blame. They're the ones who backed us into this corner. You were in the bar last night. You told me those stories going round. It's the insurgents in Paris with their riots and their lunatic agenda. They're the ones to blame. Where were they when they should have been supporting their Government? Brawling in the streets. They left the Government no choice. They're the ones who forced it on us—not the Prussians.'

Crécy, who had hoped to dazzle with semantics, cast about for a way to redeem himself. He had always found detachment useful with its presumption of superiority, founded or not.

'You'll have a seizure one of these days,' he said.

'I'm telling you . . . '

'No, please. Don't tell me. I agree with you. Fully. This was an armistice that had to be made, and was made, with honour. I just hope the new Government knows what people are calling it. That's all.'

'Well.' Strange how gaining agreement was never quite what one wanted, no one left to spar with. Gagnon looked into his glass. 'Well. You and I will call it what we like—' it being too trivial, after all, for his attention '—at least we'll be able to do business again.'

Crécy's doubts persisted despite what he had said, but who would want to draw another barrage this morning? The outcome of their arguments, he noticed, depended on the time of day. Did Gagnon perform better with a drink inside him, or did he himself do worse? He was surprised too at the robustness of Gagnon's defence of the Government. Gagnon, who had been the most bombastic of them all a couple of months ago, who sounded bombastic still, even when he was defending this caving in (yes, that was what he, Crécy, called it, but in private now). But then Gagnon in a tight corner always was a pragmatist. When the inevitable came, wasn't he always the first to climb over the barricades and do business?

'Isn't that right, Courtebois? Business resumed.'

'Bloody Reds,' said Courtebois. 'You won't get any business done at all until the bloody Reds are dealt with.' Courtebois had his own ideas on honour and glory and felt that he could gladly kill to prove it now that the enemy no longer wore a shining Prussian breastplate but a worker's dirty blouson with a red sash round his waist.

Both the other men paused. Eleven in the morning was early for blood.

'It's what we're up against over there,' said Courtebois, justifying, indicating with his head the window, by which he hoped to imply the docks and the entire situation over at Le Havre.

Crécy and Gagnon could not agree that insurgents were the trouble over there. There were difficulties, to be sure. Whole shipments of food bound for the starving in Paris were still sitting in the holds of American and British vessels in the harbour. It was the fault of the authorities. The men to unload them could not be found or at least could not be hired without dispute, haggling over the means of payment, wanting cash on the spot,

which no one was prepared to give—not for Parisiens anyway.
And so the food was beginning to rot in the damp holds while the
authorities in the fuggy offices quibbled—and while men like
Gagnon glimpsed still more opportunities too good to miss. He
already had several of his own shipments successfully unloaded
and sent on their way in boats small enough to negotiate the
choked river. Now with the cooperation of the harbour master
and of Courtebois, the shipping merchant who would come in
with him, he proposed bringing at least two of the foreign ships
across the Seine to their own port. Commission from the owners,
who would the sooner have their ships back in service, and from
the French Government, which would be saved the embarrass-
ment and expense of dumping rotten food, would not be difficult
to exact. Success would only mean more contracts.

Courtebois was happy with the plan, except the part that
included Alan Bridges. The English were as bad as the treason-
able Reds, were in fact, it was obvious to anyone who cared to
look, in cahoots. Where, again (the question could not be asked
too often), was the headquarters of the *International*? In London,
where else? Case closed. Yes the English were certainly as bad as
the filthy revolutionaries, themselves ten times worse than
Prussians—who after all were leaving. Yet here they were with
an Englishman in their midst, and Gagnon—never quite conven-
tional—about to take him into his family and, what was worse,
into his most vital affairs. He had listened to Gagnon's rationale:
Bridges would be useful; in negotiations with British shipping
agents he would be skilled enough to close a sensible deal. As
long as he wasn't involved at the other end, was Courtebois' private codicil. That would be too much: feeding the insurgents of
Paris. It was with them, he felt sure, that Bridges' sympathies lay.
He had heard about him in La Madonne the other day. When the
*mobile* had started talking about blowing out the insurgent's
brains, Bridges, so Vavin reported, had got up and walked out.

'And what does your *Englishman* think about the armistice?'
Even the idea of Bridges gave Courtebois' voice an edge.

'*My* Englishman? My daughter's Englishman soon. My

Englishman is not a political creature. Ask him what he thinks of the coming elections and he'll ask you who the candidates are.' Which made everyone feel clever enough to forget Bridges and turn their attention back to their current pastime of predicting the outcome of the election. Thiers was the man. Never mind his list for peace. Thiers was the outright winner and altogether the best man (bearing in mind the paltry abilities of the others), in fact the only man (given that there were none as able as themselves in the running) for the job.

*All night the cathedral fell, the stones tumbling, turning like leaves, towards the earth, shaking bishops from their perches, undermining the stability of saints. The stone angels from the corners flung down their trumpets and flew about in gritty consternation, chipping their wings on the descending masonry. Janik tripped on broken stones, ducked and ran again. Between the stacked grey granite of the high houses the streets were narrower than she had ever known them and more tortuous. The walled city had become a maze and it was in motion, the cobbles grinding like teeth underfoot, cornerstones shifting as streets redirected their paths to collide with grating thunder, or veer again in a flash flood of rock back towards the cathedral, which continued to fall. Cowed by the rumbling of destruction and too exhausted to run again, Janik crouched in the rubble. Under a shower of slates the gargoyles howled their pleasure at a descending archdeacon, who fell horizontally with perfect composure, falling asleep. Above, on a buttress, the great griffin screeched and Janik shook. Undreamlike angels hazardous as brickbats battered the dusty air above her head. Janik prayed to be crushed quickly. She covered her head. When she looked up again there was silence. The cathedral was gone and Bridges was standing in the emptiness, his legs and boots grey with dust, small bits of rubble and shards of coloured glass around his feet, and, Janik could see, behind him in the distance, the*

THE AIR WAS riotous with wind. Elisa had lain awake most of the night listening. As soon as it was light she drove the photographic equipment up to the churchyard, she and Marguerite like grave-robbers in the early dawn, the pine box between them, the tripod clanking. Janik had asked to be married in the sailors' chapel above the town—not the eccentric overturned hull on the western hill, that was more than she dared to suggest, but the venerable Norman church that looked down on the harbour. It was not what her father had wanted. A daughter of his deserved prominence; Sainte-Catherine in the centre of the town was fitting. Until he remembered her collapse at the convent. Perhaps it would be as well if the wedding were private, close. If necessary, if all went well, he could instruct Felix to make a detour on the way back to the house, to go down and along the harbour and up again. For all to see.

At the church, the grass was wet and littered with bits of twig, but the rain had stopped. The priest would not have the stuff within a yard of the porch. The women left it there under a tree and went back to the house. Elisa went first to her daughter's bedroom, while Marguerite began to draw off the water that had been heating on the range.

'Janik.'

Janik when she slept flung out her legs and arms in disarray, sometimes engaged the pillow with her teeth. Daily, on waking, she would be astonished at the abandon of her nights and would rearrange her limbs at once.

'Janik, you are a bride today.' But Janik, unbridelike, grunted. Elisa shook her shoulder.

'You cannot sleep any longer.' She did not like waking her,

resisted it for its implications of lambs and altars. 'You cannot sleep. Not today.'

And Janik at last remembered, waking, gathering her limbs, brushing her hands over her face, taking away the dirt of a wild place. 'Marguerite has heated water for you. We shall not have long.' She bent to kiss her as she sat up, She smelled like a child still. 'I'll come back when you're ready.' She stepped aside at the door to let Marguerite through with another kettle of steaming water for her bath. 'And there is rose water,' she said, turning, smiling in the pain of it, afraid too of the dangerous innocence. The dried and powdered Janik would be safer, in her perfumed petticoats. Elisa went to give orders to the two schoolgirls who had come to lend help in the kitchen, and in a little while Gabrielle, too, arrived. When she felt brave enough, Elisa went up again, taking with her the lumpy bridesmaid who, with the fat hands of a baker, twisted and knotted the fierce hair. And the solemn Janik in quiet submitted.

Elisa and Gabrielle stood back to view their work.

'I am not quite ready.' Janik picked up a small crucifix on a gold chain, kissed the cold ivory feet of the dead Christ and passed the chain around her neck. Elisa fastened it and thought of blood. She kissed her daughter on the cheek. 'I must go now,' she said. 'The doctor and Tante Clothilde will be here and I am not quite ready. You must stay here until we are gone. I shall need a little time to arrange everything.'

She went to her room. Paul was tying his cravat. 'Elisa,' he said, putting out his hands. A compliment for himself would have been welcome but he said, 'You look magnificent.'

Elisa confronted her reflection in the door of the armoire.

'Are you happy?'

'Of course.' She tugged at her jacket, discontent. It was not clear whether she was thinking of her dress or of the day.

'That's all that matters. As long as everyone is happy.' And Paul went out, perhaps to enforce it.

When he had gone, Elisa stood for a moment in front of the

mirror without moving. The dark, wine-coloured dress, the velvet jacket. Paul had arranged for her to have it made years ago in Paris. She did not wear it often. Madame Gagnon, mother of Janik. She heard the doctor arrive, Clothilde's loud voice, but she did not move. At last, when she had looked long enough, she opened the wardrobe door and reached to the back of the high shelf, past wraps and collars until she found her Kashmir shawl. She slipped the blaze of colours across her shoulders and went downstairs.

The day was wild and bright, dashed with white for this wedding, the white clouds scudding, the ribbons on the trap fluttering, struggling to come untied. And how constant the smile of Paul in his satisfaction, who saw his plans finally taking shape, his unnatural daughter made acceptable this day. He settled Marguerite and Gabrielle in the doctor's barouche, and Elisa climbed in to sit next to Clothilde. His conviviality gusted after them as they bowled away. Paul waited by the trap for his daughter to come down. He ran his hand over the shining leather of the seat, pleased with the way the sun glanced from the polished surface and the brass bindings.

'You have done a good job. Thank you.' He nodded his approval to Felix who stood at the horse's head, an anchor for it in the wind, though its side did ripple and its mane lift. The carpenter had reappeared two days before. He had gone straight to the boatyard and set to work, lighting the stove so that he could warm a pot of varnish. Unhurt, he was nevertheless subtly changed by his months away. He was, if it could be possible, deeper in his deafness, and his eyes when he blinked were slow, as if they would stay closed.

Felix smiled his acknowledgment and lifted his eyebrows without commitment; his labour on the trap had been an act of friendship not of service, but he did not try to explain, would not have, even with speech, Monsieur Gagnon, as he was, closed in his own state of deafness, stuffed to the ears with satisfaction. For here now came his newly natural daughter, stepping from the house into the bluster of bright air, her veil pluming upward, tugging at the red hair, her dress billowing to carry her to her decreed destiny.

The bay Felix was holding skittered, almost shied at the whiteness of the apparition that was about to mount the step behind. Paul Gagnon handed his daughter up and took his place beside her.

ALAN BRIDGES THAT morning was riding in from Trouville, where he had had business with Tante Clothilde to attend to. Tante Clothilde herself lived in the town, but she had a number of small parcels of land in the vicinity and it was one of these, on which stood a small cottage, that was to be Janik's wedding present. Bridges, who had been pricked with an unpleasantly voyeuristic sensation as the wedding preparations began in earnest, had taken it upon himself to leave the Gagnon household during the week before the wedding and visit the property, ostensibly with a view to assessing the repairs that might be needed and determining for himself whether or not to keep the tenants. In fact, although it rained for most of the journey there, the air was tonic, the scenery fresh. Paul Gagnon's mare was highly strung but fast, and Bridges had not all winter had such freedom. He visited Tante Clothilde, who made him welcome and after two days put her house and her servants at his disposal, having friends to visit before the wedding. And when she left, there were the lights of Deauville, which could not be ignored. After his initial visit to the cottage he did not go back again. It was little more than a farm outbuilding, except that there was no farm to speak of. The tenants could stay. He could not see what should or could be done to stop it falling down around their ears in time. It was nonetheless a sound addition to his precarious income.

On the morning of his wedding, Bridges put on the clothes that Tante Clothilde's servants, an old couple as much married to Clothilde's service as to each other, had variously cleaned, brushed, pressed, and polished the day before, and set out to ride back. He could ride forever over the flattened grass. Brilliant clouds captured and released the sun. It did not occur to him that he was riding towards anything, not, certainly, towards a married life. It was a morning of change, that was all, and the bowling clouds perfectly matched his mood.

Above the town he stopped at a farm to tidy up and accepted the breakfast of sausage and soup. When he left, seagulls were wheeling and banking against the steep air, falling away suddenly to imaginings of fish below. There was just time, he thought, for one more run across the top.


GERARD MARÈCHAL AT the church door, flicked non-existent dust from his lapel and smoothed his hair. He looked at his watch. His proximity to danger in the war had plumped out his bitterness with self-satisfaction, and he had been large enough to accede to Bridges' somewhat untoward request to stand beside him as his best man, the bachelor of honour. For Marèchal, after sending volunteers by the hundreds to meet the Prussian lines, had himself seen action—or said he had; his service had been brief and mercifully bullet-free. Only twice had his unit received the call to arms; the first time they had not been needed and the second time he had had the good fortune to have a heavy rock fall on his foot during the repair of some earthworks. He was, he knew, somehow ennobled, entitled now to scoff at Prussians and scorn unworthy Englishmen who had not seen action. He looked at his watch again. The man was behaving true to type, he thought, but he managed to sound cordial when Bridges at last, with many of the guests already in the church, rode up.

'Good morning,' said Marèchal. But Bridges seemed not to hear him. He was watching the doctor's barouche approaching. He dismounted and a boy ran up to take Gagnon's mare.

'Good morning,' Marèchal repeated and had to take out his watch again.

'Oh, it is a glorious one,' said Bridges and grasped him by the shoulder and shook his hand. 'Let us go straight in.' He did not offer any excuse for his lateness. It was a cut to match the watch and Marèchal said nothing.

ELISA SAW THE two men disappearing into the church as the barouche pulled up. The doctor offered to help her set up her developing tent on the grass beside the church, but Clothilde was eager to go in and take her place.

'Thank you. But I have Marguerite,' said Elisa—and the dubious help of the yard boy, Anselm, who was not nearly so simple nor, as Elisa well knew, so willing.

'I can manage,' she said. 'Please do go in. We shall not be long.'

So they erected the tent and opened the cabinet, setting out the slide holder and the trays on the folding table. It swayed a little in the wind, making the bottles clink together on the rack. The smells intrigued. Anselm had instructions not to touch and was left to watch.

Elisa and Marguerite went into the church.

Bridges and the unfortunate Marèchal stood close together, though there was no reason to confer. Elisa was sorry for Marèchal, who should never have been asked to perform this function for the bridegroom. But Bridges must not have known that he had asked for Janik and been refused. And Marèchal's pride would not allow him to tell. Why yes of course, he had said. It would be an honour. I am most flattered, sir. And Elisa then had felt protective, as with an ungainly child, but there was nothing to be done. He had even bowed.

She walked as quietly as she could down the aisle with Marguerite, but she knew that Bridges would turn round and he did. He had his eyes on her until she reached her seat in front of the doctor and Tante Clothilde. She let Marguerite, who always sat with the family, in first and slipped quietly in beside her, but had still to acknowledge, and looked up, inclining her head under the tilting, ribbonned hat, and Bridges had still to reply, bowing, murmuring, Madame. He was playing his part not quite seriously, an actor who did not belong to the company, indifferent to the outcome of the play. She was glad when the footsteps of more guests arriving trod away the sound of his voice.

The space behind Elisa began to fill with the rustle of skirts and whispers. Elisa, sitting beside Marguerite, realized for the first time that she had no role at all to play. She was a spectator.

The organist stopped his uninspired meanderings and began a processional. Alan Bridges, standing now before the altar, turned his head just enough for Elisa to see that he was half smiling. Elisa looked towards the altar and held onto her missal as if it were the rail of a ship. The notes of the organ were filling all the air beneath the roof and heads were turning to see the entrance of the bride, expecting, having heard reports of white silk, hoping, to be dazzled, and one or two preferring to be outraged at the immodest notion of declaring purity in so blatant a fashion. But she always was strange. The ethereal veil silenced whispers. It was a shock and no one knew quite what to make of its gauzy suggestion of heaven. Elisa too, though she had helped to cut it, to fasten it, was not quite prepared. She would not look, did not want to see the blaze of hair burning beneath the white smoke of veil, did not want to see the daughter's eyes that would be downcast, relinquishing all hope of angels. She did not want to see but had at last to look and caught, as she did, the wide-eyed stare of private panic. Her daughter, she thought, might as well be approaching the guillotine. But Paul! Here was her husband broadly beaming, a human sun, as if he were a young man and this his very wife upon his arm.

Then Tante Clothilde began to cry in lugubrious, hooting sobs, and Elisa found herself grateful, as she was for Marguerite punctuating the ceremony with her inane reflections on the priest, the veil, the sunshine, the boots—keeping her from fixing on what was happening before the altar. And then a handkerchief was necessary for Marguerite, who did not have one, and no more than half a minute later it was 'Madame' and her arm was grasped hard and suddenly, making her turn in surprise to her left again, towards the urgent whisper—'Madame, the kiss'—so that, distracted, she missed it.

But here they were now and facing the congregation, and Bridges was supremely pleased, his eyes narrow, his smile, for Bridges, out of control, and Janik, too, was smiling though her smile was of another kind, closer, with the lips drawn slightly apart and her teeth, Elisa knew, clenched. For Janik had looked in the shaft of sunlight and there were no angels when she needed them. Janik, holding onto Bridges' arm, had never felt so alone.

Paul Gagnon, beside his wife for the first time, put her arm through his. He covered the back of her hand with his and shook it fiercely, signalling, she supposed, that he too was greatly pleased.


OUTSIDE, THE GUESTS fluttered and flapped about the bride and groom. The wind whipped ribbons and lifted hats at random. Elisa removed her hat and laid it on the grass. She did not trust her camera to fix this group. In the centre, the white airiness would lift and wave until it was anchored. Hands bobbed up to hats, to feathers that tickled. The hounds that had run up after the gig of Picard the corn merchant ran among the legs, their whips of tails inciting disorder. Elisa went into the tent and made the plates ready, sliding them wet into their holder to carry them out to the camera. When the group was as ready as it would ever be, she ducked under the black broadcloth and slipped a plate into the camera. In all the movement while she was trying to focus, her daughter's eyes and Bridges' had been constant: Janik's fixed somewhere above the camera, towards the sky; Bridges' looking straight into the lens, looking directly at her. It was as if his eyes were in touch with hers, as if no one else were present, least of all a wife. She made the exposure.

When she gave the signal to relax, the group dissolved, melting into kisses and embraces, and had to be reformed for the second plate. Now they were experts and challenged the camera,

tilting chins, straightening shoulders, laughing when it was done,
applauding Elisa as she emerged from under the cloth.

Paul would have had her admired and gracious beside him, but it was not possible.

'I shall not be many minutes,' she said. 'It must be done straight away.' And she carried the plate holder back to the tent. But she was only finishing the first plate when already they were calling her. She left the photograph in the tray of hyposulphite and went out, blinking against the sunlight. Paul Gagnon, not content with the part he must play in this group, was anxious to see the couple back at the house where his role was more impressive. 'Come on, come on,' he said. 'The newlyweds are leaving.'

Elisa, with her hands held up and away from her daughter's dress, leaned forward and her daughter kissed her in a womanly, an unchildlike way and said, 'Mother.'

'Now Alain,' said Elisa, turning to her son-in-law. But she saw the smallest movement in the muscles around his eyes and had to stop and offer instead her hand, smiling ruefully at the stains of silver nitrate.

'Love her,' she said. But Bridges laughed; he might have misheard.

'Madame, I thank you,' he said. 'And Monsieur *mon beau-pere*.' He shook hands with Paul. 'How can I thank you enough?'

'You can come and eat a good breakfast,' Gagnon said, showing the obligation, as far as he was concerned, to be all on his side, although later, far from dismissing the question, he would with the wedding wine inside him be more honest, and when Bridges asked again reply, 'You can give me a grandson, Sir, that's how,' laughing and clapping shoulders, but serious.

Then Bridges with his bride climbed into the ribbonned gig and took the reins, while Paul Gagnon went over to the mare and all around the guests began to remember they would have to hurry if they wanted to join the ride back. And in the confusion of horses backing into traces and starting out of them again and dogs with the wind in their tails and the strange iron three-legged one-eyed beast still staring at the space before the yew, in all of this there had to be and was a high-spirited creature that spooked at the sight and threw up its head, its legs following, and clawed at the air until its hooves, finding no purchase, clambered down the invisible paddles of a revolving wheel to hammer on the tent and pull it over, the glass inside smashing and the liquid from the trays seeping into the earth as the vanguard of the wedding party vanished over the brow of the hill.

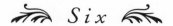 *Six*

THE TRAIN JOLTED and stopped again. Bridges sat, half lay, with
his legs stretched out across the compartment and his eyes closed.
Beyond the window was an unploughed field, lumpy with clods of
grass and strewn with cabbage stalks. Sometimes the train did not
move at all for more than half an hour. Janik stared out at the dismal landscape. The sun on the dirty window blurred everything.
But they had seen the destruction. They had passed through ham-
lets where no one was in sight, where houses had been gutted and
bedding and broken furniture lay about outside. In one place, the
contents of a house had been piled up outside—carpets, chairs,
mirrors, books—fuel for a bonfire no one had had time to light.
The shutters of the house had been wrenched off and the windows
had been broken. A grey horse stood in the front doorway, the
house open behind it, and watched as the train went by.

And yet how unwarlike, these Prussians. At one stop several
of them had taken over the stationmaster's office. Two of them
were playing dominoes outside in the sun. There were Prussians
on the train, eating sausage out of brown paper in a carriage all to
themselves. Here was an anomaly too troubling for conversation
in front of strangers, the brutal destruction everywhere apparent, and everywhere the far-from-savage soldiers, relaxed and

cheerful, chatting, reading—soldiers courteous even, if they crossed one's path. And so Bridges dozed and Janik watched for signs of sufffering and savagery.

By the time the train reached Rouen there were Prussian soldiers everywhere. The town had become a Prussian garrison. Perhaps because he was English, Bridges had no difficulty getting about as long as he dealt with Prussians. They went at once to the Port Authority and delivered Gagnon's letter. When they went in search of lodgings it was not so easy. The place was crammed with Prussian soldiers and every hotel was billeted; the hotel keepers and landladies alike had a way of shaking their heads without so much as an apology. The English, after all, had never loaded a single rifle when they were needed. It was late when finally, in a dark street, they found a place to stay. Madame *la patronne* said she was sorry but there was only one small bed. *La fille* was welcome to the cot behind the stairs—when Monsieur had finished. She would not charge for that. Bridges considered walking back to the station and taking the midnight train on to Paris, but Janik was tired and Bridges convinced himself that she had not heard. He signed his name and Madame made a bad joke about the Prussians and their English friends and took them to the bottom of the stairs. 'My ulcers are bleeding,' she said. 'You go on up. To the top. You don't need me.'

So they climbed a narrow twisting staircase to an attic room with the door standing ajar. They had to stoop to enter and the door would not close behind them. Bridges lit the lamp. The bed was disconcertingly small. 'We can go back to the station,' he said. But Janik was dealing with a private panic that was making her teeth chatter. She shook her head and began to take off her wrap. When Bridges came to help her she said quickly, 'I should like to pray first.' Bridges, who had not thought to be so precipitate, laughed but said, 'Of course. *Madame* Bridges—*Mistress* Bridges. And I should like to smoke a cigar.' He took one out of his pocket.

'I mean together.'

'Well certainly. We have everything to be thankful for, apart

from this room. My mistress, my lady.' Thinking, if she continued she might well put the seal of celibacy on this, their first
night.

'I mean to pray for a blessing.'

The thought appalled. Bridges had always assumed that
heaven had the decency to look the other way at such moments.
He raked a patch of his memory for something appropriate, but it
was bare. 'We have received the sacrament of marriage,' he tried.
'We are blessed already.'

But she was not happy. Her eyes implored. Anything but
tears, thought Bridges, anything. He knelt. The words *For what
we are about to receive* malingered on his tongue. He could not
speak.

'In the name of the Father . . . ' She was prompting.

And so he said the Lord's prayer.

Her clothes were easy to remove; she helped, it being her duty,
and then lay very still underneath the covers. He closed his eyes
and Elisa stood in her spattered dress with its pattern of melting
stars burned across the silk. He had not known a woman so still
as Janik, and yet she was soft and his hands met with no resistance nor his mouth (nor would she have shrunk from his eyes,
but he kept them closed), so that in the end he knew it was nothing but magnanimity and it would break him. He bit then,
gnawed at her collarbone to make her writhe, to make her
protest, biting her shoulder, her elbow, fighting the urge to close
his teeth on her breast. So that at last she did move, her wide
mouth on his neck, her teeth closing.

Afterwards it was difficult to sleep side by side in the narrow
bed. Bridges curled up on the floor with his coat. There was not a
sound from Janik. He wondered briefly whether they had delivered themselves to the hands of a spy-catcher and whether the
woman would cut their throats in the middle of the night. And
then he fell asleep.

Outside, the Prussian soldiers were loud as they went from
bar to bar. In Paris, the first of the Prussian troops were pulling
out. They had had their day. They had marched in victory under

the Arc de Triomphe itself. And every one of the soldiers in the provinces wished he could have been there and contented himself instead with conquering barmaids and dreaming of home.

✍

AT MIDNIGHT PAUL Gagnon said good night to Doctor Escher. He would have liked him to stay, for Escher had stories to tell. He had spent the latter part of the war working with the American *ambulance* just outside Dieppe. Since his return he was prone to bouts of empty despair. Sometimes the prospect of his past spread as his future before him was more than cause for dismay: the goitres that continued to enlarge, the cataracts that continued to thicken, the TB there was no containing, the women who bled and would not stop; soldiers who lived or died—though most of them died—were preferable. Today he had enjoyed the wedding, seeing his friend happy, but the long perspective opened by the event left him feeling chill. He needed to continue the night alone.

Gagnon was disappointed but determined. He sent the schoolgirls home, tired of their endless coming and going with glasses and with plates. Of the guests only Crécy, whose wife had left earlier, and Courtebois remained to accompany him on his dogged journey to the bottom of the bottles. He was happiest when the empty bottles stood shoulder to shoulder in the centre of the table. To have them removed one at a time was not as satisfactory.

And tonight it seemed they would need to form a whole regiment of bottles. They had dispensed with the subject of the wedding early, and the women, and the character of the English, turning out their mental pockets for something good to say. They were (at least) an independent nation. There was that. They carved (most of the time) their own path. And successful. No denying it. To a degree. (And at whose cost?) But there, not every nation. Certainly. And the ships. Well no one could deny the ships, a topic safer than the natives, who might lead one at any moment to offend one's host. But the ships at first proved not a good idea. They plunged the table into the doldrums and lay for a while becalmed, their bows pointing back in the direction of the war and its outcome while the shameful inactivity of the French fleet was pondered. But then the tide turned and the conversation rode upon the flood of possibilities that came with peace. There again were the British ships, but this time standing off Le Havre, low in the water with their shipments of food. The opportunities. And Gagnon's own chartered vessels ahead of them all. And then the work still to be done on the Seine. With the scuttled English colliers at the bottom outside Rouen. Exactly. Everything was an opportunity. That was a fact of life. It was all work. For those who were willing. No one could argue with the fact that there was work out there.

Elisa got up and left the table.

Crécy and Courtebois agreed on the work. Not to mention their host's skills. It was said, and did Crécy need to repeat it, that at Rouen they were desperate. No one, however, would do the job since it was the Prussians who were paying with the indemnity taken from the citizens themselves. Courtebois thought they ought to look further afield and laughed, and so did Gagnon, having upstairs a copy of the signed contract he had charged his son-in-law to deliver. Without delay.

They heard Elisa go up to bed. It was a signal for the men to slide forward on their chairs, abandon the formal right angle of the seat and settle in, their legs flung out stiffly and their backs braced against sleep, against losing their grip on the world's affairs.

Crécy fired another opinion into the increasing fog of the conversation: the new Government was at least led by a realist. He had heard Elisa Gagnon say earlier that President Thiers was nothing if not a realist and had pocketed it away until the right time. Which was now; these two would agree to anything. In fact another bottle could be opened while they all endorsed it. Thiers, said Crécy, had wanted as fervently as the next man to be rid of the Prussians—only he had the courage to assent to the terms that would achieve it. Courtebois began to find everything too much at this time of night. He shoved his hands deeper in his pockets, let his behind slide further forward on the seat of his chair. Oh the Prussians. One grew tired, but then they had been around for too long altogether. But the Reds . . . Now this was a danger, a very real danger that had been ignored. As soon as Crécy stopped twittering he would raise the subject. He got up to fetch another bottle of calvados.

UPSTAIRS, MARGUERITE HELPED Elisa off with the damaged dress. They hung it from the door of the wardrobe and Marguerite made a concert of small pitying sounds.

Elisa would not join in. Marguerite fussed at the fabric.

'But you will be able to do something? Madame Bedard can mend anything.'

'I used to think like that. That everything could be mended, put right.'

'Well? She is very good.'

'But there is always a scar. Sometimes you just have to leave things. Develop a blind spot.'

'Can you mend the photograph?'

'The plate was not broken.'

'But that is good news.'

'No. It's over there.' Elisa pointed to the glass plate beside the chest of drawers.

Marguerite frowned. People liked to make her a fool. The glass was black.

'You said it was broken.'

'The easiest thing to say. Everyone wanted to know if the photograph was all right. I could not save it in time. Some of the trays were upset and one of the bottles broke.' Though her tray of hyposulphite had been there in the ridiculous fallen tent, arrested at the end of its slide along the collapsed shelf, enough solution in it to save what she saw, had she wanted to: the dark faces looking out from the glass, their white hair already dead, their eyes, his eyes, his eyes looking into hers as she knew they had, though it was the camera he looked at; but it was there in all its appalling risk for everyone to see so that she could only be glad when the dangerous ghosts chose to disappear as she watched, sliding back into the blackening glass as she crouched there under the cloth of the fallen tent, the shouts and the confusion of feet outside, unaware.

'It is a shame.'

'Yes. Everyone wanted to see.'

'Monsieur Gagnon is very sad.'

Monsieur Gagnon in fact, and Elisa knew it, rather hoped his wife had learned her lesson now and the irritation of her pastime would be over.

Elisa propped the plate against the wall and began to get ready for bed. But when later her husband came to her heavily, clumsily, as he always did when he was drunk, the black pane assumed a presence of its own within the room and the image on the plate began to etch itself behind Elisa's closed eyelids, so that as she lay half smothered by the drunken bulk that worked itself to a kind of death upon her she saw the face of Alain Bridges looking at her, knowing her. And she saw her daughter's gaze, turned away.

FELIX WAS WAITING outside the church the following Sunday. He had the developing tent in a handcart. He drew Elisa closer and to Gagnon's dismay began to open it up to show her the improvements he had made in the repair.

'This is not necessary, surely.' How to whisper to the stone deaf? Gagnon was driven to hiss. Others heard and came closer to inspect the contraption.

Gagnon chose nonchalance. 'It isn't worth it. You might as well give it up. There are better ways to employ your empty hours I would have thought.'

'None that gives me so much pleasure. Don't worry. I shall be out of your way this afternoon.'

She turned to Felix and bowed. It seemed necessary. Felix smiled and wheeled the tent away to put it on the seat of the trap.

To his relief, Gagnon saw Crécy and his wife approach with Courtebois and the doctor too, who perhaps had only come to socialize. And Gagnon was an important man again. Since the wedding he had not been able to hear too often how magnificent was the breakfast, how fine the wine, and now, that particular subject's interest being all but exhausted, there was Paris. For Gagnon had news.

'Paris,' he said, like one who knew, 'will survive. She is wounded yes, but the new government will restore her.'

But Courtebois had his latest scapegoat and never missed an opportunity to haul it out. 'Paris is full of Reds.'

'Rabble,' said Gagnon. 'Nothing but rabble. They can do no real harm.'

'Tell that to those who died in January at Buzenval under Prussian fire, at the Hôtel de Ville under French fire,' said Escher. 'Anyone with a rifle can do real harm.' And knew what he was talking about, his head still filled with sights and sounds he did not want.

'But these things are not new. And in a time of war . . . '

'Civil war next,' said the doctor. 'That is what they are saying.' But found no support. Gagnon's view was too easy to agree with on a fine spring Sunday.

'The Reds will settle down. When the last of the Prussians are gone, the Reds will settle. My daughter's letter says the cafés are all open, and the theatres. What can be so serious?'

And so they could ask him just how it really was, and he, the lucky possessor of the word, could tell them: the price of chicken, the way the lamp posts had been twisted by the bombardment. Though Madame Crécy would have preferred limbs.

Elisa, coming close enough to hear, said it was not a place for sightseeing, and the doctor, who himself had seen enough, was in silent agreement.

Madame Crécy knew how to make her appetite look reasonable. 'You would not then, Madame Gagnon, see a page of history as it turns? This, to be sure, is a sight.'

'I think there are sights better left unseen.'

'But Madame, with all respect, you yourself say you are a photographer. A photographer, is he not a witness?'

'Yet with still the power to choose. One is not compelled to see. The act itself may sometimes be complicit.' But this too dark now for a bright morning in the open air, with the coffee and rolls warming in the kitchen at home.

'Which is why photography may not be a woman's art at all,' said Gagnon, thoroughly satisfied at the outcome. 'As I said. We must be on our way. Madame Crécy, gentlemen.'

And Gagnon, whose wife had once excited envy, not to mention other deadly sins, began to feel himself considered, if not with pity, then sympathy. For who would wish upon themselves a complicated woman? And photography was not an inexpensive pursuit.

Monsieur Harmon, whose wife only sketched, thought himself lucky.


MARGUERITE ON THE way back from Mass was despondent. She herself would keep to the house when they got back, her mistress too demanding by far. Marguerite come here a moment. Oh yes, that was always how she started. Just take that off. Yes, that too. There. Shivering in the cold. But the last time at least she had a good chenille tablecloth to wear. Warmer than the lace curtain she had had for Iseult. There. No, leave it off this shoulder. Just like that. Good. And the brass curtain rings on a piece of silver upholstery braid. There. Banding her forehead. A little lower. Not cold are you? Good. Jephtha's daughter. With bangles. On a chill February afternoon in the glasshouse. Lovely. Three or four plates she would use, sometimes more. And all the washing still in the basket and soon it would be too late to hang it out at all. Marguerite, you're perfect. Folding up the tablecloth, wondering if Jephtha's daughter had to do the laundry too. No. Better to lie low when Madame was having an afternoon. Safer. She liked to cooperate but. But. And there were limits. Monsieur Gagnon coming in to find her posing in Madame's chemise, giving him ideas. And those lace curtains. Which were questionable, she thought, to say the least, and could only mean Iseult was something of a whore. No, there were limits. Though Madame would never see it that way. It made her feel uneasy to think of the things Madame felt free to ask. Why did she get those angel pictures out again last month? Little Janik in nothing but a pair of angel wings. She just hoped Madame was not reviving the idea. No telling where it would end. The work it had entailed. Had Madame killed the swan? Marguerite could not remember, but it had been there in the yard still warm when she came out. Marguerite, I need your help. She used to say it even then. Sit on the neck Marguerite. All your weight. Marguerite knew how to get the wings off. She wouldn't have done it that way. Madame had the filleting knife and had slit the skin under the wing, but then the bird had seemed to come to life and it thrashed and kicked with the force of a goat so that Madame had to take the axe again to its head. When it was still she took the knife and carried on cutting the ligaments. All right now. Hold on. Pulling the wing backwards and over, turning and wrenching it whole from the body. Marguerite had spat. She could taste it now. There were flecks of matter and pieces of it were in her hair. Ah, look, she had said, saved, she thought, by a sudden insight. You only need one. The child sits so, facing that way. But Madame had only looked at her as if she were simple. Hold it down hard. Ready? Yes, she made sure this time she was ready and turned her head as it came away. They had washed the two wings with soap and wired them so that they extended at an angle. Botticelli. Madame had said. Whoever *she* was. Well they had done it, and when it was done they had giggled with satisfaction. The wings now were in the attic. Marguerite hoped fervently they would stay there.

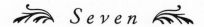

## Seven

IN PARIS, THE photographer in the Rue Saint-Honoré said anything could be managed. 'The city is ours again and everything
again is possible.' He said he would replicate even the flowers the
bride had carried.

Janik did not think it was necessary. The very idea of dressing
again as bride and groom was one she had agreed to only for her
father. It seemed somehow to detract from the validity of the
original instance. It was almost like an undoing.

'They were hellebore,' she said. 'It was what we had in the
garden at the time. You would not find it now.' Amid the velvet
and the gilt, nothing so simple. The man calmed the air with his
palms and repeated what he had said. Everything was possible.
'Besides,' he added, 'that is the beauty of the photograph. No one
will notice. Our adjustment, our minor amendments, you see.
The memory of your common viewer, even of the connoisseur,
is not as reliable as these little boxes.' He indicated his cameras
like a conductor asking his string section to rise for applause.
'And yet when our art is applied, these little boxes are capable of
great deception.' He had had no encouragement from either
Bridges or Janik, who only wanted to make the appointment and
begin their day, but he laughed anyway because this was what he

always did in his little speech. 'For us the eyes always sparkle, the cheek is always in bloom.'

An appointment was made for the next day, with the wedding clothes to be sent to the studio meanwhile.

'And might I add, *Sir*,' he said, using the English word, 'might I add that our services are presently available for your convenience at certain points of interest, at the Salpetrière, at the Porte du Point du Jour and also at Fort Issy?'

'Thank you but we have other plans.'

'A pity. It's quite the thing to make a tour and have one's picture taken at the ruins. Quite the souvenir . . .'

Janik interrupted. 'We are going from here to the Étoile,' she said.

'Ah, yes. They are calling it the Purification.' He shrugged. 'The enemy is gone. It is our duty now to get on with life. But excuse me. A young couple like yourself. That is exactly what you are cementing. Life, the future, yes? My compliments, and until tomorrow, Madame, Monsieur.' And he gave them his card, with only one tiny reminder that visiting cards were one of his most popular services.

THERE WERE FRENCH troops massing in the Place de la Concorde, battalions of the National Guard looking sheepishly happy with themselves, Bridges thought. But to be out of danger. Who would not be happy? And why be sheepish? Hard to resist not firing insanely into the blue sky. Who wouldn't? Most of Paris seemed to have turned out for this ceremony, whatever it was to be. It was impossible to get through to the Champs-Elysées. They went back instead through the broken gardens of the Elysée palace, where all the trees were down, and on through one of the narrow streets towards the Étoile. Further along they cut through again to the Champs-Elysées. Spectators lined both sides of the avenue, standing on the tree stumps for a better view. There were no troops. Five water-carts were making their way down the avenue. Behind them, a hundred or more women formed a line across the street. They carried brooms and wore their skirts pinned up; some of them were in corduroy breeches. Between the spraying water and the women, several youths criss-crossed the road, walking backwards and drizzling a liquid from the carboys they carried. The women in this procession scrubbed the paving, sometimes spat out in front of them when the crowds at the side called out to them. There was no cheering.

'What are they pouring on the street?' said Janik.

A woman beside her said, 'Condy's fluid. Stinks worse than the Prussians.'

Janik did not want to wait for the soldiers of the line who were going to reclaim this newly purged French soil and so they followed the women, keeping to the side behind the line of the tree stumps. The air began to smell smoky and the eerie silence of the procession was broken by shouts from the direction of the Étoile. Then they could see the arch itself looming through clouds of smoke. All across the vast square bonfires burned, sending up white plumes mixed with thick curdling black; men with pitchforks tended them, heaping on straw, while boys ran about with rakes to gather more from the great heap of it on the Neuilly side. At the Avenue de Friedland there was a stack of mattresses, mattresses, presumably, that had been slept on by Prussians. Three women with butcher knives were slitting them for the boys to pull out the straw and the stuffing. There were women too with cans of paraffin, making sure the fires would blaze.

Janik and Bridges watched in silence.

'It is a kind of frenzy,' said Bridges.

Janik did not answer.

'They are possessed,' he said.

Janik was watching the women with the knives. 'I am glad,' she said. 'I am glad to know they feel, still.'

The women held the knives like weapons. They might have been ripping the bowels of soldiers. Of anybody. The men were equally intent, serious in their work of burning this paltry straw as if they could burn memory, burn history. It occurred to him that the burning of straw was not going to be enough.

When they got back to their hotel, Janik was very quiet. She stood on the balcony looking out over the street. 'The poor people,' she said. 'The poor people who have suffered.'

Bridges, lying on the bed with his boots on, could not agree more about the poor people, thinking himself one of them in his own particular brand of suffering.

'Come here,' he said.

She turned round.

'It's daylight,' she said.

'It's your husband.'

She turned back again and shook her head. 'Please. Don't ask me to do what isn't right.'

'What you don't believe to be right.'

'Exactly.'

Bridges closed his eyes and tried not to think about the rest of his life.

They went out again and walked for a while along the river and then crossed to Place Saint-Michel to find a restaurant. It was nearing six o'clock and Bridges had just decided which seemed the most appetizing when Janik took him by the arm. 'Alain?' she said. 'Alain, would you do something to please me?'

He had a demoralizing dread that she was going to ask to go to evening Mass at the cathedral. 'Anything,' he said, the practised husband and in so short a time. At least they would be sitting down.

'I should like to take a cab and go back to the Arc de Triomphe. Before it gets dark. I should like to see how it looks after the Purification.'

Bridges had learned, too, how to sigh without being heard. 'Devastated, I should think, after such ill treatment. Probably needs a real cleaning now,' he said. But they went.

In the failing light, with fires still smouldering on the paving and starlings wheeling in hundreds overhead, Bridges knew what Janik had really come to see, for they stood at the base of the great arch and she could not take her eyes from the giant angel, La Marseillaise, towering over them, driving forward, with her

unsheathed sword and her mouth ugly in determination. Lost in
the drama of the stonework, Janik could not get enough of looking. Bridges walked away to sit at the base of the other side of the
arch. He lit a cigar. It was a vile statue. The eyes were mad, fixed
on a vision no one else could see. And the teeth were bared.

'Thank you,' said Janik. He got up as she came over and took
his arm and smiled up at him with her own white teeth. Which
Bridges would have liked to lick.

They took their dinner of undercooked pork in the small dark
restaurant beside the hotel, with Janik eating in an absent-
minded way and their waiter trying to eat his own dinner behind
the bar. The place had not enough people to warm it. It was a
relief to be back in their hotel room. The shutters had been
closed and the bed turned down for them, though no fire had
been lit. Bridges said they would keep each other warm. Janik
conjectured on the fuel shortage. She lay talking at the ceiling
while Bridges was undressing, was still talking about depriva-
tion, about what she would do to help if they lived in Paris, when
Bridges was turning down the lamps.

'I know you don't believe me.' And she so ready to defend,
willing to talk all night to make her case, but Bridges would not
answer. He came and stood beside her and with two deft movements, as if he were unmaking a bed, he threw back the covers
and pulled her nightgown up to her hips. She made a move to
cover herself but he pulled the covers down to her feet, then
walked to the window and opened the shutters. The gaslight
from outside shone on the bed. Bridges stood a long time looking. Janik did not see him. Janik, martyred by the light, was
drowning in an ecstasy of her own.

AT THE STUDIO the following day, a young assistant asked
Bridges to take a seat while she conducted Janik to a small dressing room behind a dark green curtain.

'You're English?' said the photographer, though it did not seem necessary.

'Yes,' said Bridges. 'Quite emphatically not Prussian. And not a Government agent or a Red insurgent either.'

Both men laughed.

'Ah,' said the photographer and shook his head. Such an opportunity, this lanky, relaxed foreigner with nothing to do but listen. There was so much to tell. But where to begin? The thing had no edges, was an accumulation of images, to be sifted, sorted. 'You would not believe. The cold. The hunger. Have you been to the zoological gardens? The animals are all gone. And then the shells. They bombarded us, you know? But of course you know.' He continued to shake his head. 'But we would not have given in.'

Bridges folded his arms across his chest. It seemed some protection against the coming onslaught.

'No, we wouldn't have given in. Never. "The Government of National Defence." That's a good one. It was the Government, the despicable Trochu, who sold us out. If you ask me, that's what he had in mind all along.'

'I didn't think he had a choice.'

The photographer opened his mouth to make some small retching noise of contempt and saw Janik appear from the dressing room in her cloud of white.

'Madame!' Professional, smiling now, the arm extended.

'Monsieur, your bride!' And he stepped aside. 'But the flowers. Louise, where are the flowers?'

Louise, holding violets tied with white ribbon, looked uncomfortable.

'No,' said Janik. 'Thank you but no. It would not be the same.'

'But with respect, Madame, no one is going to remember.'

'I think Monsieur Lipp has gone to considerable trouble my darling.'

'I shall know.'

'The trouble is nothing, Monsieur. But in my professional opinion, Madame, it is necessary—' he had begun to arrange

her limbs—'if your arm is on your husband's like so, it is necessary to have something to hold in your left hand.'

'I do not need anything to hold.'

'Madame, respectfully, it will not be quite as it should be without the flowers, as I'm sure Monsieur will agree.' But Monsieur
was not given the opportunity, one way or the other. And only
now did the photographer notice that the female party had
become angry and appeared to think he had overstepped the
mark.

'Are you asking me,' she said 'to deceive?' And everyone now
was as uncomfortable as Louise.

And so, in the studio on the top floor of Lipp's Photographic
Gallery, in their wedding garments and standing beside a plaster
column that leaned a little until Louise tucked a corner of the carpet under, they posed, solemn, all silently justifying their respec-
tive positions with regard to violets and truth.


THE NEXT DAY they took the circular railway to view the
defences and at the Point du Jour they paid for seats in one of the
cabs taking visitors out to the southern forts.

The countryside around was shorn of trees by the bombardment. What remained of them must have been carted away for
fuel because there was simply nothing there. It was as if they had
been blown out of the ground and carried clean away.

Inside Fort Issy, the visitors inspected the remains of gun
emplacements and looked out through the embrasures to
Châtillon where the Prussian guns would have been firing on
Paris. A soldier of the line, too old, surely, to fight, had set himself up as a guide. Heavy shelling, he said, could in no way be
compared to gunfire. It mutilated the human body beyond
description. It carried off the head and blasted the torso to shreds.

'I cannot imagine the men here,' whispered Janik. 'And the
stones falling.'

'And the cold,' said Bridges.

Outside, some small boys had been waiting for them. They

had a barrow-load of shell fragments. They were selling them for five sous each.

'Look, Monsieur, this one's like a duck.'

'You can get them for two at the Point du Jour,' said Bridges. But the boys had already turned to the next visitor.

'Hey!' said Bridges, and gave the thinnest boy a franc. 'Get some bread and share it with your friends.'

'Monsieur?' The boy turned his back towards Janik and spoke to Bridges so that she would not hear, unwrapping something from his pocket. 'I've got one here with hair still on it.'

BRIDGES SAID THEY had seen enough of battle grounds. In the next few days, with the weather allowing the possibility of spring, they walked. They strolled the boulevards. They crossed and recrossed the river. They meandered through the Luxembourg Gardens, but these, like the Botanical Gardens, had a ravaged, dismal look and evidence of the shelling was all around. They walked the quays and they watched the river from the bridges. There were fishermen on both sides. The gardens of the Tuileries were still in use as an artillery park. Janik said gardens were really neither here nor there. She was standing near the entrance off the Place de la Concorde, looking up at the great winged horses. Bridges said if she wanted statues they should go to the Louvre.

At the entrance, a notice declared the palace open to the public and at the same time apologized for the absence of the paintings which had been removed before the war to Brest for safekeeping. They made their donation, to go to the victims of the siege, and walked through the great rooms. Janik refused to believe that the children and the old people of Paris could not have been similarly removed to safety before the fighting began.

'Think how matters would have changed,' she said. 'The men left to fight and the healthy women, without children, to assist them. The forces against the Prussians would have been almost doubled.'

Bridges said it could not be that easy, families leaving one
another. While the voices in the dark water came back to him, the
names flung out like ropes, mother to son, son to father.

'They could have been ordered, for their own good. And for
the cause of the war. Think of the food that would have been
saved. There would have been no need to surrender.'

They were standing now in front of the Winged Victory. The
force of the headless figure drove itself against perception, insist-
ing on invincibility, overwhelming evil, like wind over a ruined
city.

Janik whispered. 'It is a woman.'

Bridges moved on. They all were, all these abstractions. He
had had enough of marble torsos altogether.


BRIDGES WATCHED HIS wife push her food around her plate.
She would take her fork, lift it, and stop and look around again,
frowning to herself, thinking, all the time thinking.

'Wonderful chicken,' he said. 'It melts.'

'But you have to wonder.'

'What?'

'Who else can eat like this?'

'All of these.' Bridges, with his mouth full, waved his fork in a
semi-circle taking in the crowded room.

'No, outside. The food queues are dreadful.'

'That is only because we keep walking where the food is dis-
tributed. Take another route and we would not have seen it.'

'There is something to see on any route, on every route you
take.' She scraped all her food noisily to one side of the plate,
mashing it into a messy heap. 'Look at that funeral.'

'Yes. It was unfortunate.' Could not, in fact, have been more
ill-timed, Bridges thought. Casting its pall. It had been a wonderful morning until then, airy and light. They had been walking
along the quays and they were turning back again across the
Place de Grève when they heard drums. A funeral cortège had
entered the square from the other side. There were five coffins in

all. Four of them belonged to children. There were women cry-
ing, men and women shouting, but most of all there were
National Guardsmen, armed and angry. Some of them ran onto
the steps of the Hôtel de Ville and when the column came to a
halt, one of the men began shouting back at the crowd, working
it. Bridges had not wanted to stay but Janik had insisted. A soldier on the steps was shouting something about rents, about how
all their children would starve the same way.

'They starved?' said Janik.

'Not these,' said the woman beside her. She stuck out her chin
and drew her finger across her throat. 'The father,' she said. 'But
a man can be driven to madness. And he made his peace. He did,
he made his peace. Folded their dead hands, he did, then he shot
himself. Through the mouth.'

The soldier was still shouting. 'If this is a crime then who
is the criminal? Who is? Who is?' Over and over. So that the
crowd had seemed of its own accord to draw the name of Thiers
out of the air, and suddenly a funeral was not nearly as com-
pelling as the thought of bringing down a government. Bridges
had had to shake Janik by the arm to make her move on with
him.

'But these things go on, have always gone on.'

'And it is our duty to bear witness.'

Bridges shook his head. 'Gawking. How would you like that if
you were starving?'

'You are being deliberately trivial.'

'No.' Though he knew he was. 'It affects—it effects—nothing. The sole effect of your bearing witness has been to ruin your
dinner tonight.' Thinking, 'my' dinner.

'And I should eat in the face of their hunger?'

'This morning wasn't about hunger. It was about grief and
rage. It was an impotent rage that brought to pass the death of a
whole family.' Cross now, savage with the mess left on his plate.
Cross enough to inflict a little pain himself. 'And it's an impotent
pity that looks on.'

She was silent.

'Seriously, what can you do about it?'

'You know I can do nothing, not me by myself. And I am not a Parisienne. But these. What about all these?

'They try.'

'Not all of them Not all of the time.'

Bridges pushed his plate away. He had been enjoying his dinner, to start with. He called a waiter and ordered an apricot tart.

'There is a Mass,' said Janik. 'Did you see?'

Bridges had not seen.

It was for the war widows, she said. It was the least one could do. And it wasn't far away. At the Madeleine. Only a few minutes.

They left the apricot tart.


THEY WERE ONLY just in time. The church was very full with only a few empty seats at the back. The further the better, Bridges was inclined to think, who, though he was sorry for the families at the front, leaning on each other in their grief, had not the slightest wish to spend his evening with them. He followed Janik to a chair, sat down and leaned to speak to her, but she was on her knees already, her eyes fixed on the window above the altar. Even when they stood for the priest she did not look round. The priest came in with two acolytes and a straggle of particularly dirty-looking servers. He had rough red skin and grey hair. He jerked his head compulsively to one side as he walked. As if he were a dog tugging at a rag; Bridges sighed and sat down at the first opportunity. He began to consider their next day's outing. An early breakfast. If the weather was fine . . . He had got as far as the Bois de Boulogne, though the priest had only reached the Preface, when the doors at the back burst open. The sound of boots made every head turn. There was a woman and behind her five men in National Guard uniforms. The woman was wearing pantaloons tucked into high boots and a worker's blouse belted with a gun belt, a red sash across her breast. She had a rifle crossed at her back and she held up another in one hand in a gesture that called for silence. The noises from the street came in through the open door. The priest turned back to the altar. The woman brought the rifle down and slung it onto her shoulder and then she let her boots ring on the flagstones, made them ring, as she stalked down the centre aisle. The priest kissed the altar and turned, twitching. The acolytes looked to each other for help. The shorter one began to arrange the altar vessels like a servant in a dining room not wanting to be seen to listen. The priest was at the top step, speaking out now to the soldiers, who seemed the lesser threat. 'What is this? What is this? What do you think you are doing?' His words were like birds loose in the church. No one knew what to do with them. And the woman now was at the pulpit.

'Good people of La Madeleine, Citizens, I shall not keep you long.'

Already at the back of the church the Guardsmen had removed their *képis* and were starting down the rows of chairs.

'You have suffered. You have come here with your suffering. But you will not put an end to it sitting here in this mausoleum. You are praying at the gravesite of liberty, the tomb of justice.'

The priest was making to go down the steps but the taller acolyte put a hand on his arm. It did not take much.

'Turn to the *Comité Central* for an end to this oppression. Are you followers of Jesus Christ? Do you love your neighbour? Then you must fight for your neighbour. Show your love. Give to the *Comité* as the *Comité* knows how to give, yes, its very life, to you.'

But it was not necessary to ask. The caps were filling with coins. After all, the men were armed and the woman was clearly a lunatic. 'My sisters and brothers,' said the woman as she came down the steps. 'My sisters and brothers,' and she reached out as she passed the first row of the congregation, which made some of them reach back and take her hand until, on her way back to the door, she might have been a *toucheuse* and every one of the faithful, sick or not, ready to be healed. The acolyte had let go of the priest's arm but the old man did not move.

'From the Red Virgin!' the woman called from the back of the church, the rifle raised. An actor now, her audience in the palm of her hand. *'Vive La Commune!'* and she swung the rifle down, firing a shot to the ceiling before she walked calmly out, leaving the congregation with ringing in their ears and the priest with his influence permanently injured.

Janik picked up the spent cartridge case that rolled to her feet.

'WELL,' SAID BRIDGES outside. 'Paris is full of surprises. Have you recovered?'

'Me?'

'From the shock, I mean.'

'Oh, it was not shock. Surprise, yes. You had the word the first time. But not shock.'

'Outrage, surely?'

'Not at all.'

Bridges looked at his wife.

'I think, on the contrary. She was inspired. She was Christ in the temple.'

Bridges doubted. But could see it would be futile to say.

Janik took his arm. 'Thank you,' she said. 'Thank you.' She would have liked more than the thin smile he gave in response, more than the ten francs he had given the soldier. She would have liked his heart as well as his money. She would have liked conviction. ' "Whatsoever you do to the least of my brethren . . ." '

'Well whatsoever you do, don't go quoting scripture. These particular brethren would have you shot for that. Accidentally, you understand.'

'I don't believe it.'

It was not the first time that Bridges had noticed how Janik's beliefs and disbeliefs always cleared her a straight path. He, on the other hand, always saw a profusion of paths, none of them straight, and preferred on the whole to resist taking any.

That night beside his wife, Bridges had never felt lonelier. She had let him make love to her with her eyes wide open, unblinking. He was unnerved. He wanted to see what she was seeing. He supposed that it was angels. He did not see the bare-headed woman with the red scarf crossed over her breast, the rifle across her back and the black boots striking the flags.

## ﹌ *Eight* ﹌

ELISA HELPED MARGUERITE prepare the dinner for their home-coming. She tossed out the daffodils Marguerite had picked and instead put rosehips left over from the winter in an earthen jar. She liked the odd mixture of the barren thorn, the bursting fruit. Marguerite tried hard to find them appropriate.

'For Janik that is just so,' she said. 'Her hair like fire.'

And her heart. Elisa did not know how her daughter endured it. The burning. Without end. And did Bridges feel the heat? She smiled to think of him returning scorched, astonished. Who had been an idle river.

They boiled a ham with some bay leaves and there was young asparagus to eat with cream. Marguerite had made a tart and a *crème anglaise* too, in honour of Bridges. Gagnon ransacked his cellar, grumbling happily.

Elisa wished they were not coming back. And there was no one she could tell.


'MOTHER. FATHER.' JANIK held her parents briefly, kissed them each distractedly on the mouth and on both cheeks. Bridges stood by and smiled.

Janik, who clearly had much to tell but was not going to, stood back. Which left the others to surmise, Gagnon with his arms outstretched and nothing to fill them, Elisa expectant, looking to Bridges. And Anselm all the while carrying in the boxes, setting them in the hall. If he had carried in the hymeneal sheets and displayed them, the atmosphere could not have been more stifling. The breath, it seemed, was momentarily trapped in their bodies, though Gagnon at last did laugh, talking about taking Paris by storm, slapping upper arms—which always filled a gap, he found. 'And not only Paris,' he had to risk, laughing with satisfaction, happy with his choice of son-in-law.


BRIDGES, ELISA SAW when they sat down to eat, had not changed at all, though she had hoped, unreasonably, he would. Janik, on the other hand, had re-established some of her old ways. She watched her across the table. Janik was filled, she brimmed. There was something portentous about her bearing. She carried herself with her shoulders drawn up and her nostrils flaring as if to feed the momentous thing inside her. It was not the smug self-satisfaction of the bride. It was possession. She was enraptured. But not with her husband, that was clear. When she leaned on her husband's arm, when she sat beside him, he was forgotten. Her eyes focussed on the distance. She might have seen through walls. And Bridges might have been one.

'So,' said Gagnon, 'Paris has not yet fallen apart in the hands of those incompetents?'

Bridges smiled. 'I'd say Paris was doing quite nicely, in the circumstances.'

'Paris will not fall apart, the *Comité Central* will see to that.' Janik was fierce.

'Not your opinion, surely, is it?' Gagnon asked Bridges. But Bridges would not be drawn. All Frenchmen were dangerous in debate.

'Oh,' he said, 'governments come and governments go but there will always be Paris.'

'And any government can find support in Paris. People are fickle,' said Elisa.

'I can't agree,' said Gagnon. 'It is only this idea of a Commune that creates a mob. It's like a sewer sucking in the rabble, the filth. Paris is a hothouse for fanatics. And that is precisely it. That is exactly why we need the Government to do something about the foetid atmosphere. Something drastic.'

Janik looked sharply at her father. Bridges, Elisa saw, put his hand on her arm. Gagnon was in full flight. 'Forget the Paris Guard and their communistical ideas. Look at the soldiers of the line, look at the forces of the Republic, the Zouaves, the Breton *mobiles*. They were superb in defence of their country. And they will be again.'

'Perhaps you would like the Emperor back from England?' said Janik.

'Why not? Take a dory and bring him back, eh, Alain?'

And what could Bridges answer to this pointless banter, though he was glad there was an end to the fulminating. He looked to Elisa for help.

'I think the two of you should have gone there in the first place. Never mind Paris. London is the place,' she said.

'Ah, but you are forgetting. We have a business to run,' said Gagnon. 'Life is not all cherries, eh, Alain? However sweet. There were opportunities that were not to be missed. And there will be more. You wait and see. I'd keep that army well equipped if I was in power. Boots on their feet and beef in their bellies. Just . . . in . . . case . . .' He brought his fist down in a slow grinding motion on the tablecloth and looked to each in turn, soliciting support or perhaps laughter.

Janik got up and left the table.

'If you will excuse me,' said Bridges, and followed her.

Now Marguerite had room to make a statement of her own about the rhubarb, which was still too tart despite the sugar and the cicely, while she watched Monsieur and Madame raise eyebrows over their daughter: he as if to excuse, to say it must be a strain, all said and done, surrendering one's virginity, one's personal Paris to the foe; but Madame perhaps sharing her, Marguerite's, own private opinion that there was more here than meets the eye. And what was this about, this freakish display from the high-strung child? Who should by now have softened into woman.

'The rhubarb is just right,' Madame said. 'I wish you would not fuss.' But Marguerite liked to.

UPSTAIRS, JANIK RAGED against her father and grieved for a precarious ideal and for its terrible vulnerability. Bridges stroked her hair and advised discretion. Her father was a strong man, he said, and it was not always worth the effort to oppose him. The troubles, anyway, were miles away. It was really nothing to do with them. And then it was necessary to hold her even tighter. He wondered if his breath upon the crook of her neck where she smelled so sweet might be calming, but she raised her shoulder to squeeze him out.

'No,' she said. 'It can't be right to do nothing when there is so much need. So much work to be done. People waiting to be helped.'

'And people waiting for their pudding.' He was not sure as he closed the door behind him whether he had wanted her to hear.

Elisa watched Bridges take his seat again. She would have liked to know how matters stood. But Bridges was giving nothing away but his customary smile.

'Now,' said Gagnon. 'Tell us how it really was.'

ELISA KNEW HE would come to see her. It was why she had gone to the glasshouse. She was, she thought, like a dowdy guinea hen picking its way to a covert, hearing the grasses snap behind her. She looked for things to do. There were the pho-

tographs of Marguerite. They bored her. Marguerite as Echo
meeting Narcissus. 'Desire, Marguerite. Don't you know what it
means?' Marguerite as Persephone. 'No, Marguerite, you are not
sad, you are not afraid. You are innocence itself. You know nothing.' And Marguerite indeed did not know, being innocent of all
classical allusion unless it were to Atlas or Hercules, their names
stamped on rival brands of scrubbing brushes. Melancholy was
her speciality and so there were Antigones and Ruths and Iseults
in droves. But Elisa now was irritated by the knowledge that the
expression was assumed. The photograph was like a mirror,
catching the observed and the observer both so that it was a dou-
ble image, the observer always present in the consciousness of
the observed. It was there in the eyes. She would have liked to be
able to take a photograph unseen, to come all unannounced,
unnoticed, upon a rage, a heartbreak, and trap it on the solid
glass like a fly on glue-paper.

She turned her attention to technicalities where the mystery of
process was still intact, a reliable distraction. She went to find
some eggs. There was no one outside. She had to rummage
under bushes and into plants, for Marguerite was avid in her egg
collection every morning, hating to see them wasted on what she
called a pastime. When she had enough, Elisa took them into the
glasshouse and separated the albumen. She put it to one side.
Then she filled a beaker with water and began to stir in some
chunks of salt. She stirred for a while, standing with her back to
the door, imagining a footfall behind her, a shadow across the
light. Bored with trying to hurry the solution along, she carried
the tin cup of yolks outside and whistled for Tor. Four whole,
heavy yolks slid out fast onto the path for the dog to lick, its tail
waving. The fifth, which was slightly broken, she held back and
then, tilting her head and closing her eyes, drank it herself.
Before she had opened her eyes she knew he was there.

'*Your health!*' he said. He used the English words and his voice
sounded distant and amused.

'And yours,' she answered and smiled and would not be put

out. 'I'm sorry I have none to offer.' And was at once put out by her own words, which made her think of the one egg yolk sliding and their two mouths sucking at the lip of the cup.

'Was it good?' She had stood in such a way.

She laughed. 'It was only an egg.'

And now he went inside and roamed the length of the bench, observing, picking up the whisk, the salt jar.

'What is this? *La cuisine? La chimique?*'

'Something much newer. The science of light.' But thinking in her turn, What is this? Rudeness? Amiability? Though she knew it was neither and would not admit.

'The eggs then?'

He tipped the bowl of albumen, watching the transparent masses slide through each other, and thought of her with an egg yolk in her mouth. There was an outrageous innocence about the image. It was carnal but only in the manner of an infant. Or an animal. He could not reconcile the two. The images, too, slid about.

'They are good for you.' She tipped her head back as she had when she drank.

And the two images combined in perfect hedonism.

'No, look,' she said. 'I'll show you. I'm preparing the paper. Are you interested?'

'No,' he said. 'But show me.'

'These are the papers I will use to take prints from the glass. One needs an emulsion that will make the silver nitrate stick. So it is quite simple. This is a base I prepare with albumen and with a salt solution. So.' She was pouring and mixing, concentrating. He watched her face.

'Are you happy?' She had put down the bowl quite suddenly to ask it.

'You know.'

'Tell me.'

'You know your daughter.'

'And?'

'She has changed.'

'Yes, I've seen that. But then she has not changed. It is Janik.
She has only changed back. It is how she always was.'

She took up the whisk but he stopped her hand.

'She is obsessed.'

'Yes. Perhaps possessed.'

'She does not want a husband.'

'Then you must make her.'

He moved round behind her and she waited for the touch of his hands. He whispered.

'When I have her I think of you.'

He was touching her neck, her face, close to her ear. And she did not say it was not possible, that he must not. Instead she reached up and closed her fingers round his.

ALAN BRIDGES, BLEARY and dishevelled, groaned and squinted at the light. He would have liked more sleep and thought how Marguerite, bringing the water earlier, must certainly have supposed a night of lust. Half the night he had sat up with Janik, watched as she was consumed by her own passion, saw how ideas burn more fiercely than flesh. She did not love him, did not appear even to want him. Once she had said, 'I want only to serve God.' Rejection was never so simple, nor so bleak. Bridges had stayed awake, had wondered how he had got into such a situation. Who had thought himself so honeyed over with luck, had scarcely believed. But who all the time had been holding only a magician's gift, exploding now into smoke in his hands. A rigged offering from fate. This breakfast, he thought, might as well be a wake for marital felicities. And there was his host, his father-in-law, as irrepressible as ever in his cheer.

It was a sunny morning, his family was at his table and Paul Gagnon had made a decision. For him, peace or war made little difference. The world continued to turn his way and life to prove that one good thing always led to a better. The reputation he made for himself at Le Havre during the war had assumed a life of its own. After the armistice there had been the work at Rouen clearing the river. The English colliers that had blocked the channel just below the city had not moved for Prussian engineers nor French, but for Gagnon had stirred, bucked with the slowness of planets, and lifted themselves, giant bears dancing to the strange gravity of the marvellous contraptions he raised above them. Gagnon made his mark.

At Rouen an agent from Paris had sought him out. There was work, he had said, for a year to come. It was not in Gagnon's mind to work there for a year, but the most urgently needed work was always the most profitable and the agent had implied that the gain would be great for the successful completion of the most difficult job, a submerged locomotive on the Marne. And so this morning Gagnon had made up his mind. He would go at once to Paris. Everything his son-in-law had told him since his return piqued his interest. It was not to go and ogle the defeated, not that. He was not a morbid man. Nor to profit from their misery. But to see the great forts and the destruction wrought upon them, to see the stones that still stood, in spite. No one could say it was not arresting. Here were the works of man subjected to all of man's most dire contrivances. He had an urge to walk among them. It was, besides, time. It was time for him to, what should one say, have a little holiday. There was Alain, not so much younger than he. No, not so much at all really. On his honeymoon. Dawdling with the young and dimpled, the delightful, his daughter. Was he jealous? Well, yes, call it jealousy if you like or, no, envy. Yes, he was envious. That was it. He envied him that excitement of the new. Nothing to match it, that first taste. Not that this was Alain Bridges' first taste, no—he was not blind— but his first taste of this particular apple. The sweet spurting surprise. He could almost drool if he thought about it too long. Not that he was given to depravity. Far from it. Hadn't he redoubled his attentions to his wife since Alain Bridges' arrival in the house? But his wife. His wife did not deserve it. She was as con-

trary as water and could be relied upon only to make him mad.
There were nights when she turned her face away and held her
teeth together. Enduring. That's what it was. Supporting. Yes,
supporting him. Arching her back dutifully, stoically. Oh, give
her a goddamn martyr's crown. Christ, he hated her for that. And
then when he hated her most, he wanted her, but it was no good,
she lying there, all her self running away, seeping away through
his fingers and he could not hold it, like water, seeping away,
leaving him stranded. But the other nights. That was the matter.
On those other nights she was different again, rushing at him,
hurling herself against him, like waves breaking. And sobbing
too. He could drown in her depths. And might have if he had still
loved her. But he was saved. He had had enough. Enough of her
half-brained pursuits, her 'art.' Elisa with her head stuck under
the black velvet half the time, clumping in and out in all weath-
ers, looking like a peasant, skirt hitched up around her and
chicken shit on her boots. Elisa keeping the servants from their
work, letting her dinner go cold on her plate because she'd had a
sudden thought. She wasn't interested in him. And wasn't that a
licence, of sorts. No, not of sorts. It was a licence. Besides.
Besides. There were a hundred reasons to go to Paris besides the
one he had in mind. And he was able now to do such a thing.
Alain was a capable man. He could run the business perfectly
well, he and Felix together, Felix who simply worked whether
one was there or not.

Gagnon was good at besides. Life never ceased to be accommodating. Unfailingly it provided him with justifications for
whatever he wanted.

'Good then. That's settled. I shall go,' although he would have
liked a little more interest from the others that March morning as
they breakfasted together, but his wife was preoccupied with her
coffee, cradling it, cupping it and inhaling with purpose as if she
were trying to cure a cold, and his son-in-law was intent upon his
bread, sculpting *confiture*, nodding only, agreeing, nodding.
Neither did his daughter exclaim as he would have liked. But

then, she was a woman now. He waited but she did not respond at all, only set her mouth, he thought, in a pout and began to push the brittle crumbs around with her finger.

'If the order from Bertrand Fils comes you can go ahead.'

The jam now was dripping from Bridges' bread. 'Right. Right,' he said, and took some more.

'And you should see if those two cutters of Maréchal's brother-in-law are still in the dock. You know he was wanting to sell one.' Gagnon mashed his bread between his teeth with mechanical ferocity. He ate with audible squishings and grindings. 'What I was thinking of was the traffic to and from Southampton. There is a great activity now, you said. It could be the time to strike.'

The world was at his feet. The Prussians had come and over-run his country and left it in turmoil solely, one would think, to provide him with a few more ventures.

Alan Bridges fastidiously, illogically, scraped the jam from his bread and began with equal attention to put it back on again.

Elisa watched across the rim of her cup. Janik's finger had ploughed a perfect circle through the debris. She had the look she used to have when she made up her mind not to cry.

'I'm coming with you,' she said.

Alan Bridges, the over-attended bread halfway to his mouth, saw that Elisa was looking straight at him. He did not look away. His father-in-law, at last having some response, though not the one he had expected, was fully occupied.

So now it seemed that the magician's trick was not yet finished and the smoke might yet clear to reveal something altogether more delightful.

There was no moving Janik, though Gagnon was trying. Clearly he did not want company. He was a busy man, he said, and would not be able to attend to her in any way, so how did she propose to get about? Alain, she must realize, could not be spared on any account.

But Janik had an answer for every objection. She would only trouble him on the journey, she said. After that, she would go to the house of her godmother. Gagnon raised his shoulders in a gesture of impatience and looked at Bridges. Bridges took his wife's hand.

'I think we should go out for a walk.' he said.

Outside, the high live air elated. The wide sky made Bridges want to shout. He chose his words carefully, shamelessly, knowing in advance their effect. He spoke about duty and Janik spoke about a higher duty; he talked about responsibility and Janik talked about sacrifice. He stopped short of talking about love. 'My duty is to take care of you,' he said. 'I'll come with you of course.' It was not what she wanted. Her face was wretched in its misery, ugly. Bridges knew what it was she did not want to say. She did not love him, did not want him. He waited. After a little while she said, 'In such a time of trouble, I want only to give myself to the service of God, to his people. Do you understand?'

'No,' he said, 'but you are free to go. You know that. Just don't stay long. Let us say two weeks, no more than three. You must promise that. And you have to write. Every day, if it is only a line.'

'I will write,' she said. 'And I do promise.'

It gave him a start of excitement to hear it made. He wished he had not asked for it. It produced the thrill of the schoolboy about to step into trouble, and he disgusted himself. Opportunity was one thing; creating it quite another. It took away his appetite.

'BUT THEN IT is not what I would have wished for my son-in-law,' said Gagnon that night, folding a shirt (in such a way, Elisa thought, that he might not want to put it on once he unpacked it). 'To have his wife run off at once. Does that look good?'

'With her father?'

'No, but that is not the point. Not the point at all. Is she discontent? People will ask themselves.'

'She is just strong-willed. You know.'

'But they don't understand that. Just don't go telling them she's gone to Paris. Bridges has a reputation to maintain here. No one respects a man whose wife has gone off the rails. Say she's just going to Trouville. That her aunt is sick.'

'I don't think you have to worry.' She could have said more but would not, for her life, seem to sue for her daughter's absence. 'We tried to dissuade her. We did our best. Both of us.' It seemed a good idea to make some things clear to start with.

'And Alain.'

'Exactly.'

'Well, she's stubborn. Like me. But she is on her own. I told her she can go to Agathe's but as far as I'm concerned she is on her own. I told her. I'm a busy man, I said. I shan't be there to hold her hand.' Gagnon, too, with points of his own to establish. He snapped his bag shut. He might have been sealing his plans and his jeopardized intentions safe inside.

So that Elisa now risked more. 'You should have let Alain go with her. He offered,' and watched a self she used to be approach the self she was to become, handing over responsibility for a yet-to-be-committed sin—like an empty pair of shoes left out of the packing.

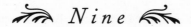

# *Nine*

IN THE RAILWAY carriage, the grimy windows showed sepia images of the spring day outside. Closed inside, Gagnon and Janik might have been travelling in different directions. 'It's like the *Lady Morgan*,' he had said. 'You have to be there when the time is right. Luck is a point of view, that's all.' So that the memory of the photograph returned and Janik knew that in all the long time since she had first seen it, first rejected it and put it out of her mind as unthinkable, she had come somehow to believe it. The sudden memory of the thing was like an unwanted third passenger beside them; she had no reply. She kept her eyes fixed on the passing countryside. Gagnon gave up his attempts at conversation and turned his thoughts to Paris. His daughter was not the most ideal travelling companion he could think of. But there was little chance that they would interfere with each other's activities beyond the Gare Saint-Lazare—if they ever arrived. For there was reason to doubt. After Rouen there had been a delay. Now the train stopped again and they were only a few miles further on. The conductor moved through the train, a weak man, this, sweaty and not quite up to it now that his job had become difficult. With each new rumour that he quelled—'No Madame, it is not an unexploded shell'—he laid the foundations for another—'Certainly, if there had been an insurrection the train would not run.'

On the platform, the station master who was also the guard had more success. He was pleased with himself. There were those on the train who thought their money might make it move. In a bluster of tartan and velvet they came down to the platform to make their assault on him. But all their urgent hissing needs to be in Paris were as spray on a rock. He was steadfast. With some effort he got them all back on board, even the large man in the paisley waistcoat with his endless, 'At once! I insist! I insist!' and patrolled the platform, eyeing the door handles, daring one to move, wishing perhaps for padlocks. A model of discretion and authority he was, a perfect meld, saving his information for those who would know what to do with it: the mayor, for instance, when he had finished getting his hair cut. For no one had even an inkling of what he knew: that the Government had fled and in Paris the *Comité Central* sat in the Hôtel de Ville.

Not surprising, then, his urge to strangle when the over-eager messenger came flying down the platform. 'The lines are open! The *Comité* has reopened the lines! Thiers is finished!'

The train then was a lit fuse, doors opening and closing along its length like sparks igniting. And the station master, the steadfast rock, now found the tide turning to swamp him with enquiries about the next train back to Rouen.

Janik and her father stood among the crowds and argued. It was obvious that she must turn back. It was equally obvious that she would not. Gagnon got back onto the train and took down her valise, brought it to the platform. Janik picked it up and went straight back to the train. A young man helped her back on board. Gagnon watched and pulled at his cravat to loosen it; a vein jumped at the side of his neck and would not stop. He walked down to the luggage van where Janik's box was stowed. The guard there would not unlock it.

There was the sound of singing. At the end of the platform some National Guardsmen had turned their rifles butt end up and hung their caps on them.

Gagnon watched and wondered whether there would be any Government left in Paris to pay him. He would ask for a fifty percent increase, and two-thirds down at least. If they could not meet that, he would take his daughter and go straight back. He would take her home anyway as soon as the job was done. She'd be all right with Agathe Fougard. Agathe probably wouldn't let her outside the front door if there was trouble.

THERE WAS A face at the window of every compartment as the train approached the station. But there was nothing extraordinary about the streets. It would have been a comfort to know what to expect. There was no sign of agitation anywhere. And then they were in a deep cutting and could only surmise. 'No turning back now,' said Gagnon, smiling at Janik. Who had not ever thought of it.

The Gare Saint-Lazare was a pleasant surprise. Gagnon, seeing to the luggage, noticed a train pulling out. If this was an insurrection then it was directed by fools. Trains returning to the provinces were sure to come back filled with Thiers' troops. But anxiety seemed not to be the order of the day. Red banners draped the doorway out of the concourse. Outside on the Rue Saint-Lazare, everywhere was open. There was a smell of bread and roasting coffee.

'Listen, my dove,' said Gagnon, overcome suddenly with a vision of Agathe in her dreary crepe offering stale cake and warm *tilleul* like urine, 'we should take a bite to eat before Agathe's. I'll send this luggage on and we'll find somewhere outside.'

Janik could not see enough. In the café she took out her pencil and her notebook and tore out a page. At a distance she could feel more than warm towards her husband. All the cafés were open, she wrote. Paris, she said, was *en fête*. The station was garlanded with red banners and all citizens of goodwill wore red sashes or red scarves. Paris had declared itself a free city. And there were flowers. Imagine! She had seen National Guardsmen with flowers in the muzzles of their rifles. (She had noticed, too, that the arms of the crosses on top of the domes and chapel roofs had been sawn off, but she did not write it.) There was no need to worry. This was a city that had cried out for justice and its prayers had been answered. *Vive La Commune!*

'May I?' said Gagnon, and took the sheet so that he could add a few lines, scribbling in between his daughter's: *Not as bad as you might think. Extr. calm. Will fizzle when they find out what work means. Thiers and some good men from V. will finish it. Be back before then. Get another shipment from Mercer's at S.hampton. Price of cheese astronomical also poultry.* He drew an arrow ending in an exclamation point in parentheses beside Janik's *Vive La Commune!*

'I'll find an envelope for you,' he said.

They took a cab to Madame Fougard's house.

Agathe Fougard, Janik's godmother, was always addressed as Tante by both Elisa and Janik. To Paul Gagnon she was Madame; there was not a man alive to whom she was anything else; even her priest was intimidated. There was no red banner floating from her window. Perverse always, Agathe Fougard had draped her window boxes in black crepe. She had the shutters closed already, or perhaps she had not opened them all day, so that when Janik and her father were shown in it took a minute for their eyes to adjust to the gloom.

As if announcing her, the clock struck.

'God bless us this hour,' she said and made the sign of the cross as she came in. She walked as if she were treading something unwanted into the ground and in her voice there was a residual irritation, like grit that cannot be sluiced away. 'Sit down. Are you tired?' Though surely she could not care. 'We'll have a *tilleul*.'

Gagnon said he could not stay long.

Madame Fougard looked at Janik.

'So you have come to work in the *ambulance*. They're all dead.' Though whether she meant the patients or the doctors was not clear.

'No, Tante Agathe. I have come to work among the poor.'

'They would be better dead.'

'Oh come now,' said Gagnon, risking informality and why not? With this woman the least exchange was a game of dare. 'Madame, you know you have a heart of gold.'

The clock ticked.

The tea was lukewarm. Janik imagined that the dinner too might be waiting, already prepared in the kitchen. Cold.

'Well it is up to you,' Madame Fougard said. 'There are the deserving and there are the wicked. You shall see. And why aren't you wearing something on your head?'

Gagnon belched, thought it best to say 'Thanks be to God'—just in case—and smiled at Janik from behind his cup. The woman was a dragon. He could not imagine her condoning Janik's going out alone. Janik would be safe with her. From the wicked godless poor. From even fire and pestilence with such a protectress.

Madame Fougard turned slightly away from Gagnon to address him. 'I think it necessary for you to know, Paul, that accommodation in my house—God be praised I have a roof at all—is cramped, very cramped indeed,' her rusty ribbons agitated, her lips doing their best to cover the yellow teeth.

Gagnon smiled smoothly, shook his head, eyes serenely closed. 'No need, Madame, no need to trouble yourself. I am staying at the Hôtel Vincennes. In fact,' such a slick escape, he put down his cup, 'in fact, I should be on my way now. You know where you may find me, my dear,' kissing the top of his daughter's head, 'though I am sure you will have no need. Madame.' He contemplated the muslined hand, wrinkled skin showing through like a boiled ham forgotten in the pantry. He shook it. 'A thousand thanks. A thousand.'

There was not much left of the day. From Madame Fougard's, Gagnon went straight down to the Quai D'Orsay. A sign on the door of the Department of Public Works read: *Business as Usual. Tomorrow.* Gagnon wondered. He doubted there would be anyone with authority to release funds to him. All the more reason to enjoy his freedom while he could. As soon as he arrived at his hotel, he ordered a warm bath. Lying in the steaming tub he considered the pleasures to come. He at any rate had money. You could get anything with money.

ELISA THOUGHT ABOUT it every day. She thought about it all day. It stopped her eating. She could concentrate on nothing else. Their eyes met, their hands. Their mouths. She imagined every detail. Standing in her glasshouse, she stared at the equipment. The only picture she wanted was inside her head, was Bridges making love to her. She closed her eyes. To want a thing so badly and it not yet known; it was not possible. She wanted to go now to find him at the boatyard. Do it all under the sad mute face of Felix. She went to the house and put on her bonnet and her wrap and went out.

The day was clear and blue. From the hill she could see Le Havre across the water, the sun reflecting from the pale stone. A thin layer of smoke like a narrow band of cloud hung above the port.

Elisa walked down to the harbour. Even the gulls seemed quiet without the wind to toss them at the sky. When she came in sight of the boatyard, she turned away and started up the hill towards the cliff walk. With the water stretching away below her she felt better.

Alan Bridges rubbed the office window with his sleeve and watched her go. After a few minutes he scribbled a note—*At the office of M. Crécy*—and pinned it to the office door.

CRÉCY LEANED BACK in his chair and savoured his calvados. The Englishman, he saw, had finished his and was cradling a few dregs for the sake of decency.

'Another.'

He reached for the bottle.

'No. I thank you. This is very well, thank you.'

'Well then you are a moderate man—and that can only be good for Gagnon.' He laughed and feared he may have been misunderstood, for the Englishman sat on the very edge of his chair and could not seem to control his knee, which jigged up and down of its own accord, making the chair judder against the leg of the desk. 'Which is to say he is a shrewd man. I drink to the continued success of your partnership.'

'Thank you.' Bridges wondered when it was polite to conclude. 'And may it be of mutual benefit. Now—' he put his glass on the desk.

'You may call me Frédéric,' said Crécy. 'Why not? Gagnon and I are old friends. From our youth.' And it was not time, surely, to get down to work again already.

'Thank you.' Bridges was getting up. 'Now if—'

God the English were boring. Crécy losing patience suddenly would rather say the words himself than hear this Englishman say them: 'Good. Now if there's nothing else—?' He got up, brushing the front of his jacket though there was nothing there except perhaps the last crumbs of his hospitality, which, without a proper response, had become an irritation. He held out his hand. 'Monsieur Bridges. Until next time.'

'Indeed. And many thanks Monsieur Crécy.' For concluding at last, he might have added. Though his handshake was firm, was warm enough. Irritations were nothing, now that he was free to go. He could embrace the world.

ELISA WALKED UNTIL she came to a place where a long collar of cliff had fallen away, leaving a ledge that formed a lower path, protected on the landward side. She climbed down. Along the path there were isolated pockets cut back into the cliff, places where one could rest, slightly off the track, and take a breath. She stopped at one of these and leaned back against the chalky stone, watching the horizon fade and reappear in a blue haze. She imagined a shadow falling across her from the path above, saw herself turning, saw the polished leather of his boots, the bits of dead grass sticking to their wet surface. She would smile. You found me. And he would grin, drop to his haunches. He would hold out his hand.

The imperturbable sea. The sky. She could have wept. To have unpicked the fairy tale of faith. For here it was, the grace of God painted so blue that she could not mistake it. Extending immutable and calm. And now remote. But the mercy of God was infinite, wasn't it? His grace limitless? There was only one sin, Janik had told her, parroting doctrine, only one sin that could keep a soul from God: the sin against the Holy Ghost, the only sin that could leave a sinner stranded beyond grace. So even the ultimate transgression, the Unforgivable Sin, was then a reassurance for toothy twelve year olds. For who knew or could imagine what it might be, this trespass, this infraction against a spirit, a disembodied distillation of white? And—ignorance a welcome defence against blame—who would be foolish enough to ask? Except Janik. Janik with her tiresome persistence had to know. And Elisa had answered that she could not imagine. But now. Now, when she had almost forgotten all about it, Elisa knew: it was a turning away. And more than that: it was the knowing, knowing without a doubt that she would turn her back forever on the infinite blue.

THE DAILY LUNCHES at La Madonne had been resumed. As he left his office, Crécy, as he always did, tested the temperature of the air before he put on his hat. Today he remembered something else and turned back. Halfway up the stairs he called out, 'Gil, when you lock up, take the second page to Paul Gagnon's yard. The Englishman forgot to sign it.'

La Madonne was noisier than usual. The table at which the friends usually met had been pushed up against the wall to make room for a large party of *mobiles*.

'Have you heard?' Marèchal's timing was wanting, as always.

'No.' Nor was Crécy interested. Harmon and Marèchal

and Courtebois and even Vavin were already there. The spot with the least room had been left for him. He sat down, puffing conspicuously.

'You see who they are?'

'I see they've taken our place.'

'They are on their way to Versailles. There is to be a march on Paris.' All of life was a competition for Marèchal, even the bearing of news, as if some special honour accrued to the first to tell. But the *mobiles* had finished all the mackerel and it was only the irritation of their presence and not the prestige of their novelty that he acquired. Crécy ordered sole and turned with emphasis to Harmon.

'The doctor has gone back, I hear.'

'To Paris, yes.'

'They say the *ambulances* have disbanded. If the fighting starts it will be a shambles,' said Vavin. 'He's mad.'

'Gagnon, too,' said Courtebois. But no one could agree on Gagnon's whereabouts, and the only point of accord was that wherever he was he would come back smiling.

Crécy was not pleased. His sole was soggy. And now here was Gil and he had the document, squeezing past the backs of the *mobiles*.

'Good.'

Gil shook his head. 'He was not there. I did not think I should leave it.'

'He said he had to get back.'

'He wasn't there.'

'Augh.' Crécy shoved the letter under the side of his plate. 'All right, Gil. I'll see to it.' He felt like saying something malicious but there was nothing that would not reflect on Gagnon too.

Marèchal announced that the English were unreliable, but no one seemed inclined to take up an assault on an entire nation. He tried again. 'Monsieur Bridges might not be such a wise choice of business partner after all.' And now there was interest.

Crécy pointed out that he himself had always advised caution. Harmon disapproved of Marèchal's calumnies but it was not in his nature to say so. Instead he made excuses for his friend as he did for the rest of the world. For Harmon was gifted with a well of love which not even his work could turn brackish. He forgave men and women their faults more readily than their debts. He suggested that Marèchal would say as much of any Englishman, and Courtebois said if Marèchal wouldn't then he would. And not only unreliable. How about untrustworthy?

And here was an opportunity for Marèchal who now could say, 'Remember? Remember what I said?' Though no one did. 'Just a little while ago, in this very restaurant?'

Harmon sighed, waiting for the stale business about spies to be revived. 'But the Prussians have gone.'

'I never said he was working for the Prussians.' Marèchal chewed in a way he hoped was enigmatic.

'Somebody did.' Courtebois could contribute with confidence, having agreed at the time with the somebody, whom he could not now remember.

'Not the Prussians.' Marèchal quieter, quieter. More and more mysterious.

And at lunch tedious. Some still had business in the afternoon and there was no time to waste on riddles. They turned their attention to their plates. Except Courtebois, who suddenly understood and leaned forward and pointed at Marèchal with his fork.

'You're right, you know.' Making the others again look up. 'What organization, what *international* organization do you suppose is pulling the strings of the Commune?' He mouthed the word as if the Versailles men might jump up and attack at the mere mention, but they were fully engaged in a ribald joke with *le patron*. 'And where—where would you look for the headquarters of that *international* organization?'

Marèchal, capable only of mindless, vaguely aimed mischief, had thought of none of this before, could not himself answer Courtebois' question, but nodded sagely and murmured, 'Exactly.'

'Well in London. Of course.' Courtebois carried on eating. His case rested. But his melodrama was too much and the laughter from the next table was infectious.

'Of course,' said Harmon. 'That's why he wasn't in when Crécy's boy went round.'

And Crécy collaborated because it was time for some cheese. 'Yes,' he said, lowering his voice, conspiratorial, a stage whisper now. 'He went out . . . for lunch.'

'. . . to a Red Club,' said Harmon.

'No . . . to England'

And they laughed and dismissed the prospect of the Englishman now that he had entertained them.


SHE WAS AT the back of the chapel, kneeling on the floor behind the last bench. She had not lighted any candles. Thou shalt not. There was not even a commandment for her sin. Adultery was easy. Thou shalt not commit adultery. A commandment that could be broken like a china plate; and she was ready to break it—there was nothing that could not be mended. But this, this unforgivable sin. There was no name for it. To turn away from the possibility of grace. Thou shalt not. Thou shalt not even think of such a thing. Except that she had. She had seen the infinite. And now she was to live the unimaginable, must embrace her sin. She wanted to pray. But who to pray to for the courage to complete a sin?

She did not look round when Bridges pushed open the door. At first he did not see her in the darkness and then he went and stood a little behind her.

'Elisa?'

Still she did not look. 'Kneel down,' she said.

But Bridges was not about to pray. The world outside had been sucked away and they were adrift in this shell, on this sea of darkness and silence. Words might have been a help, had he any. Then his limbs did bend and he knelt behind her, over her, his mouth on her neck.

IN THE CHURCH of Saint-Eustache, an orator, a woman, stood in the pulpit and argued for the abolition of marriage. It was not what Janik had come to hear. She was not sorry when some of the crowd began to shout her down. The idea was too new. The woman climbed down, red faced, her teeth biting up all the unspoken words. A young man was next. He turned his fragile face to the hostile crowd, wire spectacles pinned close to his eyes like badges, hair cropped like a convict's. He carried his cap rolled up, holding it with both hands. The crowd settled down, his voice so quiet, his look so learned, he must know. He told them what they wanted to hear. They had grasped the future and now they must keep it. Never before had the people seen such swift and sure success in the fight against the tyranny of power. But now the real work began. They must organize. Were the poor hungry? Then they would feed them. Were the children in the factories tired and wretched? Then they would rescue them. No one else was going to do it. No one. They must organize and they must organize now. There would be fair and just elections but meanwhile let every man work to help his brother; let every citizen strive to build a benevolent, responsible community; justice and dignity were theirs at last. No one could take them away. And if Thiers came to try then they would defend them to the death—in the streets.

In a little while Janik had signed a paper and agreed to present herself that afternoon at the old Guard Rooms, where a district headquarters had been set up. One of the women taking names took off her red scarf and gave it to Janik, kissing her on both cheeks. She put the scarf round her neck. It smelled of leeks.

Janik would have liked to pray. Since she could not pray in the church she went outside and sat in the gardens, folding her hands in her lap. The red scarf was not a good idea. Some National Guardsmen wanted to sit beside her. She folded it up and pushed it into her pocket.

There was birdsong. She closed her eyes. She saw the leaves of the trees shimmer and catch fire, saw the trunk and limbs spiral in

tongues of flame. And at last there were wings. They beat about
her head and face but still she sat. They fanned the air above,
grew larger. Whole quarters of the sky shifted as they slammed
together. Janik wanted to lie flat to escape their thunder. Where
there had been trees there were churches and palaces roaring in
flame. The dense smoke lit by the flames billowed. She opened
her eyes. There was light everywhere flowing like water, over,
through. She was in the light and of it. She was the light. The
presence of the angel was beside her.


'I SHOULD HAVE known,' said Madame Fougard. 'You are no
more sensible than your mother. What motives led you to attend
a scurrilous meeting in the sacred precinct of a holy church I cannot imagine. I have left the fare for Le Havre on the table and I
have written to your so-called husband to expect you.'

That afternoon, at the old Guard Rooms where she went to
sign her name, Janik asked if there was somewhere she could
stay. The freckled woman behind the desk said that her sister had
a room. It was not very far.

Janik returned for her bags.

'I shall not expect to have to speak to you or even about you
again,' said Madame Fougard. She turned her cold, furry cheek
away and Janik was not sorry.


'A DECENT SMALL room at the top of the stairs,' the freckled
woman had said. It was small, certainly, and it was at the top of
four flights of stairs, but it was less a room than an area of the
sister's bedroom curtained off to help with the rent. And
Mademoiselle Cliquot was not alone. She slept, or more often did
not sleep, with her lover from the National Guard. Mademoiselle
Cliquot, scrawny, with greasy hair said, 'You mustn't mind us,
dear. We make a lot of noise.' And Janik was unable to sleep. She
tried not to mind but it was difficult. Extraordinary sounds issued

from Mademoiselle's throat and made her think of the Gadarene swine. She had to say an extra prayer when it was over.

In the first few days, Janik worked hard for the committee doing nothing she had come to Paris to do. She compiled lists, she queued up for sausages, she went to buy ink, paraffin, string, she cleared out a store room, and at last she was sent to help distribute clothing and dried beans in a dingy quarter of Belleville. She gave the scarf away too. When she returned at night to her room behind the striped curtain, she wished she was in the immaculate cell of Madame Fougard's spare bedroom. Her new friends urged her to go out with them in the evenings. There was always a meeting. Janik stayed behind to write a torrent of exclamations to her husband. The poverty! The misery! The sickness! She did not say The anger! or The bitterness! She did not say that Denise, who talked to her of a new order and of justice, had a rifle and wore it even at the baker's where she worked. She said the food queues were perhaps getting shorter and that people said the city had never seemed so peaceful since the judges and the police had been dismissed.


THE MAYOR OF the 2nd Arrondissement was an impatient man. He flicked his hand two or three times in the direction of the chair as if to say that Gagnon might sit, he did not have time. He paced and talked, looking at his watch, checking the window.

'I'm so pleased to meet you,' he said, though it was not apparent. 'Your skills are well known.'

Gagnon had time only to cough.

'But we shan't be needing them for this job after all. Things have changed. You've seen, of course, that things have changed.' He gestured to the window as if Gagnon might see the demands of the *Comité Central* written on the building opposite.

'So.'

He sat down and folded his arms. His gaze was unwavering.

Gagnon realized that the man had held his attention since he came in. He had not had time to look about the room and take

stock. It was not often he was at a disadvantage. Clearly he was
being asked to declare his interest before matters proceeded.
Ambivalence might not be a bad idea.

'You could still, however, use my services, I take it?'

The mayor gave a slight, noncommittal nod.

'Your situation cannot be easy. Restoring peace when there are
those who would destroy it. The city needs cleaning up.'

The mayor nodded again. 'Obviously some arrondissements
are in more need than others,' he said. 'Let me give you an
address. You'll find someone there who could make use of your
skills. A gentleman of the best intentions.'

Gagnon laughed and said intentions never paid bills. At which
the mayor remained stony but got up and went to his desk, wrote
a promissory note contingent on completion of the work to
bediscussed, let Gagnon see the amount, and then promptly tore
it up and put it in his pocket. 'My word is good,' he said. 'Like
your work.'


ACCIDENTS IT APPEARED had to happen. The man at the address
the mayor had given him did not reveal his name to Gagnon.
Something must be arranged, he said, if the good standing the
mob enjoyed in certain quarters were to be reversed. There was
a weapons manufactory on the outskirts of Belleville. Such a
building could almost be said to be a bomb waiting to go off.

Gagnon's evening was quite destroyed along with his equanimity. There was the mayor's promise. A sum he could not have
dreamed of. For such an easy job. And yet it was not the sort of
work he relished. Against the Prussians, yes, that was one thing.
He had done such things. But against his own countrymen?
When someone could get hurt? No views, however despicable,
could justify it.

The next morning, in the Rue de la Paix, certain citizens
marching on the side of order fell beneath the guns of a rough
bunch of the National Guard. Gagnon heard the story more than
once. The proprietor said the National Guard had fired the first

shot; the waiter said it was the demonstrators themselves. No one could say for sure. By the afternoon the names of those who had fallen became known: a doctor, a retired colonel, and others, one of them a shipping agent Gagnon had had dealings with.

Now he felt better. He would be doing Paris a favour to take the mayor's money. He went back to discuss the details of the proposed accident. A young man, built like a farmer, broad and stocky, was introduced to him. Obviously it had to be done, this new man said, in a way that would bring the greatest amount of discredit to the supporters of the National Guard. Yesterday's unfortunate occurrence had been perfect in that respect—but so many useful people lost . . . it was a shame. Nevertheless, it had provided them with a new idea, he said. Next to the weapons manufactory there was a convent, Notre-Dame-de-la-Croix. The nuns passed through an adjoining alleyway each day when the Angelus rang. Look at it like this: they were all on their way to heaven anyway.


AND HE HAD only thought to test the water. The sudden depth, the blackness, and the need to get out fast alarmed Gagnon. He had tried to walk away, had raised his price thinking they would never agree, thinking he could pick up his hat, say sorry gentlemen, shake hands, perhaps, wish them success, regret the fact later on the train, safely going home. No one could have been more surprised when they agreed to his price; no one more than Gagnon who never had learned in all these years that he always got what he wanted.


MADAME FOUGARD WAS as acid as an unripe plum. The child had gone, she said. She said she had only an address, and proffered the square of paper by the corner, three redundant fingers raised, horns to ward off evil.

At the Rue des Bergers, the woman downstairs said try the

headquarters. 'The district headquarters,' she said, spitting a little so that Gagnon had to move back. 'They've set up in the old Guard Rooms.' She muttered, *'Vive La Commune!'* and shut the door. Gagnon hammered until she opened it again.

'Can you read?' he said taking out his pocket book. She shook her head. Gagnon scribbled a note to Janik to get her bags and meet him at the café at seven o'clock; 'Where we ate before Agathe's,' he wrote in case the note reached other hands. He held it out to the woman. She did not take it. When he had counted out twenty-five francs, she took it and shut the door.


WHEN JANIK ARRIVED at the station café she did not have her bags with her. Gagnon, who had been waiting, drinking one absinthe for every ten minutes she was late, felt a volcanic rage building.

'You can go without your bags,' he said.

'I'm not going anywhere.'

'Listen.' Gagnon leaned forward across the table. 'This is not a time for martyrs and saints. You don't know half of it.'

But she would dispute. 'I know,' she said and would not bend. Or break.

'I'm telling you. I know. The siege was nothing, a fête, compared to what is round the corner.'

'And why do you know?'

'I just do. And what I have learned would turn your hair white, my young lady.'

'Have you raised the locomotive?'

'That's not important.'

'But have you?'

'There is other work to be done.'

'For Versailles? For the Government of National Defence?'

'For order.'

He might have said for corruption, or for tyranny. She was disgusted.

'Well. You get on with your good work. I'll get on with mine. We don't have any more to talk about.' She moved to get up.

He reached and missed her arm and instead clutched awkwardly at her sleeve cuff to stop her.

'At least get out of that filthy hole.' He was giving her money now, pushing it at her, clumsy again. 'Agathe won't have you back but you can get yourself into a proper hotel at least. Get out of that quarter.'

'It's not filthy and anyway all the rooms are like that.'

'It's not the place for someone like you.' He slurred his words in his attempt to cajole. 'You are too pure, too good.'

She looked at him and despised his drunken sentimentality. 'Well it's too late now for the convent. You married me off, remember?'

He caught a look that brought her back to him, a child again, vulnerable.

'Ah, my precious, my only one,' he said.

She bent over to kiss him and smelled the absinthe, said, 'Stay there. I don't need an escort.'

As she walked away he was conscious of a desperate lurching fear. It came at him like panic and entered with a cold plunging fall from mouth to bowel. Suppose she thought again about it . . . Suppose . . .

He was running, stumbling on the iron legs of the chairs, running, trying to seem not to run from the café with a treacly lack of speed. He did not want to call her name. He grabbed her arm, catching hold this time, and stopped her, stood gasping, the first word beaten back with the need for every new breath. 'Don't!' he said. 'I didn't mean it. Don't go to any convent. Don't even go near one. Take it from me. The mob, you know,' and it relaxed him, this sudden inspiration, 'the National Guard. They could attack at any time.' He was pleased with this fabrication, the way it served a dual purpose, shifted the blame.

She was dismayed by his behaviour. 'All right,' she said quietly and patted his hand on her arm. 'All right.'

GAGNON WAS SOBER as a stone when he met after midnight with the young man in a small room over a tailor's shop in the Rue de Saint-Martin.

By morning the details of his plan were in place. When he walked back just before dawn past a battalion of the Guard assembling in the Place de Grève, Janik was no longer a problem. Alain would remove her. Paris was no place for a young woman—a wife! Paris was no place for anyone. He would send to Alain and Alain would come right away and get her. If she wouldn't obey her father any longer, at least she would obey her husband. He could come and get her. By the time Bridges got the letter, the job would be done and he himself would be on his way back. The business wouldn't suffer. Elisa could take care of things.

A layer of pink mist lay on the surface of the Seine. There were early fishermen setting up under the Pont Neuf. Gagnon went down and walked along the quay, the walls of the buildings all along the north side were taking colour from the rising sun. They glowed. Everything was manageable. Everything worked out. The whole exercise would be worth it. Though he did not actually smile, all the muscles of his face realigned themselves. His fee had doubled twice in twenty-four hours.

MARGUERITE COCHARD, STAYING at the house in the absence of Monsieur, knew all about it. Marguerite knew all about everything. She was profoundly disgusted but not surprised. Her mistress was aberrant. Anyone could see that. How it had gone unnoticed by so many for so long was beyond her. By Monsieur even! He was a man who knew what's what. There weren't many up and about before Monsieur Gagnon. Nobody could pull one over on Le Gagnant. And yet she knew he didn't know. Only an idiot would leave a woman like Madame with a reprobate like

*Mister* Alain Bridges. Where they did it though—Marguerite had to concede that her omniscience was not quite complete. She had watched, oh yes. Not exactly spied on them, just, well, kept an eye. They were never alone. Well, not for long. No one was that quick, that desperate maybe but not that quick. During the day, every day, Madame worked in the glasshouse. But the glasshouse was in full view of the kitchen window and, as she said, she always kept an eye out. But if Bridges ever left the office it was not to visit the glasshouse. And anyway she, Marguerite, was always backwards and forwards, in and out. They knew that. They wouldn't be so foolish. So that left the nights. Of course she didn't lie awake all night, didn't pretend to. But that wasn't to say she hadn't sat up late in the box room where they kept her bed. She couldn't read, had never learned. She sewed. Caps with ribbons. It wasn't easy in the lamplight; the stitches had to be so small. But once she got started time disappeared. Several nights she'd been up until two, three o'clock. And not a soul. She'd listened. And anyway she was the one who made the beds. She'd have been able to tell. Oh, they'd smooth out the sheets and all that, take precautions. But that wouldn't alter the smell. There was a smell of it. It was unmistakable. It was like foxgloves just before they turn. It was the way men smelled. She knew anyway because of that time with him, with Monsieur. That had been years ago, her first year with them. Madame pregnant. She did him a service. There was nothing in it. Except that she had the money for new shoes next day (for which she was more than grateful, don't be in any doubt about that) but, as she was saying, that time she had nearly had a fit. Walked into her room that night and *smelled* him. Hours afterwards but he might have been there in the room standing wagging that thing in front of her. She'd washed her linen the same day and she remembered because it had snowed and when she brought the sheets in they were frozen solid and she'd had to bang them on the edge of the table to get them to fold over. But to get back to the point, she was up before anyone. So when they found time, or where, she couldn't say. But they did. There was not a doubt in her mind.

She'd watched them at dinner. She'd watched their eyes.
Madame would look up from her dinner and he would be looking
at her but she'd look down again straight away. None of that
business you'd expect between adulterers, no smirking over their
guilty secret, licking their lips. But there was still something. The
way Madame sat there looking at her plate. She might have had
her skin peeled off her. She looked as if there wasn't one place on
her that wasn't raw. And him. He just kept on eating slowly but
he was just as bad. Looked as if he might push his plate away at
any moment, discover that he'd been eating something rotten all
along. Yes that was it. It wasn't exactly what a person *could* see. It
was what a person knew was bound to happen, what a person
*might* see at any moment if they continued there much longer. It
was he pushing his plate away, sliding it right to the edge and it
tilting, toppling to the floor, leaving the knife and fork stuck in
his hands, desperately silly; it was she looking up, her mouth
opening, the expression on her face like someone watching a man
fall overboard, or watching herself and him, the two of them out
there, drowning in the fog and nothing she can do about it.

## ⫍⫍ *Ten* ⫎⫎

WHEN JANIK GOT back to the lodgings, the others were out and not expected to return. The old woman downstairs stopped her in the hall. She was excited by something nasty and could not wait to tell it.

'Didn't you hear?' she said. 'Everyone was talking about it. There was fighting at the Pont de Neuilly this morning. And all the little girls from Notre-Dame-du-Ciel coming back from their Palm Sunday procession. But the Government *mobiles* keep shelling and they don't stop and the sisters are crazy anyway and they tell the little girls keep walking and do you think the *mobiles* stop?' Such a moment to stop now and puff on her pipe and enjoy the young girl's face. 'There were legs and arms blown into the water. Heads.'

Janik tried to get by, turning her face from the smoke.

'Well now everyone wants blood. That's where they've gone.' She jerked her pipe towards the stairs but Janik wasn't looking or listening. 'They've gone to the meeting. They want revenge. And they'll get their blood. You wait and see.'

Janik shut her door. She threw her cape and her bonnet on the bed and knelt down to pray. She tried to pray for the souls of the schoolgirls. Instead she found herself praying for courage. She

imagined herself being given a rifle. Louise Michel, the Red
Virgin, was handing it to her.

It was not until she was ready for bed, standing in front of the mirror, that the thought came to her. It was as clear as if it had been written on the glass and yet it was not outside her, it was not detached; she knew it with a completeness that she knew only in her visions: her father, too, was out for blood.

It made her sit down. It was as if all other thoughts had been merely water flowing through her, fluid, commingling, and now they had parted suddenly, leaving the single shocking thought like the bones of a skeleton stark against the mud. She could taste the salt bones of it against her teeth and she knew it to be true. Her father was working for the Government. He was taking money and it was stained with blood. She remembered the photographs, the face she had not wanted to see, the knowledge (real, then, it too) of the man's falling, of her father's watching him go. And thinking of this, she remembered more: the way he had put the cost of the men's wages above the life of the falling man; the way he had married her off to improve his business. Someone was paying him well to stay here, in Paris, or he would have left. But no one was rebuilding; and if his job was not to salvage the locomotive, if that was no longer important, what was?

She sat down on the edge of the bed and folded her hands in her lap, certain that the answer would be given to her if only she waited (*you wait and see*) and was quiet enough. 'Just you wait and see. You wait and see.' Her thoughts fell away from her one by one. She sat quite still. The smell of her father pervaded the room, his breath returning to her perfumed with absinthe. She heard the sound of his iron chair falling on the marble floor. He was clutching at her arm. He was saying, 'Don't. Don't go near the convent.' And so the truth did begin to seep, like a stain through bandages.

She stood up and began mechanically to dress herself again.

The old woman, having heard the stairs creak, was at the door when she went down.

'Yes?' Believing as she did that all people wanted ever was absinthe or laudanum, she could always offer something.

'Where did they go?'

The old woman tipped her head back, stretching the loose skin of her neck. She leaned back a little as from a horse that might bite.

'You too?'

'I have to see them.'

'The Headquarters. At Saint-Eustache.'

Janik closed the front door. The gas was still lit at the end of the street. She had not ever been out alone so late. There was no one in the street nor in the next one, but everywhere she caught the sounds of people about, sometimes shouts, sometimes the noise of wheels and horses, music once. As she got nearer to Saint-Eustache, she began to pass others, couples and groups of men. A knot of soldiers stood at a corner under a lamp and smoked. As she approached, they assessed her in silence, resumed their conversation when she was close enough for them to see she was respectable. She began to almost run, not wanting to draw attention to herself but wanting like a rabbit in the open to take cover.

There were five National Guardsmen on the steps of the church. She nodded briefly and said 'Citizen' and one of them stepped aside and opened the door for her.

Its tremendous creak gave the impression of a great machine that had cranked all heads in her direction. The woman Michel was in the pulpit, the sound of her voice ringing under the vaulting. Janik nodded to left and right, resisting the urge to genuflect, and whispered 'Citizens,' as perhaps she might have crossed her fingers for luck. She slid into a chair at the back.

She found it harder than before to understand Louise Michel. The woman was possessed. She raged against Thiers' Government that trod on the necks of the people, she bled for the little girls that had fallen under its guns. But her eyes had been opened. What she had witnessed was nothing less than a dream of justice fulfilling its glorious destiny, the monster of Religion falling victim to the monster of Government. And it was up to every man, every woman now to rise up and mow down both

monsters so that Frenchmen would never again be called upon to
open fire on brother or sister, son or daughter.

Janik tuned to the young man beside her. 'What convent were they from?'

He pulled his sleeve across his nose and said, 'Notre-Dame-du-Ciel.'

'The one in Ménilmontant?'

'No. That's another one. That's miles away. You're talking about the one next to the factory where they make the ammunition. Notre-Dame-something-else.'

The woman's voice had become tiny. The man's words—*where they make the ammunition*—had left a silence that was expanding around her, over her. The stone of the building was retreating from its pressure, stretching, expanding upward, outward, making the distances inside grow vast. The blind bat of the woman's voice was lost beneath the distant ceiling and the congregation was reduced to dust motes on the floor. Nothing now but the terrible silence of the certain knowledge while what had begun as a seeping of truth flooded, filling her head, filling the church.

'De-la-Croix.' The young man nudged her rudely and she looked at him puzzled.

'Notre-Dame-de-la-Croix.'

'Oh, yes. Thank you.' She began to shiver. She told herself she could be wrong. But she knew about the convent; it wasn't far from her lodgings. And she knew about the factory from one of the meetings. It had been set up by the Government during the war. When the Government fled to Versailles, the insurgents seized it. And her father was working for the Government. Her father would not say what he was doing. It meant nothing, none of it—until she closed her eyes and summoned her father's voice again. And there it was, its urgency keen enough to cut through the thickness of drink: Don't go near.

And now people were on their feet and applauding. Janik got up and clapped.

The young man leaned towards her and said he could show her the place. Now. She shook her head and moved away, joined a crowd of people trying to talk to the woman, Michel. When there were only three people left, the woman turned to her. Janik could only whisper.

'I want to talk to you. In private.'

Louise Michel knew all about burning needs and how they can be fanned to zeal. She took hold of a piece of Janik's cape, finished with the others, and drew Janik away with her as if she were a child to the sacristy.

'There.' She closed the door behind her. ' "In private".'

Janik looked around at the other men and women in the room, some talking, some writing, a man perched on the table edge, smoking.

'They're all right. They're all committee members.'

Janik's voice would not return. She whispered. 'I have to speak to you alone.'

The two men standing nearest, they might have been coalmen, in National Guard *képis*, stopped talking.

Louise Michel sighed. She looked under dark eyebrows at one of the men. The shorter one, who was stocky and appeared to be covered in soot, nodded and ground out his cigar.

'Come on then,' the woman said to Janik and led the way to the priest's closet. The sooty man leaned against the door jamb outside. Louise Michel indicated the chair and Janik sat down. The woman stood in front of her with her arms folded. Janik coughed but her voice was not there. The same hoarse whisper came from her throat.

'You have to watch the ammunition factory.'

'We run that powder factory. We've got thirty-seven tons of ammunition coming out of there daily.'

Janik's chin was shaking ridiculously. She tried again.

'You have to guard it.'

'It is guarded.'

Now her mouth worked like a poorly managed puppet, her lower jaw wagging up and down and no sound emerging.

The woman crossed her arms and drew in her breath impatiently.

Janik jammed her jaw shut. Her teeth clattered. She closed her eyes.

'Someone is going to blow it up.' Her voice was level at last, almost normal.

'Come in here,' the woman said to the man outside then. 'Say that again. Listen.'

'Someone is going to blow up the powder works. I know who.'

BRIDGES OPENED HIS eyes and it was as if he had not slept at all. He did not understand how he could have let himself be twice the loser in this strange game where the rules slid and shifted. His wife had used him. She had not been interested in him, ever. He was just a way out for her. How it must have suited her that his thoughts were elsewhere. He had used her, too. He knew that. He had never pretended to himself to be anything other than callous. He had been resigned, and happily, with relish even, to his own damnation; it seemed to him an attractive way to perish. And yet—and this is where the game took a turn he had not predicted—he had not perished; he had not embraced his fate. His wife had apparently found what she wanted, which was all kinds of trouble and meddling in the world at large, and he had nothing—through no one's fault (and this was the bitter part that left him such a brackish taste) but his own. Lying beside Elisa on the grass that day in the lee of the chapel—she would not stay inside—he had closed his eyes in the pain of not taking her. At each other's mouths like newborn babies learning how to suck, they had cried together, tears running in their throats, blood from his bitten tongue. They could not even kiss, had lain back. She was shaking. Their clenched hands a turk's head of knuckle between their hips. And then yesterday afternoon she had come to see him at the yard and it was as if she had walked out of her woman's body, her body as lover and mistress and sinner, and walked in to her husband's office spotless, her husband's wife, her daughter's mother. She had a letter from Gagnon in her hand and she spoke to him as if nothing had passed between them.

'He says things are bad. Janik should not be there. He says she is only endangering her own life. She has to come home.' Even her voice was different.

'Why isn't he bringing her back?'

'He says she won't listen to him. You will have to. Listen. He says here—'

He stopped her. He was not altogether lost. 'I'll go,' he said. 'Of course I'll go.' She had tears in her eyes. She was muddling at the letter, a handkerchief, her gloves. 'Don't worry,' he said. 'I'll look after her.'

At dinner she had been calmer. She had sat across the table and eaten little, spoken little. He told her he had made arrangements to leave early in the morning, to go over to Le Havre and take the train at once. Looking at her, he thought he saw gratitude. And he had considered how events for him seemed not to be paid out in a line in sequence and in consequence but seemed to slide on the surface of a seamless band of twisted ribbon, sometimes on the underside, sometimes the upper, and what he had thought to be a cause might turn out to be an effect, an effect a cause.

He heard Elisa moving about downstairs. She would be again Madame Gagnon, the woman she was yesterday, mistress of the family, the house. Ah, Alain, good morning. Everything is on the table. Damn the table. Damn Elisa. Playing parts. Walking all over his heart. Damn her. Damn her whole bloody family.

He got up and shouted to Marguerite, who should have had his water ready for shaving. Dressing, he imagined Elisa at the door, made fragile by the weight of the heavy pitcher, half smiling, saying, It wasn't me, yesterday, it was another woman. Here I am. I have come back. To you.

But it was unmistakably the toe of Marguerite's boot against the bottom of the door.

'Monsieur.' She wondered why he should be so rough taking the pitcher from her hands and treated herself, when she was out of earshot, to a short address, wishing him a good long sleep on the train since he obviously had had none in the night—or perhaps it was just his lack of breeding starting to show through, she wouldn't be surprised.

Bridges cut himself. He went to breakfast with a piece of lint stuck to his chin. And Elisa said it. 'Ah, Alain. Good morning.' So that all he could manage was, 'Madame.'

She looked round quickly and there was, though he did not look back at her, the smallest frown between her eyebrows as if she were trying to say she knew he was speaking in code but she could not break the meaning.

He sat down and ate his bread without tasting it. Elisa came and slipped into the chair opposite. He would not look up.

'Will you be ready if I have Anselm bring the gig round?' Her voice was fragile, infinitely careful, her words as tentative as footsteps across thin ice, as the hands of a nurse on a wound.

He looked up and saw her head inclined, waiting for his answer, her eyebrows lifted, her mouth in the shape of a smile, though she was not smiling.

They were the bereaved, and mourning would not have been amiss.

'No, it's all right,' he said. 'I'll walk.' He wiped his mouth. 'I'd like to walk.'

He got up from the table. In a little while she heard him in the hall. She panicked. Marguerite watched her coldly as she rummaged the shelves in the pantry to find some cake. Without saying anything, the servant held out a small tin and Elisa took it and put the cake inside.

'Just a moment.' She was calling now, almost shameless. She arrived slightly out of breath as he stepped outside. Now, more foolish than she had ever been, she held out the tin.

'Here,' she said, without meeting his eyes, his mild astonishment. 'For your journey.'

He put down his bag and reached out with both hands, pushing the tin back towards her, his hands for a moment over hers.

'I don't need anything,' he said. He closed his eyes briefly and when he looked again she had turned away.

ON THE FERRY to Le Havre, Bridges watched the buildings of the town recede. The rising sun was turning the grey slate to shell. Bridges thought about the evening he had left England, the windows of the port taking fire randomly as the boat moved away. He was always moving away, never left behind. He thought about leaving for good. He wanted to believe it would be easy to sail away. To walk along the dock on the other side, past the railway station, and continue to where the Atlantic ships were berthed. Walk into the shipping office, lay his money down. Only he had none, or barely enough to fetch his wife. For, thoughts of desertion notwithstanding, Bridges had to fetch his wife. And whether it was for Elisa's peace of mind, for Janik herself, or for the last of his self-respect, it was hard to say. Perhaps it was just that he knew he could not leave. In any event, he had to get to Paris. And afterwards?

At Le Havre a porter said the Versailles troops were carrying out manoeuvres just west of Paris. They could close the line any time. Bridges went to buy a paper and read that a loyal army of 60,000 was ready to storm Paris.

The news of Paris itself was conflicting. Bridges could not make it out. There were reports of arrests, of summary executions, but there was also a report of the proceedings of the Commission of Trade and Licensing, and notices of a new performance of one of Bouilhet's plays.

When the train began to move, Bridges was attentive. The damaged landscape was unchanged. He wondered why the thousands of demobilized soldiers had not been put to work on the battered villages and towns. Instead it seemed they were all at large and itching for a fight. With each other.

'Ah, yes,' said the older man in the seat opposite. 'It's bad. France is in pieces and there are traitors at every turn.'

Bridges managed a vague combination of vowels that sounded suitably indignant and opened his paper again.

By the time they rolled into the Gare Saint-Lazare, he was thoroughly alarmed. Outside Paris he had seen enough of Government troops manoeuvring to know that if they were

coming in, he and Janik should be getting out. Just over the
bridge at Clichy, a small contingent of the Guard had boarded
the train and searched it carriage by carriage. Bridges was taken
to the guard's van for questioning. He told them he was secretary
to Mr. Gladstone's Minister of Treasury and saw with relief that
they could not formulate a question to follow.

The station was crowded. At one of the gates, someone had
fainted and a woman in a uniform was haranguing the crowd to
make way for a doctor to get through.

Outside, the air was still warm from the spring sunshine.
Bridges decided to walk to Madame Fougard's house. It could
have been an evening in May, though no one was promenading.
The cafés that were open were not full. Those people who were
in the streets were there, it was obvious, for some purpose.
Bridges quickened his pace.

MADAME FOUGARD HAD retired for the night, said the girl who
opened the door. No, she did not think she could get her up. She
never got her up.

'It is most important,' Bridges said. 'It is in connection with
her niece, my wife. I need her address.'

'In that case,' said the girl, 'I know she will not get up. Come
back in the morning.' She closed the door.

Bridges had the letter from Gagnon in his pocket. He decided
to take a cab to Gagnon's hotel. The proprietress was sorry.
Monsieur Gagnon was not staying with them. He left yesterday.

The cab driver had gone.

Bridges was tired and hungry. He walked for a while until he
came to a small restaurant with rooms above. He ordered a cutlet
and some coffee and went to bed.

'MADAME FOUGARD IS not up,' said the girl when Bridges called
again the next morning. But Bridges' patience was exhausted. He
put one hand to the edge of the door, said, 'Excuse me,' and

　stepped inside, about to say he would wait. Madame Fougard appeared at once from a door to the right.

'Sir?'

Bridges bowed, though he had intended only to nod. 'Alain Bridges, Madame Fougard. The husband of your niece.'

Madame Fougard primped her lips a little more tightly and turned on her heel. Bridges followed her into the dark salon.

'Thank you, Monette,' she said when she had sat down. Bridges remained standing. After the maid had closed the door, she waited for her footsteps to recede to the kitchen.

'Your wife,' she said. 'At large on the streets of Paris. Your wife, sir, is no niece of mine. I have had her name removed from my will.'

'Madame—' Bridges spread his hands helplessly against the approaching flood of rebuke.

'And you are no husband. I sever her.' But apparently it was not enough for she had to continue. 'Absolutely and in every respect. You may not call on me again, sir.' She got up. 'Goodbye.'

'Madame, with respect, I have come merely to obtain her address.'

'Good day.'

'Madame, please. I have come to save her.' Inspired, Bridges crossed himself as the old woman turned round.

She, however, was as sharp as razors, and as unforgiving. 'Liar,' she said. 'See the girl.' And went out.


AT THE RUE des Bergers there was no answer. Bridges was wondering what to do, when he saw Janik. She was walking quickly, as she always did, with her head slightly raised as if against insults and her eyes cast down, the eyelids almost closed so that it seemed as if she were sleepwalking. She had almost reached him when she looked up.

'Alain,' she said. And was not put out. Her clothes, thought Bridges, though they were the same she wore at home, looked

unkempt, uncared for. Her hair perhaps had not been tidied that
morning.

'It is open,' she said. 'You could have gone in.' She pushed the door and it opened to a dark hall.

'Wait here,' she said. 'I'll be down in a minute.'

'Janik.' Bridges was smiling. She lived in another world, needed reminding that she had a husband. He reached to hold her back and stopped. She had turned abruptly—her shoulder evading his hand.

'Please,' she said. 'I'll be down in a minute.'

'Janik, for God's sake.'

'Please,' she said again. 'It is not suitable.'

Bridges waited. His slow rage, against Janik, against Elisa, against the family, France, returned.

Janik came down again and they went out. They walked until they came to the canal and stopped there on the bridge. Janik kept her eyes on the dark water.

'What is wrong?' she said, braced, as if waiting for a blow.

He did not expect the question. 'I have come to take you home,' he said. 'Your father wrote to me.'

'Where is he?'

She turned too quickly. Her voice was too urgent. He did not understand.

'In here. In Paris,' he said. But she knew this surely.

'Have you seen him?'

'No. I arrived last night. He wasn't at his hotel. I tried to come and see you straight away but I couldn't get your address.'

She had turned to him, her mouth half open, ready to speak, but she slowly closed her lips on whatever it was she was about to say. She turned away again and looked down at her hands resting on the iron railing. She was making the smallest shaking motion with her head, like someone frail or old. Bridges remembered how he had thought of her during the war as a woman deranged, someone to be spoken to with care and extra kindness.

'Why?' he said. He put his hands over hers.

She shook her head. 'I wanted to speak to him. That's all.'

Only if she kept very, very still, Janik thought, could she control her fear. There had been arrests. Just this morning. She had heard from Mademoiselle Cliquot and her young man. Two Government agents had been discovered in the armory. Another in the ammunition factory. The hostage law was in effect, they said. Government men would do very well. No one knew the names. They were not important. All night she had worked at the local office. Hoping to hear more. In the early hours some National Guardsmen had come in drunk. The sooty man was with them. They had just left the Mazas gaol where they had escorted the prisoners. He caught sight of her and lifted her onto a table. 'A heroine,' he had declared and passed round his bottle. 'Let's drink to vengeance. Give them the roasting they deserve.' He laughed. And then he had waved the bottle under her nose and laughed again when she had covered her mouth and gagged. 'Another virgin!' he said, she gagging, not on the alcohol but on her own stupidity. She was betrayed by her own judgment. She could not imagine how she could have believed that he would ever be safe. She had been so sure and yet now it was all so obvious. It was inevitable that he would be arrested. She must have seen that. How could she not have seen it? Had she then wanted it? He was not there. Bridges had said he was not there. She was sickened by the terrible, irreversible nature of the consequences of her action. The pain of it made her want to cry out. She stood very, very still. Holding on. Telling herself yes, of course he had caught the train for Le Havre last night. Of course.

But Bridges now was appealing to her as his wife. What was he saying? He was in earnest. She had missed it. 'I beg your pardon?'

'Today. Now. Get your bags and we'll go straight home. My love?'

And because she could never go home, she drew her hands out from under his, carefully, so as not to dislodge the panic. She shook her head.

'Your mother—' began Bridges.

Now things that had not previously even loomed in her consciousness suddenly became clear to Janik and she looked up. 'Go back,' she said.

And here was Bridges' child-wife, a woman, looking at him, looking into him. Keeping her eyes on his she said, 'Go back and look after my mother.'

Everything in her eyes said she knew and was steadfast in the face of it, and because she did not flinch, the knowledge of it did not demean her. So that to be her equal, Bridges had to say it.

'I am in love with your mother.'

Still she looked at him. She said. 'I know.'

For the second time she had humbled him. He felt no shame but sadness that he could not start from now, could not start again and know her only from this moment forward.

'Is that why you came here?' he said. 'To get away?'

She shook her head. 'No. But it is why you have to go back without me.'

He moved to touch her. 'I can't leave you here.'

And then she was angry but looked away quickly to save him. 'I have found what I want here.' For even Janik could rub out a little of the truth and add the details she preferred.

'Janik—' and Bridges, not knowing how to say he was sorry, said instead, 'Please.'

'I am alone here,' she said. 'It is what I want.'

He was at a loss. He needed time. He told her he would come back in the evening and talk again when she was quieter. Though a rock could not have been more still. He kissed her on the cheek.

He walked away, not sure where he was going or what he should do. He wanted to do the honourable thing. It was why he had come to Paris. Elisa had made it easy for him. He had been angry. He had wanted to bring her back her daughter, his wife, almost to spite her. But how this aging, this aged child-wife overturned his plans. To live with mother and daughter and they both know? That was beyond him. He could not leave her in this lunatic city—and he could not take her back. Emigration loomed again. If he presented himself to Janik with two tickets in his hand?

In none of this did Bridges consider his wife's last statement to be true.


JANIK WENT BACK to her room. Bridges, she thought, would go back to her father's hotel. She knew her father would not be there. In a vast calm she renounced all scrambling after events. If she could have lighted a pyre of her intentions she would have climbed on top.

But still it was important to evade this poor man, her husband, who could not hear what she had to say. For the second time in two weeks she packed her bag and then quietly she closed the front door behind her and began to walk along the street, just as before, with her eyes cast down.

The sooty man had a headache. He did not appear at the local office until three o'clock. Janik stood up when he came in. She had her bag beside her.

'Well saints and bloody holy sinners,' he said. 'Jesus bloody Christ.'

She put out both her hands, palms uppermost. He thought perhaps he had not woken up.

'I have nowhere to stay', she said.

## *Eleven*

CRÉCY STRETCHED HIS legs out under the table. The group today was reduced to four.

Courtebois said, 'He is a man of honour, our doctor,' and felt something of the reflected nobility of it.

Marèchal sat across the table with one arm stretched out, his hand toying with a knife in a way designed to telegraph his superiority while he declaimed against Prussians, Parisien scum, and perfidious foreigners in turn. Beside him, the lenient Harmon forebore. Their dishes arrived and were subjected to the customary ritual—the prodding of the filet and lifting of skin, the discreet sniffing. Crécy was annoyed that he had not chosen the mutton, as he was first going to do, while Harmon, who had, sighed with anticipation over the rising scent of rosemary.

*'Bon appetit.'*

'And to our friends!' said Harmon, raising his glass.

And they began their meal.

'So. Who will be next to go?' Crécy tried to forget the beef, rubbery under his knife.

'We should all go,' said Courtebois. 'It wouldn't take much to get them out, but if no one else is doing it then let us. We fought the war to save Paris. Now we can fight Paris to save France, eh?'

His cleverness gave him such pleasure he had to disguise it by champing hard on his mouthful and looking like a man of the world.

'Oh, they'll climb down.' Harmon. 'Give them time.'

'That's not what *Le Havre* says.' Crécy had no patience with vague sentiments; always he put his faith in facts. 'Gets worse every day, apparently. Eight hundred dead so far.'

The figure crashed among the lunch dishes like a musket ball and had to be repeated.

'That's what it said. Eight hundred. Starting with Generals Thomas and Lecomte and it hasn't stopped since.'

'But now you're making it sound like war. It was supposed to be all back to normal, everything running smoothly. Look at Gagnon. He's there now.'

'Anywhere there's chance of profit.'

'As far as I know he's helping with the reconstruction,' said Harmon.

'For a fat fee.'

'Why not?'

'I could think of a reason why not.' Marèchal was looking at his remaining pieces of carrot as if they were communards with their backs against the wall. But obscure comments that were supposed to radiate significance were all too common coming from Marèchal, and his friends went on eating. He tried again.

'I could think of a very good reason.' He piled the carrots carefully on his fork and ate them. He was consuming the last secret in the world. They would never, ever know. Until they asked.

'Well?'

'A certain Englishman.' And now he was cleaning up the evidence with his bread.

'You can't leave it alone, can you?' muttered Crécy, not liking to see his friend demeaned by another's malice.

'I wouldn't have left the Englishman alone, not with my wife there and his own out of the way.'

'Ah,' Courtebois was going to enjoy this lunch. 'You find Madame Gagnon attractive, do you?'

'I didn't suggest that. I didn't suggest anything at all.' Marèchal poured himself more wine. 'Perhaps I was talking about reasons for not leaving the business.'

'Or perhaps you weren't,' Crécy said.

'I find her attractive,' said Courtebois. 'That's why I never get asked there.'

'That's why you never get asked anywhere. You're a liability around wives.'

And Courtebois laughed most loudly of all.

Harmon waited. 'I think you might be mistaken, Gerard,' he said gently to Marèchal. 'I don't think the Englishman is even there.'

But this was dull indeed and provoked no interest except from Marèchal who, if he was going to have his thunder stolen, expected to know the reason.

'Oh?'

'Marguerite Cochard was bringing us some photographs Elisa Gagnon had promised. She said he was going to get his wife. He took the Paris train yesterday morning.'

Crécy looked up first and then they were all looking at Harmon.

'The Paris train?' said Marèchal. 'Madame Janik Bridges is in Trouville.'

Crécy smiled, his friend's name cleared but not Bridges'. And didn't they all know the Englishman was never quite above board?

'Be interesting to see if he brings his wife back,' he said. 'Won't it?'

Marèchal's coffee tasted good after all.

MARGUERITE SAID, 'THERE.' She put another cup of coffee down and took the first one away. It was cold. 'Why don't you drink that and get on?' she said. 'It won't do you any good, you know, sitting there. Her neither.' Elisa took the cup but continued to stare out of the window, watching her daughter fall and fall again under the feet of horses, the rifle fire of soldiers. Rehearsing anguish, rehearsing grief, she could try to ignore the thought that all uninvited had come to squat obscenely in a corner of her mind. But it was not enough. She had not articulated it, would not look close enough for that, but still at a distance she recognized it. If Janik should die? It shook her sense of who she was, what she was capable of. And then Alain, too, was at risk. 'I am going to Sainte-Catherine to pray,' she said. 'For her safety. Will you come, Marguerite?'

In the church it was hard to concentrate. Rumour of disturbance spilled into danger, gathered to a flood, and swelled to rivers of blood in the street. She left Marguerite to light candles and went outside.

Madame Crécy saw her and crossed the street. 'My dear,' she said. 'My dear.' She held her hand. 'What a time for France. What a time for us all. I, too, have said my prayers for your husband's safety. Rest assured.'

On the way home, Elisa told herself that he did not need her prayers. It was not that she did not love him that she had not prayed for him. Paul could look after himself. Self-interest had sent him there; it would bring him back. But Janik. She was the stuff of martyrs. And she could see her again with her strange, somnambulist's walk, walking through the yelling crowds, the wounded men. And Alain. Careless to the point of foolishness. She would not think of Alain. She told herself that Janik was not insane; she was courageous with a courage she herself could never know. She believed it; she would pay homage to it. Yes, that was it. She would make a testimonial. She would give it to Janik when she came back. She would come back.

'Marguerite,' she said. 'We will make some photographs.'

Marguerite, a few steps, behind pulled a face. 'I have to finish the beds,' she said.

'Yes. That's it. You can bring down the green cover. It's nice and dark.'

THEY DID NOT finish until late in the afternoon. Once Judith put down her sword and went in grumpily to put a piece of hock on to boil. She trailed a corner of the green coverlet in the greasy liquid that she spilled, noticed it, and said, 'Good.' Enough was enough. If anyone called at the house today she would die of shame. Her mistress was behaving like a madwoman. Asking her to pose with a sword. Good God. The thing was almost too heavy to lift. Where she'd got it from God knows. And never satisfied. No Marguerite. This is a man's head, not a chicken's. This is not something you do every day. Right about that, anyway. And then, Look, Marguerite, I'm Holofernes. I'm asleep. Lying down on the floor right there. You're going to kill me. So you might really want to. Now how do you look? But it wasn't just that. That's how she always was. No, it was a craziness about her. Frowning all the time, and in a hurry. Like someone who has lost something.

At five o'clock, Elisa was not happy with any of her work. She wanted courage. She wanted the thing itself. These pictures told stories. They told stories about courage. She wanted the thing that existed independently of the world, independently of the self. The thing that disregards the self yet is the very self, invincible even in death.

She propped the last of the plates against the wall. The light was low and very beautiful. It caught the plates and printed the stone behind with shadow.

Marguerite was in the kitchen putting up her hair. There were vegetables in the sink and a basket of dirty laundry on the floor, on the chair a pile of folded linen to be ironed. The cats were licking at the place where the hock had boiled over.

'I'm going out,' said Elisa. 'You have some soup. I'm not hungry.'

Marguerite, fastening her hair, only rolled her eyes a little.

Elisa walked and tried to think. The picture she had been trying to make was a cheat in every respect. It was not, could not ever be Judith. Nor was it a tribute to courage; in making it, she was not honouring Janik, she was saving herself from her own worst thoughts. For still she did not know how she would live when they returned from Paris, all three.

That night she could not sleep at all. Marguerite was sitting up sewing. She was making bonnets to take to her sister in Lisieux. She hummed quietly. For almost two hours Elisa listened, hearing the humming stop, start again. Then she heard the boards creaking, quiet movements. Marguerite softened by the meditation of her hands. Even her footsteps had changed. So Marguerite went softly to bed and the house at last was still. It made Elisa, soundless and wordless, cry. Her eyes, her nose became wet. She was dissolving without changing even her breathing. Her wretchedness was all loss, all longing. The two were the same.

She had kept the thought of Alain at bay since the morning. Now she remembered: with what deliberation he had put down his bag and put out his hands to push back her gift, with what careful accident he had let his hands cover hers. And then she could not stop but had to go back to when they lay outside in the lee of the chapel, their temples touching, his breath on her mouth, and before that, inside the chapel, he behind her, his body covering hers in a most obscene, most holy act of desire.

She got up and lit a lamp, took it over to the plates that leaned against the wall by the chest of drawers. She knew which one it was. It was at the back. She carried it over to her table by the window and laid it down, brushing the surface of the glass as if to clear it. Its blackness was cosmic. She pressed her palms over it and sat holding back chaos, willing his face to appear.

BRIDGES HAD SPENT an hour trying to compose a cable to his brother. He spent the next three trying to send it. All of Paris had something urgent to communicate. He had no doubt that his brother would send the money. The word *Canada* would thrill him with relief. Alfred had never been comfortable with him just a channel-crossing away. And so he asked for the money for two single outward passages and named the shipping agent in Le Havre who could receive it. He would take Janik back. He could remain in Le Havre while she packed her things at home. Gagnon would bluster and fume. He was prepared for that. But what could the man do, ultimately?

It was this plan that Bridges had begun to formulate in the confusion of the telegraph office. But even as it took shape he knew that Janik would not come. He knew that what he was really doing was leaving. And all the time, in the back of his mind, came the question: And Elisa? Over and over until the words became a figure, became Elisa herself. She standing, calling to him, and he not answering.

When he had at last sent his cable, Bridges went to find something to eat. He was not hungry but he needed time to think. He drank his wine slowly, hardly wetting his mouth at each sip. At last he paid his bill and got up to go. He walked, making more time for himself and his ridiculous proposition. Why should Janik come with him? Why indeed should he want her to? The idea of the two tickets would not be dislodged, and he was standing with Elisa on the deck of the transatlantic vessel, both of them pretending to watch the coast of France diminish, both of them waiting to go down to their cabin, taste the sea-spray on each other's skin.

Janik was not at her lodging.

'You can come in and wait,' said the woman, and Bridges could not tell if she was leering or mocking. 'You her father?'

And perhaps because Bridges had no wish to be her husband, he said yes.

The old woman made a little ugly shape with her mouth to show she did not believe and then led him up the narrow stairs and unlocked the door.

'What——?' Even in the dark, Bridges knew something was wrong but the woman was already on her way down and did not hear.

Bridges unfastened the window and pushed open the shutters. The room was empty. The wardrobe door stood open.

He went down and shouted to the woman. She came out scowling and Bridges was angry with her puckered bladder of a face, angry with her smell, her dirty house.

'The room's empty. Where's she gone?'

'Eh?' The woman too was angry, her rent hightailing away over the pavements to better things. She shoved Bridges in the ribs and pushed past him up the stairs.

'I said she's gone.'

But the woman had to see for herself, stoke up her fury.

'Ah, the bitch. Hey!' She could not get down the stairs fast enough. So that Bridges unconsciously, never mind his anger, had to reach out to steady her before she overbalanced at the bottom stair.

'You. She owes me thirty-six francs. Come on!' She moved round, placing herself between Bridges and the front door, holding out her hand and digging her fingers repeatedly into her palm.

But Bridges' patience was at an end. He took hold of the woman by the shoulders and moved her, like a small piece of furniture, out of the way.

Her abuse followed him down the street, her language an education, or would have been had Bridges been able to translate more than the single insult: *Anglais*!

He spent the rest of the afternoon criss-crossing Paris. Again there was no answer at Gagnon's address. Janik's godmother would not receive him. Never had the Atlantic appeared more enticing. And yet Bridges could not entirely abandon his responsibility, or perhaps he could not quite recognize that his child-wife had grown.

It was not difficult to find the central office of the *Comité*. It was draped with red from every window. Still he did not know what he would say to Janik.

There was a young man at the door. Bridges said he had come to find his wife. The young man said he should see one of the women at a table inside.

They did not know a Madame Bridges and continued to sort papers.

Madame Janik Bridges? Madame Janik Gagnon?

The woman on the right looked up quickly. 'Mademoiselle,' she said, and her glance was what Bridges had crossed and recrossed Paris to find, for she telegraphed in that single glance that Mademoiselle Bridges had cut herself off from all such outmoded institutions as husbands.

She held back her breath as if what she was going to say would be a cause of the utmost anguish.

'Mademoiselle Bridges is not here,' she said.

The older woman beside her was more blunt. 'She left with Corporal Patry.' But she did not look up.

'I see,' said Bridges. 'Where can I find her?'

'I'm sorry. I can't help you.'

Bridges went over to one of two upright chairs with green leather seats and sat down. The second woman looked up over gold-rimmed spectacles and glared mildly. Bridges waited. The implications of his position crowded in on him like unwanted baggage and he began to see his situation as others would. He saw that he should feel dishonoured. His wife had run off with another man. But it was his liberation. He had never believed in honour; it was as alien to him as glory. These were concepts dreamed up by men like his brother, elaborate codes that served their purposes, not his. He had been robbed of his honour, yet how could he be robbed of something he did not believe in? He had been robbed of his wife. But she had gone. Simply. He had a great desire to get up and walk out. It was what she wanted. There was no honour in trying to stop her. And yet if he did not appear to try . . . if he appeared not to try? He saw Elisa in the hallway, saw her anxiety turn to anguish. He had to do something. All right. He would get her address. He would arrive at her door. Monsieur le Corporal Patry would open. He, Alan Bridges, esquire, would take him by the neck of his tunic and hit him full in the centre of the face. He would take Janik away. No. He would arrive at her door. He would wait inside for this Corporal Patry to come. He would take him by the throat, he would crack his head against the wall, hard. He would take Janik away. Or he would arrive at her door . . . In none of this did Janik have anything to say. He knew she would not come with him. Whether or not he hit her lover, or where, was quite beside the point. It was for Elisa that he had to look for Janik, for Elisa that he had to be seen to try. Through it all he saw dimly how in the end he would be free, for Gagnon surely would be glad to see him go. He put his head in his hands. What had begun as a brilliant escapade, an erotic adventure *en famille*, was about to devour him, devour Elisa's regard for him and leave him face to face with his own obsession.

Eventually the woman with the spectacles got up and went through one of the doors on the right. She appeared to have forgotten him.

Bridges went over to the desk. The younger woman had grey eyes.

'Mademoiselle,' he said and looked at her from under raised eyebrows. It was a look he had found useful before. 'Please can you tell me where she is? I only want to say goodbye, to wish her well. I'm leaving France for good. I may not see her again.' While he talked, the young woman scratched the blotting paper with the nib of her pen, glancing up once or twice. He finished speaking and waited.

'I think Corporal Patry took her to the house of Citoyenne Michel,' she said.

'And who is he?'

'Citoy*enne* Michel,' she said and began to colour at the neck. And as she scribbled the address, already with misgivings, Bridges saw again the woman in the church, her boot heels striking the flagstones, her pantaloons like a hussar's, the coil of hair that had come loose and was hanging between the crossed rifles at her back. Her strut and swagger. And Corporal Patry of Bridges' imagination peeled himself from the wall and shook his head like a dog stung by a bee. Bridges wanted to laugh.

'Thank you,' he said. '*Vive La Commune!*'

All that night the young woman worried in case she had been duped. She hoped that Citoyenne Michel's bodyguard was wide awake. In the morning when Louise Michel strode in, her young friend following, the woman with the grey eyes was more than a little relieved.

GAGNON NEVER UNDERSTOOD why, when he went back to his hotel, there were two men waiting in the room. They took him straight to the Mazas. Misfortune was a mystery to Gagnon, something like a closed prison cell itself. Past which it was always best to walk with a brisk pace, pretend it wasn't there. If by mischance one found oneself inside and the door locked, the only way to act was as if it were all perfectly normal. But how hard to appear normal standing in front of these two men at the table, listening to one of them read the report: '. . . two nuns, and nine children.' And Gagnon had a strange sensation, his body reacting to the words as if to shed them. It was as if his own flesh were falling away, a cascading of skin, hair, tissue, falling, rippling down from the top of his head, falling away, but he, Gagnon, left sitting there naked, exposed as it fell, its falling changing nothing, his eyes and ears wide open while the man described the scene. But he did not have to describe it. Gagnon could see. (And again it came.) The disposition of the bodies and the parts of them. And the survivors. For whom it was perhaps worse. The interrogator closed the report. 'Better dead, really,' the man beside him said, 'than be left like the wretched little soul that couldn't move, looking at what had happened to his friends.' And proceeded to tell. Gagnon, to stop the flow, talked volubly, not caring if the man was making it up, wanting only to stop him, shut him up, mixing lies and truth with abandon and giving away names as fast as he could in return for promises of freedom. He had heard all he needed, had heard the rumours, too, about hostages, had never been so scared. But when his interrogator hit him in the ribs, then the closed door of his misfortune opened just a crack. When he was returned to the cell that he shared with a cardinal's clerk, the sense of falling flesh came again, this time with a wave of nausea and a dragging sensation in his bowels. He fouled the floor. They brought him a bucket and some straw and he cleaned it up. He saw his chance. He asked, as the price of supplying one last name, to see that evening the doctor who was checking the hostages.

Doctor Vaupier was a weasly, worn-looking man but he listened, pulling yards of red and yellow fabric from his bag, apologising for the lack of bandages, but the casualties, you know. And the war.

'Yes,' he agreed, winding the coloured cloth round Gagnon's ribs, 'yes, it was only a question of money.' Release could be purchased certainly, but the difficulty lay in getting word to this friend of his, this notary, where did he say he was from? Ah. He stopped winding. It was so far away. 'But don't give up,' he said. 'Don't give up. I'll see what I can do.'

'Do you know a Monsieur Gagnon?' he asked twice before his colleague, Doctor Escher, heard. 'Gagnon. He said he's from your town.' Doctor Escher was tired and Vaupier talked incessantly through every kind of medical procedure. It took a while for the information to settle.

'Certainly I know a Gagnon,' he said. 'But I can't imagine what he would be doing in Paris. Or in prison.' Nevertheless, to set his mind at rest, he went. And there was Gagnon. With a bloodshot look to his eye and with his ribs bandaged, but unmistakably Gagnon.

The doctor went to an office to negotiate. He was surprised at the readiness of the officer there to release his friend. They walked back down the long corridor together. At the door of the cell the soldier paused. 'Yes. He can go,' he said. 'He's told us everything we wanted to know.' Both Escher and Gagnon pretended they had not heard.

'Well!' A hackney cab drew to a standstill for them outside. 'Just as always, everything turns up for you, just at the right time.' It seemed the right thing to say. He did not like his friend so utterly without himself.

With the danger of a Government attack imminent, the *ambulance* at the Palais de l'Industrie had been reopened and it was here that Escher brought Gagnon. He found him a bed in a small room with no others. 'Rest,' Escher said. 'That's the thing.' He said he'd get him into a proper hotel for that. He sat and waited.

Gagnon laughed, if it could be called that. He held on to his side. 'Yes,' he said. 'I'd like to know how I got here too. Don't ask. Shall we just say I took one step too many?' He laughed again, beginning to reappear, Le Gagnant, under his bruises, and shook his head, still not believing that it had not come out as he intended. 'I tell you it is a wonderful thing to have friends.'

'If they are in the right place at the right time, eh?' And with the right sum in their pocket book, but would not be so churlish to add, just now anyway. For Gagnon's release had cost Escher dearly, insurrectionists being, almost by definition, penniless. But his friend had been lucky too, there was no doubt about that.

Before Gagnon was asleep, the doctor looked in again.

'I checked at that address,' he said. 'I had one of the lads go round. He said your daughter's gone. They told him she left a day or two ago. With a young man. So you needn't worry any more. Sleep easy.'

BRIDGES SPENT MOST of his journey back with his head in his hands. He had gone to the house as he had planned and he had seen Janik. The house was guarded and he had been made to wait in the street, with all the time the sound of boots on the wooden floor upstairs. When Janik came down she was wearing pantaloons and a red sash. It seemed a foolish thing to ask her again, and Bridges did it only for Elisa's sake. Janik's refusal was absolute. More than ever, she had the air of one possessed. Or in possession. There was no more questioning. She was in command of her own fate. She had found something she had been searching for and she was not about to let go. It was her fate and she was in command. Then Bridges might have been jubilant, might have hugged her in gratitude for righting their momentous mistake, but was enraged. It was as if a wife were to leap into the fire. To cheer you my dear. As if he could ever again enjoy warmth.

'You cannot.' He must have said the words, twenty, thirty times. He cited all the stories he had heard since he had arrived in the city, each worse than the last. But she was adamant. She behaved as if he were keeping her from important business, and she looked from time to time towards a black-haired, grimy-featured youth who finally was moved to stump across to them and suggest that it was time for all non-party members to leave. He pushed his chest out and buffed at Bridges like a mother duck to make him move, and Bridges itched to really hit him but was not a fool. The two guards waiting for a chance to fight someone, anyone.

So Bridges said, 'Goodbye,' said, 'Kiss me. I insist.' And her lips burned his cheek so that he had to look again, to see, confirm. Yes, she was all on fire, her eyes, her face, and it was not for him.

The train was very crowded. It seemed as if the whole of Paris was running away. There was talk of a fresh siege. They said Thiers would blockade the city. There were troops enough outside already. The insurrectionists were scum, filth. A shame it would be to dirty the streets with their blood. Though some favoured rivers and others torrents, they were all agreed upon the blood. Bridges rested his forehead against the window. They were travelling through a valley where apple trees were showering their blossom. The new grass seemed suddenly long. He did not know how Janik could turn away from such simplicities. The taste of wine on the tongue. The warmth and smoothness of skin on skin. Who would not choose it over cold abstractions? He was afraid for her, perplexed at his fate which seemed to have given him—who never thought to manage anyone—some part in shaping hers.

But he would not stand by to watch her wrestle with her chosen angel, witness this martyrdom she called upon herself. She had divorced herself from him. He was crushed by the irony of it, for in doing so she had divorced him from Elisa. Impossible now to stay in France. The precarious tableau kicked to pieces. He did not know what he would say to Gagnon. The man would rage certainly. He could weather that. But Elisa. He rolled his temple against the window. Elisa.

The woman next to him looked sideways at him, turned down her mouth and pushed the impossible hoops of her skirt away from his legs to show she disapproved of drunkards.

ALFRED BRIDGES KNEW how to pull strings, make people jump to it. He had his banker send a wire personally on his behalf. He could not have his brother off too quickly—or too far. Before Alan got off the train there were two tickets for Halifax made out in his name and waiting in the shipping office in Le Havre.

ELISA WAS IN her room when he got back. It was late. She could hear him downstairs talking to Marguerite. She could not hear Janik.

Marguerite went to the bottom of the stairs and called. 'Madame? Monsieur Bridges is back.'

The silence filled the house.

'I'll come down.'

Bridges was standing in the drawing room waiting for her. He was looking down as if he had just noticed that his boots were dusty, and when Elisa came in he did not lift his head but turned it to look at her, the hair falling across his eyes. The thinness of his smile telegraphed his message.

'She's not coming back.'

'Is she all right?'

'She's fine. She's—she's fine. She's well.'

Now here was a terror between them more intimidating than any wedding vow. He might have taken her to the edge of a gulf, leaned out, or led her to a caged animal, put his hand on the bolt. But she did not see it.

'Where is she? What is she doing?'

'She's working for the Commune. In Belleville. She's not coming back.' Opening the cage a little more, letting the beast come out, crouch in full view between them. Touch me. See what happens.

'But you tried . . .'

'Of course.'

'And Paul?'

'I didn't see him. Neither did Janik.'

Why couldn't she see it, feel its breath. In a moment it would lick her feet.

'What will happen?'

He made a slight movement. She must know as well as he did. 'She's in danger.' It was like a shrug and he regretted it.

'If I went to get her . . .?'

He shook his head. 'What you have to understand,' he said, 'is that this is what she wants. She's happy. Whatever happens now, you have to understand that.'

And the beast could have been devouring her alive because her face was drawing down and her mouth was working horribly and Bridges could have died for it to be for him, but knew it was not. It was for Janik, this wrenching of the heart.

He made her look at him. 'She is happier than you or I will ever be. That is what you have to remember.'

And Marguerite at the door summoned up disgust and enjoyed it.


THE NEXT EVENING, when Marguerite had gone, Bridges laid the tickets on the table between them.

'She has what she wants.' His hands were shaking.

'I want you. But not this.'

'This is all we have. I can't stay, we can't stay. Not now. We have to leave.'

'You can't leave. You are her husband.'

'Elisa, she knows about us.'

Elisa closed her eyes and shook her head. 'There is nothing to know.'

'She knows that I love you.'

And even now it seemed they needed Janik, for Bridges had never spoken it out, still did not.

'So we are damned.' Her smile invited drowning.

And so they sat across the table from each other, their palms down on the scoured wood, the tickets for the passage to Canada forgotten between them while with meticulous desire their eyes drew the clothes from their bodies and their naked feet trod them in a pool and together they stretched themselves on the cold linen of her bed and shuddered at each other's touch.

But they sat too long, savouring, because the boy that Escher had sent down on the early train (that might well be the last to run, the doctor feared) was already at the door of the harbour master's office, was explaining to the harbour master's clerk how Monsieur Crécy was not in, how he had been told to find him here to give him the message, how the message was urgent— and Marèchal now was reading with excitement the letter not addressed to him, was reaching for his scarf, saying I'll deal with this, and was taking only minutes, so keen he was, so pleased to have a drama by the throat, to be up the street and approaching the front door. Marèchal in the thick of life at last. Nor would he be deterred by the silence following his knock but had to go round and come in through the gate at the side of the house and push open the door to the kitchen: 'Madame Gagnon? It is my duty to interrupt you. I have most important news that cannot wait.' Braying, the man a donkey.

So that she must leave her mind licking at the vision like a wound and get up and let her visitor in, showing him the chair.

When she sat down again she sat exactly as before. Pressing

her palms to the table hoping to find again the thing that had passed between them.

'HOW DID SHE take it?' It was not curiosity; Harmon was concerned.

Marèchal took a deep breath and savoured the moment. He looked from one to the other.

'You might as well ask how she did not take it.'

'What do you mean?'

'He was there. Bridges. He was sitting at the kitchen table when I went in. Only one lamp alight. I said, "Look, Madame, I have some very serious news for you concerning your husband." She went and sat across from him and she put her hands flat on the table. Just like this. She was looking at me as if I was twisting her arm and then when I said, "concerning your husband," she looked straight at him, Bridges.'

Courtebois exhaled his cigar smoke on a gust of derision.

'No, I'm not imagining it. It was like a door banging open—if you can say a look is like a sound. I think you can. Especially in this case . . .'

'So then what?'

'Well then I said that there had been some kind of misunderstanding, that he had been arrested, suffered some kind of hurt, but that he was all right and the doctor had secured his release and that he was coming home when he was rested. You'd think she would have said something, or been upset. Well she didn't say a thing. And he, well he never moved. Never spoke. She sort of put her hands up and brushed her face, as if she had a cobweb or something. Then she put her hands down again. The same way. Just like that.'

'It was the shock,' said Harmon.

Crécy agreed. 'She needed a close friend for that kind of

news,' he said. 'What bad luck too that it had to be you. I'll get my wife to call in on her.'

Courtebois, though, wanted more. 'She can't have said nothing.'

'No, she said, "And he's all right." I said, "Yes, he's all right." She said, "Thank you. I'll just sit here a bit." So I left. They were both still sitting there. Probably still are.'

And Harmon, moved to excuse them, said, 'People need time when it comes to bad news. You never know how it will take them.' Who never could help being fair.

'But you don't know what was on the table. The counter-foils for two berths on the steamship *Olympia*. For Halifax.'

Harmon had had enough. He got up to go.

'Now you've gone too far,' said Crécy.

'Has he?' said Courtebois. 'What was Bridges doing there anyway? Without his wife? Didn't he go to Trouville or somewhere to fetch her?'

'To Paris.' Marèchal put his glass down hard for emphasis. The wine jumped. 'I saw the doctor's letter. There was a postscript. It said: I hope Monsieur Bridges and your daughter are safely home now.'

Neither Crécy nor Courtebois were impressed.

'Well, think about it. "Safely." The doctor wasn't talking about Trouville. He had seen Monsieur Bridges in Paris. I've given it a lot of thought,' though his thought was forming only as he spoke, 'Gagnon goes away to Paris. Bridges goes away— ostensibly, remember, to get his wife—who is in Trouville— Gagnon told us—don't forget that. He is seen buying a ticket for Paris. He is seen perhaps *in* Paris. Then Bridges comes back without his wife.'

'And Gagnon is arrested.'

'Thank you, Courtebois. Exactly. He didn't go to see her at all.'

BRIDGES WOULD NOT give up. At breakfast he put the tickets on the table again.

'Next week,' he said. 'She sails next week. No one has to know where we've gone. We'll go over to Le Havre. Stay in a room somewhere until it's time. No one need know.'

Again at dinner the tickets were there beside his plate. She sat with her eyes cast down and he could have hated her for Janik's martyred face. She would not look. He was driven to hiss.

'There is not much time. Barely any. Paul could come back tomorrow. Any time. Elisa. Please.' And her eyes still a nun's.

'It would be like running away.'

'It is running away.'

'It would be like running away from a wounded animal. I don't know who needs me most, Janik—'

'Janik needs no one.'

'—or Paul.'

Bridges got up from the table, his face crooked with exasperation, his nose pinched. His teeth wanted to chew and tear, his legs were alive with it, itching. He paced ridiculously, then turned, slamming the table with his weight as he leaned over her.

'You bloody whore,' he said. 'You bloody, bloody whore.'

The words were boiling water flung in her face and there was no boundary between rage and pain.

'You have no right,' she said. 'I have done nothing. We have done nothing.'

He leaned closer. 'Nothing?' His breath on her, his mouth on her, his teeth on hers.

She got to her feet, pushing him away, but he was at her again and took hold of her. 'Nothing? Nothing?' repeating every gesture ('This?' his groin knocking at her hip, his hand 'This?' shoving at her breast), every caress he had ever made, however slight, making it monstrous. 'And this?' he said and stepped round behind her, unbalancing her and pushing her down to her hands and knees. 'This?' covering her like a dog, his rage and impotence working at her.

She pulled away and got to her feet, went out. Bridges listened. She was bolting the front door. She walked through and
slid the bolt on the kitchen door.

*Janik climbed the wooden steps of the pulpit. She looked down. Row
upon row of faces were turned up to her, waiting. She began to speak.
Words like bubbles of air formed and left her mouth. She could not
hear them, though the upturned faces were listening. A door at the
back of the church banged open and a gust of wind caught at all those
who were sitting beside the aisle, lifted hair and skirts, made them
turn their heads. And then the wind was everywhere, the pulpit now a
boat high on the sea, the deck of the boat higher than a roof and Janik
leaning over and looking down through the water steeple deep to a
church submerged and all the people in it alight like candles, burning.*

*She looked up from the drowned church, looked out to the congre-
gation and saw how the people sat while their hair blackened and
ignited, their clothes smouldered, catching fire at hems and cuffs,
flames at their throats like silk scarves, hands now to their faces,
hands alight pressing fire to their eyes.*

*Everywhere she turned there was fire and the noise of the wind
roared as the walls, the stone itself incredibly burned, cracking and
exploding so that flames shot along the fissures and found new routes
to take. She could hear the sound of her own voice now mixed with the
crackle and roar of the fire, but she could not catch the words that disappeared like sparks. And then she was outside and standing in an
avenue of fire, and every building in the city was alight, boxes of
roiling fire with flames billowing like torn curtains from the windows,
snapping like victory banners from the roofs, and the black smoke
gathering in palls.*

GAGNON SLEPT DESPITE his ribs. He had slept only intermittently in the three days since the explosion. Waking now in the Hôtel d'Appolon, he was pleasantly filled with a renewed sense of self. The sunshine outside was very bright. It was squeezing its way between the slats of the jalousie. He thought it must be getting close to noon. He got up gingerly, holding his bandaged side, dressed himself carefully and went downstairs to confirm by drinking chocolate and eating the best part of a loaf that he had escaped the worst life had to offer. He sucked at the soaked bread like an infant and was busy with his cup. He was alive. He was, almost, unharmed. How could he have doubted that it would turn out this way? He did not like to think of his condition of mind in the jail. It was poor and niggardly, an unmanly state of being, believing every trick the soldier came up with, pleading with God to forgive and forget. Like a child. I didn't mean it. Whimpering to himself that he would die there on the filthy floor next to the scabby clerk from the cardinal's office, who, he noticed, picked his nose with restless obsession. No, it was not a thing he, Le Gagnant, cared to dwell on. Smile on life and it would smile on you. And one adventure was, after all, more than enough for a man at his age. He had seen quite enough of Paris for now. When Escher called in again he would ask him about the trains. Escher seemed to know what was what. He took a a short walk to purchase a paper. The streets seemed quiet enough. He decided, nevertheless, to take it back to his room to read it in private. The pleasure of anticipation was good. Like the hand on a thigh not his wife's. Marguerite's. Any obliging female. He savoured it while he walked.

In his room he found what he was looking for but not what he was expecting. New evidence had come to light, *Le Reveil* said, which proved beyond a doubt that blame for the recent explosion in Ménilmontant should in no way be laid at the doorstep of the Commune. The responsibility for the resulting tragic deaths of the nine children clearly lay fairly and squarely with the remnants of the infamous government of Monsieur Thiers, a band of men so bereft of hope they had resorted to vile exercises in sabotage and barbarism in their desperate attempts to abort the common good to which the Commune of Paris aspired. Monsieur Grousset himself, the paper said, yesterday announced that the *Comité Central* was in the possession of signed statements to the effect that the atrocity had been perpetrated by agents of the disgraced government of Versailles.

The cascading flesh came again, teeming down but not away, changing nothing, leaving him intact, stark aware. But it was not his fault, no. No one could say he had killed nine children. (The stomach rising as the flesh fell.) Look. No one had asked him to do such a thing. If they had, he never would have agreed. He could not control an accident. No one could lay that at his door, he a father too, a good one. No. The world was a terrible place. Ask God why accidents happen. No. The paper was right, if anyone was guilty it was the men who had hired him. The disgraced Government of Versailles. The blame was at their door all right. Which nevertheless left him on shaky ground. Signed statements. He had only talked about engineering contracts. He had signed nothing. But they were bound to think he had. Especially the Versailles man. And he had agents everywhere. His position looked more dangerous every minute. His ribs seemed to hurt more. He lay down and tried to breathe very gently so as not to move them. He would go straight back. If they cared to follow him and ask questions, let them. He had some questions too. Like where were they when he was in jail? Anyway, he had nothing to hide. He'd said nothing. Named no names. He had the bruises to show. He'd named no names. He had never believed more constantly.

The doctor came to see him very late.

'Well, my friend,' said Gagnon. 'This is a time to call. I could have died in my bed by now. But come in, come in.'

The doctor's smile was a transitory thing, could have been taken for a wince. He sat down heavily and stretched back his neck.

'You haven't heard? The drive on Versailles failed.' He closed his eyes.

'And? That's good news surely?'

The doctor opened his eyes, looked long and hard at Gagnon. 'From what I've seen, and believe me I've seen, they bleed,' he said. 'Just like you and I.'

'But they're still scum.'

'Well you would think so,' said the doctor. He tipped his head back and closed his eyes again. 'They are fighting for what they believe.'

Gagnon snorted.

'I'm serious. Listen. Do you hear those guns?' They could not be ignored. 'Those are Government guns firing on Passy. Blowing people to bits.'

The silence was immediate and profound. Neither man knew how to extricate himself from his vision of bricks and rubble and what lay among them.

'Let me see if I can get you a drink downstairs,' said Gagnon.

The doctor shook his head and got up. 'No. We'll have to see about getting you out,' he said. 'The trains have stopped running but you can still leave with a pass. The Prefect of Police is issuing them.' Escher looked out of the window as he spoke, not wishing to see Gagnon's face, guessing the fear on it. 'I can get one for you, I think, in the circumstances. Paul Kenyon would be your legal name. Right?'

And Gagnon knew he was being protected. 'Right. Best to be legitimate, eh?'

'Now I must get some sleep. I'll be back in the morning. Meanwhile, don't overdo it.'

'Me? I feel as fit as a horse.' And would have slapped his sides but could not.

WHEN THE DOCTOR returned the next morning, Gagnon was in his room. His stomach was too unsettled to eat.

'All your business completed?' the doctor asked.

'Yes, yes.' Gagnon rubbed his hands in the way he did when he spoke of business, though to tell the truth he was far from satisfied, finding, as he had, only one half his fee deposited in his name at the bank, the other half withheld. And the clerk had been adamant. No instructions had been received, he said, none. So that Gagnon walked back from the bank with an uncomfortable sense of finally having lost control of the strings of his world, of being manipulated by—and this disturbed most of all—an unseen hand. Clearly he was expected to show himself—to return to the *Mairie* and demand his payment. He felt intuitively that it was not the thing to do, although he bled profusely for the loss of his francs which were, without a doubt, his for the job completed and for the injury he had suffered in both spirit and body. But his indignation was a frail thing beside his fear.

'Good,' said the doctor. The two of them went downstairs together.

The *concierge* settled without argument and carried Gagnon's bag out to the waiting cab.

'Where to Monsieur?'

'The Gare du Nord,' the doctor said, and would remember for years to come.

In the cab he explained to Gagnon that the bombardment was continuing at Neuilly, more fiercely than ever. There was no way out to the west but there were coaches to be had, he had heard, out at the Gare du Nord, and there seemed to be plenty leaving. No one was stopping them, it seemed, at the Porte de la Chapelle as long as they had the right number of passes.

Their progress was slow. At every turn the driver came to barricades that had not been there the day before. At the Place de l'Opéra there was a great crowd of people and no way through. The driver swore and cursed imaginatively and banged on the side of the cab with his whip handle to get their attention. Neither of the men inside could understand what he was saying through his frothing impatience. One had to assume he was asking them what they wanted to do.

'Find another way, man,' called Gagnon, to whom it seemed self-evident.

But then the cause of the obstruction came into view. A group of bareheaded men, all wearing red sashes, were leading a funeral cortège into the square. Behind them came a battalion of the Guard, their drums muffled in black cloth. The driver put the brake on the wheels and went to join the crowd. Behind the soldiers, two, then three wagons rolled into the square. They were heavily laden and covered in black, with red flags hanging from the corners. Neither the deadened sound of the drums nor the murmur of the crowd was loud enough to hide the slow creaking of the wheels.

When the driver finally returned and the crowd dispersed a little, they made their way through. The confusion was, if anything, worse. Gagnon was perspiring by the time they reached the station.

The doctor let the cab driver go, knowing he would do better to make his way back on foot. There were coaches in the station forecourt and ticket agents had set up business in the concourse. The doctor followed Gagnon inside. Gagnon went to get his ticket, relieved when, even at five times the regular price, it was finally in his hand. The ticket hall was very crowded. When he turned to look for the doctor and make his goodbyes, he was momentarily dazzled. The sun had begun to slant in through the grimy window. It blinded. And then without warning the window seemed to explode, letting the sun itself, it might have been, enter his skull.

## *Twelve*

ELISA WAS COLD. She went into the kitchen and stoked up the fire. When it was blazing she watched it with dispassion and she thought. Bridges in his brutality was not far from Gagnon, heavy and blind in brandy. It was not a wildness that she could return, almost did return that last day on the cliffs. They had been in the chapel. It had taken all her breath away when he knelt behind her. They had gone outside, lain down on the grass in the lee of the chapel. And that was different, a sacred savagery, a wild hammering at each other's souls. And she was ready. She was ready to sacrifice her soul under the blue sky but her tears made her helpless and Alain stopped. If half an hour ago it had been the same Alain, she would have gone back to him there on the floor after she had locked the doors. She would have lain down on her discarded clothes and given him all that he wanted. Instead she had gone up to her room and he had not followed. She heard him go out. It was as if they had inhabited the same dream and had woken in different places. But now nothing would be the same. And when he came back . . . She thought of Paul coming back from Paris, no longer intact himself, to find his household fallen about his ears, the wind whistling in empty rooms. And she thought of Janik walking the streets of broken stone, waiting for the thing to be done. Janik walking with her eyes downcast, her ears deaf to gunfire. Janik not looking for any angel to save her.

BRIDGES WENT DOWN to the harbour and past the muddy warmth of La Madonne where Crécy and Courtebois watched him go by the window. He carried on to Le Corsaire. It was dirtier, darker, a place where one could drink oneself stupid without being disturbed. He ordered a large brandy and nursed it sullenly for a while before he drank it down. He ordered another which he drank in the same way. The third glass he drank sensibly and began to savour the taste. It wasn't so bad, what had happened. It was in itself an affirmation, could not have occurred unless something already existed. She had already as good as given herself to him. There was no taking it away. He would go back. He would say anything that needed to be said. And he would not be angry.

CRÉCY HAD MADE a few inquiries of his own. Janik had gone to an aunt in Trouville. Bridges did not go there. Bridges went to Paris. It was just as they had thought. Someone had asked Bridges what Gagnon was doing in Paris. Bridges had said he hadn't seen him. But he, Crécy, knew for a fact that Gagnon had arranged to do some work for Thiers' government. Strange, though, that Gagnon should come to harm—and Bridges should come home. Courtebois asked if Crécy had heard what Vavin had said about Gagnon and Bridges.

'What?' said Crécy.

'Nothing. He didn't say anything. Just this.' Courtebois put his fingers to his head for horns. The two men drank for a while before Crécy spoke. 'Get him in here. We'll talk to him.'

They drank some more, agreed, no he didn't have to tell them anything.

And they could make no open accusations. Of course not. They would be doing Gagnon's reputation no favours. He wouldn't appreciate coming home to a scandal.

'But Alain Bridges can't be allowed to get away with it.'

'Indeed not. You have to teach a man like that a lesson. Bloody Englishman.'

The *mobile* nearby had been listening.

'English? The only thing the English understand is a kick up the backside.'

'And I'd give him one.'

'What's he done?'

'What hasn't he done? He's abandoned his wife and betrayed his father-in-law.'

'And screwed his mother-in-law,' Crécy said under his breath.

'And nothing can be proved.'

'Doesn't mean you can't do anything about it.' Which earned him a drink, this sign of solidarity. 'Nothing to say you can't have a *charivari*,' earning more approval.

'Shame we haven't got a mule.'

'There's horses where we're stationed.' The *mobile* downed his drink. An empty glass while he still had their attention.

'That would be just the thing for a foreigner fraternizing with rebels. To be taken for a ride on a loyal Government horse. Let me fill your glass.'


IT WAS BRIDGES' misfortune that the *mobiles* had not yet received a call to arms but were itching for action. He was sitting with Crécy and Courtebois, wondering why he had been asked to join them in La Madonne and why they were so insistently liberal with their drinks, when the soldiers could be heard outside.

'There seems to be a disturbance,' said Crécy to Courtebois.

'It seems there is.'

The two men got up and went to the door. Bridges pushed his chair back and followed. The diners at the table by the door craned their necks a little to see over the curtain.

'We're letting the cold in,' said Crécy, and the three of them moved out and shut the door. Someone outside began to chant.

'*Montez, montez, culbutez.*'

Bridges said, 'They're drunk,' and turned to go in. Something tripped him and his knee hit the step. When he looked up, Crécy and Courtebois were not there. Two of the *mobiles* reached down to pick him up.

Crécy, watching from the corner of the wall, was very drunk. It was easy to laugh at the *mobiles'* sodden buffoonery.

'Oh we beg your pardon!' They bowed, scraped cobbles with their *képis*. 'We beg your pardon, milord! Did something run into you?' While they took off his jacket, though he did fight, and turned it inside out. 'Let us straighten you up. Here, a spy should wear his proper uniform, yes? Wherever he is.'

'Never mind, milord. We'll get you back where you belong.'

'In your father-in-law's bed.'

'Bet there's nothing like it for a sore head. A sore head, eh?'

So that he was beside himself and must be hit hard and again or they could not have got the jacket back on him the way they did nor tied his hands. Crécy had to laugh now. Five of them to lift him backwards onto the horse, two to pass the rope round and under, fumbling with cord and stirrup irons.

Courtebois held the horse's head, pacifying for the irritation at its belly where the hemp went through the girth.

'There! You'll be all right now. You can't fall off.'

'All you need now is a fanfare.' And one there with his bugle obliged.

The horse lifted its tail and the *mobiles* nearest scrambled as it shat hotly and noisily. There was uproar. Crécy had tears running down his cheeks.

Someone came running from the bar with tin trays and spoons. The racket began, but already there were lights at doorways and windows all along the quay. The window of the bar was stacked with faces. One of the *mobiles* clattered up on another horse and took the reins from Courtebois, who batted at the horse's neck with his hat, making it skip sideways as it started so that at once Bridges was off balance. The mounted *mobile* cantered once round the main part of the quay and then his horse broke into a gallop or perhaps he moved it, and Bridges began

falling, slipping in a heavy arc down towards the cobbles and the
battering hooves.

The horse then without breaking its speed began a strange, contorted ballet, trying to avoid the bouncing weight, the unknown thing that it would unwittingly have pounded to death had it not been for the drunken incompetence of the guards who tied the cords, for as the saddle skewed down and under the horse's belly, a knot gave and at once one of Bridges' hands came free and the length of rope between the stirrup iron and his other hand jerked out to more than twice its former length and Bridges was almost clear of the shod hooves.

The *mobile* ran his horse around a second time. He took a wide turn and veered in suddenly. Bridges' body slammed against a mooring pin. Crécy stopped watching. On the third time round, Courtebois shouted some directions to the *mobile* and pointed up the hill. The soldier rode his horse at a run away from the noise of the quay and turned up the hill. He stopped at the big house and dismounted. What he saw, as he went round to untie Bridges, turned his stomach so that instead he yanked the buckle on the girth undone and let the saddle drop. Never before had he hurled himself upon a horse so hurriedly nor ridden away so fast, the barebacked horse running beside him now, its mane flying.

DOCTOR ESCHER THE atheist sat and prayed. Dear God. He did not get much further. Dear God. The world had gone mad. He did not know what he would say. Who should be so inured to death. He would have to have help. Get Crécy's wife perhaps. Gagnon dead. It did not seem possible. There were no words he could offer. He would rather be at work among the blasted corpses than facing Elisa Gagnon with the news. The shelling now was relentless. At the Palais de l'Industrie there were not doctors enough to care for all the wounded coming in from

Passy, some from Neuilly if they could make it. They said an armistice to bring them was going to be called. And he would not be there. And who could blame the officer at the Prefecture of Police when he had only shrugged. They had enough to do making their own arrests, he said. They had no time for murder in the streets. The whole city was being murdered. But he had no trouble obtaining a pass. Just get your friend out of the city, they said. And quick. We have enough of our own dead to bury. And one other piece of advice. Don't nail down the lid. Not until you're past the gate. So he had hired a cart large enough to take the coffin. He found a hammer and some nails in the *concierge*'s cupboard and took them, putting only two or three through the lid. Then he had an assistant help load the coffin onto the cart. And the sight was so familiar to passers-by that no one even glanced in their direction. The soldier at the gate took a crowbar to the lid, said, 'Christ!' when he removed the cloth from Gagnon's face, said, 'He caught it!' and then, seeing the doctor's drawn face, said, 'Here. I'll do that,' hammering the lid back on, not very well.

The doctor climbed back up and urged the horse on.

He made his way north and then west. Outside Pontoise, the cart hit a deep pothole and he heard the rear wheel crack. It began to rain. Then Escher, too, gave up. He drove into Pontoise and found a room, found someone to mend the cart. He prepared himself to sleep for twelve hours. The cart could be fixed but by then it would be dark. There was nothing for it but to delay until tomorrow.

'No,' said the *patron*. 'No we don't have an undertaker. You have to go to Gisors. But there's a shed in the back. For less than a room of course.'

And so Gagnon in his coffin rested that night on crates in the shed—or most of him, for the coffin was too long and the foot of it stuck out the door in the rain.

ELISA HAD NOT paid attention to the sounds of drunken rioting
that had carried up from the harbour, nor had it registered as that
until Tor began to bark and she heard the horses stop outside.
She did not feel inclined to open the door to anyone. From the
window upstairs she looked down at the *mobile* as he dismounted,
and then he was out of sight under the window, but only for a
moment before he quickly mounted again and was gone, heading
back down the hill, a second, riderless horse behind him, shaking
its neck as it ran. She went down and her curiosity began subtly
to transform itself to dread. She opened the door and knew
instinctively that it was only the first step of many. Nor was she
amazed to see Bridges on his knees in his white shirt, on his knees
in the street and leaning forward but not toppling. There was
something, she could barely see, it could be, was, a saddle, on the
ground beside him, and his coat—which had to be put on, that
was the first thing, for how he shuddered—was partly in his lap.
She crouched beside him and reached across but he made a
blocking motion with his shoulder. At the same time as she saw
that the rope led out from under the coat, she heard Bridges say,
'Get a knife.' He was blowing through his teeth. She knew for
certain then that there was more to come and that she must not
stop to speak but only do each thing until it was finished. She ran
to the kitchen and came back with a knife to cut the rope.
Keeping her eyes away from the coat that, turned inside out, was
hanging by the sleeve from his right arm, she helped him to his
feet. Inside, she took him straight to the room that Marguerite
used and sat him on the bed. She looked for the first time in his
face. He was looking at her with unspoken, unspeakable pleading
in his eyes.

She drew the coat off his arm as if she had been all her life
upon battlefields attending torn and blasted limbs, glanced only
once at what was left of his hand. She said, 'The doctor . . .
There is a doctor . . .' But he shook his head. She said, 'I'll go
right away.' But he was trying with his left hand to give her the
knife. She got up and went to the kitchen. She did not look at
him again until she had everything ready—the clean cord, the

filleting knife, the cloths, and the carbolic—and then with consent from his dreadful eyes she took him to the table.

She worked by instinct and by impulse. Because she could not bear their movement, she tied off the pulsing lines that muddled through the flesh and chips of bone with butcher string, tying it tight as if to strangle them. Then she bound the wrist tightly with a torn cloth, covered the trampled hand with another, and made her cut as cleanly as she could.

Marguerite, unlucky enough to return at the same moment, at once folded herself in an untidy pile in the kitchen doorway.

Elisa forced herself to look at Bridges. His face was pale and his lips were drawn back from his teeth but his eyes were closed, for which she was grateful.

'It. It.' But she could not join words, her mind working by itself without words, without thought, with only sensing and doing. 'It.' She closed her eyes and the words came out like beads too far apart on a string, like learning to read. 'It would be better,' she said, 'if you were lying down. For the next thing.'

She opened her eyes and he was looking straight at her, into her. There was no separation and he was not other but the same one with her in the same place where now she found herself forced to live.

'Can you walk?' she said.

He said yes with his eyes, controlling himself, not wanting to nod his head for the shaking that he sensed would start.

Elisa went to Marguerite with the unstoppered carbolic. She brushed it under her nose and Marguerite came to a stinging rush of consciousness. She scrambled up but was no use at all.

Elisa went back to the table. There was no more bleeding. She helped Bridges, now with eyes stark and his jaw rigid, back to the bed where he lay down, turning his face away as she applied the carbolic and he at last lost consciousness.

Marguerite was in the kitchen. She had looked under the cloth and was as white as it had been.

'I need you,' said Elisa. 'Light the stove outside.'

And Marguerite asking why.

'Just light it.'

And then Marguerite resisting again because now she understood.

'Please. I'll do the rest myself, just light it. Please.'

So Marguerite went outside to the glasshouse, to the wood heater, knowing at least to make it fierce.

Then Elisa came, carrying the hand in the rolled coat, shaking now so violently that she could not get hold of the stove cover but Marguerite must lift it for her to put the bundle in, which she did, releasing tremors from her hands to race through her, knocking her legs, every part of her. Carefully she moved outside and leaned against the wall, but she could hear the whoosh and hiss of the fire and she began to sweat in such profusion that the drops fell on her eyelashes while the world she looked at began to darken before her eyes like a negative image on a plate.

'You should come in,' Marguerite said. 'You're cold.' And Elisa, when the world returned to its colours, went slowly inside.

She began to scrub the table but Marguerite took the brush. 'I'll do that. You should lie down. In your condition.'

But Elisa would only sit with the palms of her hands on the damp surface.

THE PREFECT OF Police said he had seen nothing. He shook his head. He knew nothing about any disturbance.

'Madame Gagnon,' he said. 'For your husband I have the greatest respect. But this does not mean I have it in my power to reverse the unfortunate accident that befell your . . . son-in-law.'

Nothing she could say would move this man, this stone wall. 'He had been tied,' she said, and then remembered she had burnt the rope. He raised his shoulders, opened his palms, handwashing being too overt a gesture for the bureaucrat.

She went to the garrison. A sergeant there, with puffy eyes and shiny skin, said it was a serious accusation and were there witnesses and where was the complainant and what was the name of the soldier she had seen and could she identify him or his horse? She said there was a saddle. It had gone in the morning.

Glazed with calculated indifference, the sergeant's eyes stared at a spot just in front of hers. 'Really,' he said. 'How unfortunate.' And then she understood, saw with the eyes of others this stranger Bridges in the town, saw finally how she could not have hoped to keep what they had hidden. All the world must know. Well then let it be public. Let them see. She would go away with him. And the whole town could revile them, but they would do it.

When she arrived home again, she called for Marguerite. Marguerite, after everything she had seen the day before, did not question the need to go into the attic and bring down the small steamer trunk. If her mistress had taken the small step from eccentric to crazy, she would be far better on the other side of an ocean. Not that she would not be sorry, contemplating an endless vista of stiff laundry and spitting meat unbroken by outlandish interludes in the glasshouse. Though it would not surprise her if other interludes presented, once Monsieur Gagnon found himself alone.

'Madame, I have to say it.' The two of them struggling with the cumbersome thing on the narrow stair.

'Yes.'

'It does not seem right.'

'Right does not come into it.'

'But how can you say that?' Her Catholic soul affronted. 'Right and wrong. Of course.'

'It has nothing to do with "right".'

'There you are! It has all to do with wrong, excuse me.'

'Turn it sideways, will you.'

'And I shall have to confess it.'

'Why? Are you coming too?'

And they stopped at the bottom of the stair, the clasp giving way and lid flopping down, the trunk a receptacle to contain or to spill every scandalous intention, and they laughed, not because it was funny but because they would have liked to cry a little and at last did, until Marguerite wiped her nose on the edge of the lace curtain of the little window where she stood and the necessary friction was restored.

BRIDGES OPENED HIS eyes to sunlight and the foretaste of bliss that leaks from the edges of oblivion. And then the darkness overcame him. Two, three times, before he opened his eyes again, he went to touch his hand where there was nothing. Then he was conscious of his body and the terrible blackness of the irrevocable. The pain of the injuries he had sustained in the dragging dissolved in the brandy that Elisa gave him every hour, but he felt the rope at his wrist. It did not match the hideous sense of finality. He had to touch again and again to believe it.

He saw a steamer trunk being carried by the door. Later—how much later?—he saw a coffin. Muddled by the brandy he did not know if he woke or slept.

He dreamed himself inside the coffin. He dreamed Elisa beside him and they were falling through the earth.

*Ashes blow like snow across the broken walls. They drift against the barricades and settle on the eyelashes of the communards asleep over their guns. Her comrades are all asleep. There are women and men lying together on the ground. Their limbs stick out at odd angles. Their hair is dusted with white, their shoulders, their boots. She wishes they would curl themselves up. They are all awry. She goes to a young boy. She wants to make him more comfortable but his limbs are brittle and they snap like icicles inside the grey cloth. In the empty square a wind gets up and whirls the ashes round. Janik looks up and they float down past the ruined buildings and fall on her face like icy*

*kisses. She opens her mouth to them, opens her throat. Her mouth is a heart open to the sky, filling with light. Janik wakes and sees roses blooming in the whiteness. She runs barefoot to pick them.*

ELISA STARED AT the yellow pine. There were many mourners at the grave, though only one or two had come to the house. Many of them Elisa did not know. Marguerite, like a child, held onto her arm. Elisa appearing steady, but only rigid with shock.

How her husband, fixed in death beneath the boards, reached into life as surely as if he were living; in what strange, extreme fashion had he resumed control just as she had been about to slip away. For she had been intent, set. She had been packing to leave, prepared to leave him needing her or not, prepared to leave Janik on the dangerous boulevards. She had been waiting only for Bridges to come out of his stupor so that they could get over to Le Havre. And then the unbelievable. The fish-faced Madame Crécy and the faint-hearted priest at the door, Julie Harmon apologetic behind them. Madame Crécy saying, Sit down my dear, and taking out a bottle of smelling salts, it might have been a little vial of words, their dangerous vapours loose in the room, but Elisa as unlikely to swoon away as a farmer's boy. She listened as the words took shape and fell like stones on her future. And the next day, Harmon and two others and the doctor, all of them in the drawing room and the yellow coffin from which something leaked resting on the dining room chairs while in the other corner of the room the trunk stood open. The boards were not joined properly. The smell had made her gag but she had stood and breathed it. Wanting to breathe death, to catch it like a plague. Someone had tried to move her but she had refused. They left the doors and windows open while Felix worked to seal it. Elisa could hear the gulls screeching down at the harbour, their aggressive, aggrieved mewing carrying up the hill on the breeze. Harmon and the others left. Escher said, 'I heard what

happened.' Elisa did not answer. The day wore on. Neither
Crécy nor Courtebois came, but two or three others came to
stand grim-faced a moment by the coffin, their solemnity at odds
with her stark eyes, she fighting with the horror of Gagnon dead
while her mind still disbelieved. No. She would have shaken the
bloody corpse if she could to make it come alive. Come alive so
that I can run away from you. She would have shouted at its
opened face if it would have helped. And Crécy, if he had seen,
might have felt better at the devastation the blow had clearly
wrought upon the wife.

She seemed to remember Escher only as he was leaving.

'Do you want me stay?' he said.

'No,' she said, 'but I will feed you before you go.' She found
some soup and some bread and made Marguerite prepare it. Elisa
did not eat but sat with Escher at the table. He wolfed the soup,
gulping, devoured all the bread she gave him, crumbs falling
from his bearded mouth as he spoke.

'Your patient is doing well,' he said. 'But he would do better to
be away from here.' He looked up at her over his spoon. 'You
know what I am saying.' He asked where Janik was. She raised
her eyebrows slightly. 'Paris?' She was asking him.

'Madame Gagnon,' he said, 'someone will have to find her.'
He shook his head and looked down, stirred his soup. 'When I go
back . . .'

'I think she wants to be there,' was all Elisa could say, words of
any kind inadequate against the unfathomable.

When the doctor had gone and she had locked the door, Elisa
went, ashen, to Bridges and lay down behind him, her face to the
nape of his neck while Marguerite, appalled, crossed herself and
went to sit with the body.


THE YELLOW PINE was joined properly now Elisa saw.

She did not listen to the words of the priest but watched when
he threw his handful of earth. It should have been a casting down
but it was an airy gesture, theatrical, as if he were a magician and

they were to wait for an effect. She stared at the yellow wood and there were no magic tricks. And was he dead because she had wished it, because she had not prayed for him, or because she had not wanted him returning to the empty rooms, to Marguerite guilt-stricken and babbling, to the long search for Janik? At whose name she must weep. Streaming tears of apparent widow-hood, winning redemption, a little, among the solemn mourners. Janik. Who should be here beside her with her fiery vision and outlandish prayers to contend with the hopeless priest. Who did love her father and would have honoured him as perhaps he did after all deserve. For who at the grave's edge would want to say otherwise? And she remembered then her daughter's face as she had seen it years ago when Janik was lying one hot day in sum-mer in the slow water at the edge of the river; how she had tilted her head back and her face was wet, glistening, it might have been bone, her hair like red weed slicked back, her eyes closed and her mouth open, a hole into the too corporeal frame; how in her immersion in life she had presented a vision of death and how she, Elisa then, for perhaps the only and certainly the last time, had been awash with love and pity for the soul she had brought into the finite world.

Someone was pressing a handful of earth into her hand. She wished she had brought something, anything, a gift, to place in the grave. She took the earth and cast it in. Crécy watched the earth fall and was vindicated, was almost grateful. It was as if Gagnon had died exclusively to clear his name, expunge the guilt that he, Crécy, had carried, his own burden dragging behind him, since the *charivari*.

As the mourners cast more earth into the grave, Elisa slipped off her glove, her ring with it, and bent down to take another handful. She dropped the ring and the earth in together. Marèchal, who saw and thought it was a mistake, drew in his breath, but Janik's friend Gabrielle saw it too and considered it an act of love. Those who would say it was an unbecomingly previous gesture of severance, obscenely eager, saved the detail for later.

ELISA'S HAIR IS matted with dust and hangs down in a tangle on one side. The ashy paving, the snagging rubble have turned her black dress grey. She has black smudges on her face and does not know it. On the chest of drawers in the hotel room is the doctor's letter to her:

> *I have been making discreet enquiries on your behalf and it has come to my attention that the party in question is serving as a member of the 'Vengeuses' women's battalion, led by Louise Michel, 'the Red Virgin,' and active in various parts of the city in the last few weeks. I beg you, Madame, not to consider entering Paris at this time. The fighting grows daily more fierce and there is abroad on both sides such ill-feeling as to render the acts of either beyond comprehension.*

By the time his letter arrived, travel to Paris was in any case out of the question. Fighting raged in the streets in nearly every part of the city. The Commune that had controlled the city for the last two months was about to fall. Government troops were pouring in on all sides. The communards were burning their own city.

Elisa waited, sitting out the dry heat, praying with all of France for rain to save the city. As if it could put out the fires of ideology or quench the thirst for revenge. As if it could wash away the blood.

And then the following week the pronouncement: Paris is delivered.

Elisa made her way by ferry and by train to Rouen and then took a seat on the coach. All along the route to Neuilly the pall of smoke was visible. In the coach, everyone had a rumour to pass on, their own sparks sheltered in cupped hands, passed on to ignite more fires. How the communards had shot their hostages; how the Government troops had killed their prisoners. How women with blackened hands were shot on the spot as *pétroleuses*. How even children had been shot. They could smell the fires at the Porte de Champerret. And there was a smell of asphalt and tar and another smell, which made them all quiet, eyes looking to one another for confirmation, hands moving to their mouths and noses.

Elisa closes her eyes, thinks of Alain on a pitching steamship in mid-Atlantic. His coat, or a shawl perhaps, over his injured arm. The sea air would be good, she had said. Free of impurities. He would heal. She colours the pallor on him, makes him lean on the rail. She makes him look at the woman standing near. She makes him smile.

After the funeral, she had gone back to Bridges to sit by his side. He said he wanted more brandy, that his hand was hurting, and she thought his mind gone, but he said, 'No. I know. But it hurts,' his mouth held still in that awkward position so that she knew it must be true. She gave him brandy and took off the dressing. The flesh was seeping.

'If I could grow a new skin,' he said. And she said, 'A film.'

She went to the glasshouse, came back with the bottle of collodion and prepared some in a bowl.

He put in the stump of his wrist and turned it. She held his arm while it dried and she did not look at him. Who had his eyes closed on such explicit evidence of his mortal self. And it was then, sitting there, that she knew. She knew with such suddenness that it made her draw in her breath. 'You will have to go without me,' she said. Knowing that it could be misconstrued, knowing what he might think—that she could no longer love him, he mutilated—but having nevertheless to say it, fulfilling all these years later, despite herself, the old nun's words, as if they had been a prophesy from an ancient sibyl. Once in the life of each soul, a choice. Her heart plunging after Janik.

'I can't come with you.' As if he were too damaged for her to love, though she did love him now more than ever.

He did not open his eyes. He did not say anything.

'I did not ask for any of this,' she said. Meaning Janik's inexplicable separateness, meaning Paris, meaning death, revolution, vengeance, and the savagery of men, but hearing in horror her own words and knowing Bridges would think it him she meant, his injury.

Trying then to put it right. 'I was ready to come with you. You know that.'

'It is still possible.'

'And Janik?'

'Yes I have a wife. Tell me that now.'

'She is my daughter.'

'She doesn't need you.' His mouth might have been filled with bile. His words were thick with it.

'There is love.' But she knew they were the words which would kill his love for her. She wanted to hold his face in her hands, make him look into her, see the depths again, still, where they had drowned together. 'But we are all of us alone. In the end. *Tous. Tout seul. Enfin.*' The words making each of them think of the lovers' bitten fingers and the terror of separation so that they began to make each other promises in order that *enfin* would never be.

He left the next morning. She prepared everything for him, packed his clothes and tried to look forward. Bridges up and about on shaky legs, supporting his arm in a sling, learning to dress, to drink from a cup, to break bread. Felix went with him.

They left at five o'clock, just as the birds began, Felix taking him in his own boat across to Le Havre. She would not go to stand on the dock. In that chill hour.

ELISA HAS WALKED and walked these streets and still she does not know. Though she has seen more than enough. She has seen cartloads of bodies more than a week old, the stained and pock-marked walls of the places of execution. She has seen the levelled barricades and walked on a freshly made road of crushed rock, the bodies of the new dead under it. She has seen sights the doctor said no human eyes should witness. And there were others out looking. The strange English. Seeing the sights. The compulsive traffic in souvenirs, pieces of the Vendôme column, relics of battle. Once she thought she saw her. A flare of red hair lighting the darkness of a blackened laurel in the park. But the girl turned round and it was not her. And now she has had enough. Tomorrow she will go back. She will leave early in the morning. She does not need to see more. Today she has seen everything she needs to see. Rounding a corner she came this morning on a photographer's shop. There were some small boys daubing the window with their pointing. That one. No that one. In the window a display of police photographs. Communards laid out in their open coffins. There was a thin girl with wild hair—it might have been red—that spread itself to lie on the shoulder of the corpse beside her. The girl's eyes were gone. The boys were peering. 'It's her brains,' one of them said. 'It's her bloody brains coming through the holes.'

Like strange flowers blooming. As if all the visions in her head had bloomed to blot out the vision of this world, too terrible to see. Elisa had put her hands up to cover her own eyes and as she took them away she saw that they were black and she would have to wash them.

She walked back past the ruins of the Hôtel de Ville, the sun catching the stone. A photographer had set up his camera, for the fire had transformed the stone. It was whitened by the heat and

mapped with traceries of pink and green where the flames had
travelled. He would not be able to get it, she thought, and was
glad. Beauty from terror. She wished it were a lie.


NOW, FROM HER hotel window, Elisa watches the sky changing
colour. The low rays filtering through the dust and the smoke are
painting a symphony of light. The river has turned to gold. She
looks down at the last of the fires smouldering across the city and
she remembers the lights on the surface of a black sea, a ship broken on a rock and its human freight spilling into the small boats,
into other people's lives. How Alain had spilled into hers, passive
and dangerous as water leaking, entering the least space, filling it.

And if he had not? Then Janik dreamwalking herself through
convent gates, closing the door of her cell behind her, her self
wasting while the angels gorged. And Paul? She does not know.
There is still a question. It will have to be answered in the end.
The drowning man would have taken them both down with him.
And yet. Still. Ask Paul beneath the yellow boards if the account
is straight. Ask him who has come face to face with his God and
with his drowning man. She will not judge. All across the city she
has seen the outcome of men's judgments. Justice. Retribution.

She will not stay any longer. She will go back, but only to pack
her things. And perhaps Marguerite will stay and look after the
rest for a while, the glasshouse and the pictures and the equipment. For Elisa knows that she has had enough of looking. She
will enter a picture of her own making. If she can find out how.

## Acknowledgements

The author would like to thank Marie-José Gautrais, Terry Ridings, Sue Donaldson, Murray Sitter, Anne-Marie Bergeret, Penny Brand, and Peter Brand for their generous help.

Very special thanks to Audrey McClellan. Thanks, too, to Rolf and Carolyn.

Thanks as always to John.

For background material and certain details such as *The Times* advertisement, the author consulted a number of excellent works. She wishes in particular to acknowledge her indebtedness to Cassell's *Illustrated History of the War Betweeen France and Prussia* (London: 1899) and especially to Alistair Horne's incomparable *The Fall of Paris* (London: 1965, 1990), for inspiration as well as information.

## Historical Note

The Franco-Prussian war lasted from July 1870 to January 1871, the Siege of Paris from September 1870 until the end of the war. In the aftermath, a rebellion by the Paris National Guard against the French government resulted in the establishment of the Commune of Paris. The French government fled to Versailles and civil war—and a second siege of Paris—ensued. The Commune lasted for seventy-one days. It attracted an assortment of idealists, activists, reformers, and dreamers, among them Louise Michel, a revolutionary, leader of a Women's Battalion, and known at that time as 'the Red Virgin.' During the 'Bloody Week' of repression that ended the Commune and in the days of reprisal that followed, an estimated 20,000 Communards were killed or—in that century's particular rhetoric—'expiated.' Government troops had initially been reluctant to use force.